Dragon Hide

Copyright 2018, Jillian Cooper All Rights Reserved. No part can be copied or reproduced without permission from the author or publisher.

Publisher: The Wooden Pen Press, Inc
Cover: Heather Hamilton-Senter

"Ala mode," Dirk joked from the back.

A lot of St. Louis was still in the middle of being repaired. This was the furthest west you could get before hitting the barrier of the wastelands—the area of the country that the dragons turned into smoldering ash—now nothing but desert.

The East Coast was brimming with activity and almost couldn't tell that had been decimated eight decades earlier. There was trade, fishing posts, but no one dared venture to Europe or anything further east.

Unfortunately, California and the West Coast, had been hit hardest when all the celebrities turned into dragon shifters, thanks to all the chemicals their bodies had been pumped with. Botox, skin lightning, hair straightening, and everything else they did for their youthful appearance when it hit a critical level, they all changed at once. Too bad, and Oscar ceremony had never been quite as exciting as that one.

They drove through the city streets and when they got close to the steeple church that was running the bake sale, Jameson stopped the van beside the curb.

Jenna slipped off her leather jacket, and put on a canvas brown one so not to arouse suspicion. The last thing she wanted to do, was triggered a dragon change in front of innocent people.

"I'll be back in five."

As she glanced in the side mirror, she tried to avoid Dirk's gaze. It was hard, when he was always looking at her like he had something to say like there was something on his mind. There was, and Jenna even knew what, but she didn't want to talk about it. She didn't want to hear about it.

At that moment, their cargo locked in the back compartment started to make a ruckus. "Let us out of here. We haven't done anything wrong!"

"Keep them quiet would you? Maybe up their dose," Jenna said.

Yes, ma'am." Dirk banged his fist against the metal barricade. "Don't make me come back there, I will get you to be quiet."

He was such a people person.

Truth be told, shapeshifters weren't people anymore. No laws. No rights.

Jenna slipped out of the van and concentrated to walk like a civilian and not a police officer on duty.

Everyone was nervous around New Haven police, their autonomy. Regular people knew what she was and the shapeshifters, well they were her targets. No wonder they were nervous.

Jenna stepped up onto the curb and pretended to inspect the first pastry table. She loved sweets as much as the next person, the brownies the cakes, all of it looked good, but she was working.

That meant she had little time to buy anything.

The woman wearing a straw hat on the other side of the table smiled. "Fresh as of yesterday. We just got a shipment of actual chocolate chips."

Even though she was older and had lines around her mouth and eyes, there was something beautiful her. People's appearances were more natural now they had been before the war. Jenna watched the vids in school—fake eye lashes, painted on eyebrows, and their complexions shined like they were painted with a poly coat.

What was the appeal with that?

"That's great. Who doesn't like a good chocolate rush?"

The woman laughed and Jenna moved on. Positioning herself behind her target— the mother and daughter wearing matching bandannas and matching red and white polka dots skirts. They might have paired them with running shoes, but you definitely could tell how they held themselves and how they turn their heads that there was something off about them.

Jenna went up and stumbled into them, slipping the paper thin tractors against their skin. "Excuse me. I'm so sorry."

The mother laughed nervously and the daughter, who couldn't be older than thirteen, clung tighter to her mom. "Oh, it's no bother!" The mother swallowed hard. "No bother at all. Right honey?"

The daughter nodded and buried her face into her mother's stomach. The mother for her part just patted the girl's head.

Jenna's ear crackled as Dirk came through loud and clear. "Their vitals are off the chart. Nervous, heart slowing down. Blood pressure plummeting. Sure signs they're dragon shifters."

Funny, most humans blood pressure went up when nervous, but not a shapeshifting dragon.

"My van broke down over there." Jenna pointed her thumb behind her shoulder. "Can you give me just a quick second of your time? I could really use the help."

The mother's mouth dropped open and her eyes widened. "Oh…really…I'm afraid we need to be getting home. Good luck to you…"

"Momma…" The little girl cried as her body shook with fear.

Jameson sighed into her comm. "There's no way she's getting them to the van. Damn Jenna, you need to work on your performance."

"I'm on my way," Dirk said.

Jenna was happy for the backup. Her pair of dragon shifters turned and started away. Jenna followed after them. "Excuse me! I said excuse me!"

Oh, what the hell. Jenna grabbed the mother by her shoulders and spun her around, leveling her with a punch.

The little girl stood in the center of the street. All around people turned and began to take notice as the little shifter screamed in horror and her skin morphed to a radiant blue color. Blue, Jenna always thought those ones were prettiest.

But the girl's bones broke and started to rearrange, her face held the beginning of a snout. This was as close as Jenna got to a dragon transformation in two years. As the little girl began to flap her wings, Jenna pushed a button on

Chapter One

The St. Louis arch had been decimated in the first Dragon war.

Two stumps were left and the rest was ancient history. Years ago, the world came to an end. For now, humans had rebuilt cities and towns. Many people had hope, that things would get back to how they were when their grandparents were born.

Barbeques, happy times with enough food rations to go around. Maybe forget that the dragon shifters mutated off from the human race.

Maybe.

Standing on the cost of St. Louis, Jenna Morgan, a fiery redhead in a leather jacket used her binoculars to keep a close eye on downtown. The church sponsored bake sale was in full swing. Woman and children sampled delectable baked goods. Since the Dragon war, people wore simple and comfortable clothes to go about their business.

Labor was hard. Jobs were scarce. St. Louis had been one of the last cities to fall and the last to get rebuilt. Things like running water and electricity, were still new to the small settlement. So, this baked good sale, was attracting a lot of attention. And some even unwanted.

Jenna spied through binoculars a mother and daughter duo with checkered bandanas tied around their hair.

Make up for the most part had been outlawed since the war but their cheeks were rosy in and their lips held a glamorous sheen. They stuck out in a crowd.

Funny, shapeshifters usually did a better job of blending in than these two.

"We've got a couple of live ones." She turned to the black van parked behind her to the two men that made up her squad of the New Haven police force. She handed the binoculars through the open window to Dirk, sitting in the back seat.

They had been a team a long time, things happened, hell things that shouldn't have happened did. But when they are working, they were all business. Old grudges long aside.

"Jameson, pull closer to town. Let's tag these shapeshifters and keep a close eye on them, drive them away from the population so no one gets hurt."

Jameson had a blond hair and angular nose. His small handheld computer was cell phone sized and his finger flew across the display. The tech guy, it was his responsibility to update the HQ on all of their actions—and logging where the latest dragon shifters had been discovered.

Jenna took shotgun, she always did, and sat in the front seat, leaving Dirk in the back. When Jenna slammed the door shut and stuck her boots up on the dash, Jamison peeled away from the curb. He threw her a quick glance. "Bake sale, nice touch."

Jenna smiled a crooked wryly grin. "You know shape shifters. Bad ass killers, but they can't resist a good crumb topping."

her bracelet. A harness shot out and wrapped around the little girl's neck.

Her body was pulsed with electricity and the little girl gagged, grabbing at the harness and fell to the ground in a heap. The shock stopped her change and turned her back into what appeared to be an adorable, thirteen-year-old girl. But she was a shapeshifter.

Just like her mother.

Jenna turned around and tugged the harness, forcing the prisoner to crawl after her. The mother crumpled on the ground, shook her head. "She's just a baby. She's just a…"

"Monster?" Jenna offered as Dirk secured his harness around the woman's throat. "A mutant dragon creature who was responsible for destroying the world?"

"That wasn't me. That wasn't her. The blood lust is gone now. We only want to live like you."

"Except you're more beautiful than anything I've ever seen and you live forever. On blood. Human blood."

The woman gazed down at the pavement and Jenna was done talking with her. She turned her attention back to Dirk, strapping on his New Haven police uniform. "Thanks for having my back."

"That's what the team's for."

They walked to the back of the van and Jenna ignored the people at the bake sale staring at them. Dirk opened the prison compartment of the van and helped the little girl inside. Cramped as it was, she got a spot on the bench. Dirk cuffed her harness to the overhang bar that would keep her in place.

Grabbing a tube that hung down from the rafters, Dirk attached it like an IV into her hand. Immediately blood flowed into her. The little girl swayed and a small smile graced her lips.

They all wore the same dopy expression. New Haven drugs could really do a number on someone.

Jenna shoved her prisoner into the van and wasn't delicate about it. The mother's face smashed into the metal floor. "Hook her up, will you? Got a long drive if we're going to deliver these dragon bastards for reconditioning by tomorrow night."

Dirk nodded. "Yes, Ma'am."

Good. Jenna returned to the van and took her seat beside Jameson. He gave her a glance, but didn't say anything.

"What?" Jenna asked.

Jameson shrugged. "Nothing."

Jenna sighed and grabbed the New Haven Police cap sitting on the dash. She slouched in her seat and used it to cover her face. She tried to ignore the crying she heard coming from the back. Damn, she hated the crying and how human they could all look.

They were the enemy. Mutants, dragons, shifters—whatever you wanted to call them, they started the war. Humans ended it and the shapeshifters were lucky to even be allowed to live.

Time to make tracks for New Haven 56.

Seven new dragon shifters going home.

Chapter Two

May 14th, Monday Morning
The Monroe Home: 15 Candy Cane Lane

Susan Marie wasn't ready to face the world. Dreams lingered in her head as she lay cocooned inside her thick comforter. She was aware of Jeff's warm body beside her as his calloused fingers found her hips and rocked her backwards.

A playful smile curled her lips. She murmured as she tilted back so their open mouths could greet. Jeff tasted as salty as last night's dinner, and her heart quickened as his lips massaged hers.

Hungrily, her teeth pulled on his skin and she felt his desire heighten against her hip. His arms tightened around her small frame and his hands cupped her breasts beneath her nightgown. Susan's skin tingled and a long breath expelled from her lungs. Jeff kissed the nape of her neck, softly laughing against her skin. "You're awake now, I bet." His hot breath tickled her earlobe until she could barely stand it.

Susan moaned, catching a small glimpse of her sexy husband. No longer newlyweds, he still made her feel young. "In a dreamlike state, but I'm managing so far."

Outside the bedroom came the sound of heavy footsteps. Susan knew what was coming next and wanted to pull the covers over their heads. "Mom!" yelled Marie, their teenage daughter. "Jake is hogging the television remote again!"

Another set of footsteps pounded outside. "You know *Happy Days* is only on before school. I didn't want to miss my favorite episode." Jake was a year older than his sister, but they were often mistaken for twins.

"The both of you are going to be late for the bus, so please hightail it downstairs and eat your breakfast, the both of you," Jeff said, waiting for the whine and clumping footsteps to follow. He laughed and smoothed his wife's hair back. They shared another kiss. "Welcome to the real world."

"That's for sure," Susan sighed. "Why was it we wanted to have two?"

"So, Jake would have someone to be friends with." Jeff reminded her and they both chuckled. For a moment Susan laid against him, her head on his shoulder. He rubbed her arm and kissed her forehead. With great reluctance she pulled herself out of bed and dressed for another busy day in New Haven 56.

Susan had adjusted to life there pretty well over the last eighteen years. It was where she met Jeff. Without the project, she would've been dead.

She dressed in a long blue pencil skirt and a white blouse, accenting her look with pearls and a pair of heels that matched her skirt. Her hair was spiraled into a French twist, and she put a final coat of red lipstick against her pouty mouth. An expert time manager, her look was complete in less than twenty minutes.

She arrived in the kitchen on schedule. It was spacious and looked just like most of the kitchens on the block, but Susan liked how it faced the morning sun. She bustled among the framed photos of special memories and Christmas holidays while Jeff dressed to open Dusty's restaurant and pub.

Susan made the kids' lunches, stowed them in their steel lunchboxes, and lined them up on the counter. "Kids, your lunches are ready!" She poured herself a cup of coffee and placed the cereal bowls in the dishwasher.

Jeff was huddled over the New Haven *Chronicle*, reading the editorial section. Susan rubbed his shoulder while she peered at the headline: *Local Stirs Up Trouble with Protests*. As she read it, Susan's stomach tightened and her coffee lost its appeal. She placed the cup on the yellow laid-tile island. "He's going to get us all in trouble."

Jeff folded the newspaper and threw a glance back. "Relax, babe. It's no different than it was last week or the week before. We'll keep our heads down and we'll be fine." He rubbed her arm and accepted the kiss she gave him. "Got any big plans for today?"

"Nothing out of the ordinary. I might steam the rugs."

"They certainly could use it. Harvey keeps using them as his litter box."

Didn't Susan know it? "Kids!" She bellowed once more, and this time was greeted with the rushing of feet. She inspected her children as they entered the kitchen.

Both appeared well-groomed. Marie's long brown hair was tied back with a pink scarf that matched her long-hemmed poodle skirt. Jake was a good-looking seventeen-year-old with rosy cheeks. Since he became captain of New Haven's football team, he was rarely seen without his football jersey. "Well," Susan said proudly, "don't you two clean up nice?"

"You'd rarely suspect them as ours." Jeff agreed, sipping from Susan's abandoned coffee mug.

"Stop teasing us," Marie said with a roll of her eyes. "We know Jake doesn't clean up well at all."

Susan tried not to giggle while Jake's cheeks flushed and his nose turned up like a pig's. "You're going to let her talk to me like that?"

"It was a joke." Marie folded her arms in front of her. "Tell him, Mom."

"It was a joke," Susan brushed off Jake's shoulders. "And you look handsome as ever." Her smile glowed and inside a well of pride sprung a leak.

Jake's expression softened. "Thanks, Mom."

"Now off to school." Susan headed to the counter as Marie picked up her lunch, but Jake stepped forward. He fiddled with his jacket and his face turned down while he chewed on his lip. "Mom." There was a tremor to his voice. "We're out of eggs and milk. I was wondering when you were going to get new rations."

Jeff cast him a stern look. "If there aren't eggs and milk, eat something else. You think it's easy running a house with four mouths to feed?"

Marie's nose turned up. "You always eat more than your share. It's not fair to the rest of us, you know."

"Stop it, kids. No fighting." Susan sighed. "I'm heading to the market today to pick up a few more rations, but it'll have to hold us until the end of the week. We've almost used up all of our monthly spending points."

"We could eat out," Jake suggested.

"That takes money and you know there isn't enough to go around. You like this house heated and with cable TV? You like those stylish clothes on your back?" Jeff stood and shoved his bar stool into the kitchen island.

The teenagers eyed it and the air in the room thickened. "He doesn't mean it, Daddy. Do you?" Marie turned toward her brother, her ponytail lashing at the back of her neck.

"No." Jake said quietly. His cheeks reddened. "I'm happy to eat whatever Mom can cook up."

Susan patted his cheek. "Good boy. Better get off to school. The bus will be outside any moment." She kissed each of their cheeks and handed Jake his lunch. "No trading at the lunch table again, understand?" The front door latched and Susan pivoted, placing her hands on her hips.

"What?" Jeff asked, placing her drained coffee mug in the dishwasher. "He's insensitive and selfish."

"In other words," Susan said, grinning, "a teenager."

"Well, I don't have to like it." Jeff huffed. His shoulders relaxed when Susan kissed his cheek.

"He'll be our boy again once he's through this phase. He's a good kid, you know that."

"I know, I know. I guess I just remember being him, before I moved here. What a dope I was to both my parents." Jeff shook his head.

Susan rarely heard him talk about his time before New Haven, and she tried to pretend such times never existed. Her fingers twisted together and spun her wedding ring while her shoulders inched up her ears. "Speaking of your parents, we're going to meet them this Sunday for some bingo after church service. I'm making an upside-down pineapple cake."

"Not more bingo." He sighed. "Can't we just serve the cake here?"

"I love bingo and you love me, so therefore…" Something on the counter caught Susan's attention; it was Marie's metal thermos. Eyes wide, Susan snatched it and charged out the front door.

She sprinted down the street and over the residential hill. At the corner stood a group of students. The girls were dressed in proper skirts and high heels, while the boys wore pressed shirts and khaki pants. "Marie!" Susan called as the bus squealed to a stop beside them.

Marie glanced up with surprise, clutching her lunchbox in one hand and her school books in another.

"Sweetheart, you forgot your liquefied organ juice!"

Marie grinned and kissed Susan's cheek. "Thanks, Mom! I don't know what I'd do without you!"

***

Susan strolled up the concrete walkway as Jeff headed to the car. They shared a parting embrace. "Have a good day at the restaurant, sweetheart."

"I'll be home for dinner tonight." Jeff kissed her chin, his fingers gliding across her cheek.

"I can't wait." Susan's eyes sparkled with mischief and he smacked her backside. After a final wave, she headed inside to start the morning's duties.

Susan picked the cat off the counter. She sat him down on the floor and dangled a piece of yarn in front of his paws. A cute fluffy black cat, he immediately took delight in the game until the phone rang and Susan's attention diverted.

She removed one earring and put the phone to her ear. Harvey circled around her, swatting at the hem of her skirt to get her attention. When that didn't work, he meowed a pitiful sound, as if being flogged by older and wiser kitties.

"Susan here."

"Susan, hello! I have news. Are you listening?"

"I just said hello, didn't I?" Susan almost rolled her eyes, despite her disgust at such a childlike expression.

"I just needed to make sure. I have *big* news."

"Jonathan?" Susan asked. Jonathan was Megan's son and the same age as Marie. Secretly, if not exactly discreetly, the two women hoped their children would court each other so they might marry, have children, and link their families together forever.

"No, no," Megan's tone was impatient. "Two blocks away from you. A new family just moved in."

"Brand new?" Susan twirled the phone cord around her finger and held her breath.

"Brand new. Not from any of the New Havens. We can tell from their tags. You must head over there and see what you can find out. They've just begun to unload their truck!"

"I will, I will! Are they nice? What are they like?" Susan prattled on, too excited to care.

"Oh, they seem nice. Husband, pretty wife, and two small children. Remember when we were young and used to bring our kids to the park? That young."

"And they've been living on the outside all this time?" Susan asked. She couldn't imagine living on the outside with small children, always looking over her back to make sure the New Haven police hadn't caught their scent. How could anyone eat or sleep under those conditions?

"Isn't it delish? You have to find out more. See what it's been like for them. We have *got* to know. Lawrence Stark will kill for this kind of information, especially about someone so close to you, dear."

"Megan," Susan hissed, holding the receiver close to her mouth. She spun, as if to hide her conversation from an unseen watcher. "Don't tell me that you've been talking to Lawrence Stark?"

"Well…"

"Do not *well* me, young lady! You know very well that all those uprisings are his fault. I saw talk of his protests today in the paper. You're going to get yourself in hot water if you keep this up. Promise me you'll keep your distance."

Megan sighed, "Susan—"

"Promise me," she insisted with a stomp of her foot.

"Fine, fine, I promise, but only after you go and greet the family. We can meet at Pete's Soda Jerk this afternoon."

Susan glanced at her watch. "What time? Remember, I have to have dinner on the table by six."

"Three P.M. Let's synchronize our watches."

Chapter Three

Susan baked half a dozen blueberry and coffee cake muffins. Each topped with crusted sugar and cinnamon crumble. Their sweet smell carried through the house and despite her diet plans, Susan found herself munching on crumb topping.

She crafted a perfect welcome basket filled with blue and white plaid napkins and the muffins nestled safely inside. She tucked a few pamphlets she made up years ago that explained the rationing system, and a hand-drawn map of New Haven 56. In the back she tucked the drive-in schedule of movies for the month and a coupon book to her husband's restaurant.

She wrapped the handle in a blue bow and set off in her sedan. While Megan hadn't given her address, it wasn't hard to find. Other residents loitered a few blocks away. Huddled together they talked out of their corner of their mouths, buzzing with excitement.

In the small driveway of the two-story white house was a van. Three movers in brown uniforms bustled with cardboard boxes full of items from the starting package provided by New Haven 56.

Susan parked along the curb and after a check on her hair, stepped out with basket in hand. The lawn was still long, and there were dead stems in a pot that once had been beautiful flowers. This place needed a lot of work.

Who had lived here before? When Susan remembered, she shuddered.

With a deep breath, she rang the doorbell and waited with a pitch perfect smile.

A woman answered, dressed in a simple checkered dress. Her eyes were pale blue and hidden behind a pair of horn-rimmed glasses. "Yes?" Her voice was a whisper, and Susan could see her eyes were glassy, her cheeks flushed, and her hands quivered slightly.

Susan offered her new neighbor a grand smile. "Susan Monroe, and I've come to welcome you to the neighborhood. I hope you like muffins." Susan held the basket out.

"Diane." Her eyes studied the basket before her hands took it. "That's…very kind of you."

Susan clasped her hands in front of her. "Well, I know how stressful a move to a new city can be on you and especially the children. You'll have to make sure they're okay with the process, won't you?"

Diane nodded, tears glistening in her eyes.

"New job? Is that why you moved here?"

Startled, Diane blinked her eyes. "Moved here? *Moved here*? Don't you know? Don't you know what this place is?"

Susan's smile stretched like an elastic band and her heartbeat quickened. "Of course I do. It's a great community. We have friends, families, jobs. Every weekend there's a sock hop downtown. Our children can grow, thrive. So now you go on and tell me, why did you move here?"

Diane swallowed, glancing down. "So my children could grow up safe."

Susan squeezed the woman's wrist. She wore the same bracelet that Susan wore, that they all wore. The one that kept the dragon inside. "Why don't you invite me inside and I can start to show you the ropes, okay? I'll explain a few things to you. Trust me, there's a lot of misinformation out there."

"I could put on some water for tea." Diane said and pattered inside, leaving Susan to step in and close the door behind her.

Susan adjusted her skirt and heard the sound of playing coming from the living room. Peeking her head around the corner, she saw a sofa and furnishings already in place, with cardboard boxes stacked against the wall. The two boys playing on the beige rug were four and five, or thereabouts. Cute children each had thick blond hair, with bracelets on their wrists. Around their necks, Susan saw the red marks.

She gulped down a quick breath of air. How horrid the process was, just horrid.

Susan clicked down the hall and found the kitchen. Diane sat at the table beside a window that overlooked a small cramped yard. If it was big enough for a barbecue grill, Susan would've been surprised. Diane and her husband were quiet, holding each other's hands while their eyes were somewhere else. Susan knew what it was like. She knew exactly what they were going through.

She sat beside them and outreached her hand on top of theirs. "It'll be all right." Susan said softly. "You'll get through this fine. In a few weeks, you'll begin to feel better, fit in."

The husband glanced at Susan for the first time. His deep brown eyes held sadness she could feel. "We were living in Ohio. The kids just started school. We weren't hurting anyone."

Susan knew. She understood. "This is the way things are. It can be a good life, if you accept it."

"And if we don't?" He asked quietly, angrily.

"You'll go away," Susan said. "And those children, those beautiful children will grow up without a father. If they grow up at all."

He squeezed his eyes shut.

"Will the tea be ready soon?" Susan asked.

Diane nodded. "It should be in a minute."

"Good," Susan patted her knee with a big smile. "We'll sit over muffins and you can tell me about your new job. And I'll tell you all about my big Tupperware party next week. Wouldn't it be nice to get out and meet some of your neighbors?"

***

Susan sat outside at Jack's Soda Jerk with two malt shakes. It was nearly three in the afternoon.

As she waited for Megan, she primped her hair and took a sip of her beverage. She drank it slowly; the money Jeff gave her each month to spend on frivolous things was nearly depleted. In a few days, it would be a new month and she could splurge again. Susan thought a nice tube of lipstick might be nice, or maybe new pantyhose.

Many people were out that day and Susan smiled at a few she knew. Across the street, at the park, a few boys flew kites and some older boys busied themselves with hula hoops. Susan remembered being young, being able to spin her hips like that. She loved life, all stages of it, and New Haven 56 was a great place to live. Maybe how she got there wasn't so great, but after so many years, Susan was grateful for the chance to be normal, to get married, and have wonderful children.

Glancing up past her table's umbrella, Susan could see the two blues of the day's sky. One was a natural soft blue with gentle clouds drifting past. Below that a darker, ominous blue dome pulsated in static intervals, keeping New Haven safe in its bubble. Even when Susan could manage to forget what she was, that damn bubble always reminded her. She sighed and heard the quick steps of someone in woman's pumps.

Megan was a tall and scrawny woman with long red hair. Today it was pushed back with a white headband, and her makeup choices seemed a bit dramatic for running simple errands. She sat and sipped her drink. "So, so, tell me everything!"

"It's good to see you too, sweetheart." Susan smirked.

Megan sighed. "All right, all right, hello, hello. Now tell me." She waved her fingers in the air as if pushing off a mysterious uninvited guest.

"You promise you're not going to tell Lawrence Stark?"

"I…give you my word." Megan held up her hand. "Girl Scouts' honor, darling."

"And I can trust you this time?" Susan pursed her lips and her fingernails twitted against the glass counter top.

"What is 'this time' nonsense? When have I ever led you astray?"

"How about that PTA meeting last year? You told me everyone was going to be critiquing Mr. Banks."

Megan put a hand to her mouth and giggled. "Well, you were spot-on with everything you said."

"Hmpf." Susan crossed her arms. She pressed her lips together, but her eyes sparkled with mischief.

"I *promise*." Megan patted her hand. "Just tell me, what are they like?"

"Sad and afraid." Susan's face darkened as she thought about the Franklins and their small children. "He is going to work in the grocery market and she is going to be working mother's hours at the Templeton Pharmacy."

"Most do start out there." Megan rolled the straw through her fingers absently. "And they were…nice?"

Susan nodded. "I invited them to my party next week."

Megan grinned. "Wonderful! I love new people to interrogate, I mean, be *friends* with."

"Their children are small and I don't think they are old enough to know the significance of this place, at least not yet. But they were well-behaved. They said 'please' and 'thank you' when I gave them a muffin."

"Oh, that's nice. So many children are not brought up properly these days at all, you know?"

"Certainly, we're in agreement. It used to be the norm, when our two were small." Susan sighed. "Anyway, you were right. The children have the marks on them."

Megan sighed. "Oh, poor things. Poor poor things."

Susan cleared her throat. "And they brought news of the outside, but you must promise, promise not to tell!"

Megan nodded several times, her eyes going wide with curiosity. "I do, I do. I won't even tell my George!"

"Your dog doesn't exactly have loose lips, Megan."

"No, but I do tell him most everything and who knows what he barks to the neighbors."

Susan giggled. "They were living in Ohio, in a small suburb of Cincinnati."

"Like that WKRP show? Oh, nice! What was it like? Were all the buildings destroyed? Are they living in ruins?"

Susan's eyes darkened. "No," she said quietly. "Life is good. I guess economically things are tough. More people live in apartment buildings than homes."

Megan scrunched up her nose. "Apartment buildings?"

Susan nodded. "I know. Can you imagine it?"

"But they had freedom." Megan pushed on. She pointed her finger at Susan. "They could go anywhere they wanted."

She leaned in and whispered, her eyes checking for anyone who might overhear. "Looking over their shoulder, pretending to be something they're not the entire time. That's no way to live."

"And that's not what we're doing?" Megan's posture became rigid.

"Where is this coming from? We live happy content lives."

"In a bubble."

Defiance shone through her face. "I like our bubble. New Haven is the perfect place to live and raise a family." Susan's face flushed. Her fingers fumbled with the clasp of her purse and searched its content for a compact mirror.

"Look at you, Susan. You can't even talk about it without getting upset."

Susan was flustered and the words left her mouth with a hefty dose of spit. "Well, you're the one who brought it up. It's not like, not like you *agree* with Lawrence Stark is it? Tell me you haven't joined his cause."

"It's not just his cause," Megan whispered, leaning across the table. "It's the cause of all of us. Most people just refuse to believe we're anything but *human*."

Susan squeaked and dropped her mirror. "I am too. I am too! I bake, I clean, I—I take care of the children. What's more normal than that?"

"Mutant. That's what they call us." Megan's eyes narrowed. "And what's wrong with being something more? Maybe they're the ones that should be sequestered and we should be running the show!"

Megan's voice reached a shrill squeak and other people took notice. Other patrons were no longer talking but staring and across the street children had stopped playing with their toys.

Susan tried to force a laugh, sipping her float but she couldn't swallow, it wouldn't go down. "You're creating a spectacle. I think you better just tone it down."

"Tone it down? Isn't that what we've been doing for thirty years? You had it good. Your parents were brought here with you, but mine were *killed* upon capture and for what? Because they didn't want to be imprisoned here, in this perfect community? And what happened to those officers that did it? Nothing. All they had to do, I bet, was file a report!"

Susan opened her mouth to reply, but froze in silence as three armed police officers surrounded their table.

She hadn't seen them coming, had barely heard any footsteps at all. Each held an electric cattle prod in their hand. From the blue electrode tip, it was obvious they were charged. Their uniforms were black and on their head they wore hats with visors. They looked so normal, so mainstream, but Susan knew different.

They hadn't done anything wrong. Why couldn't they just be left alone to finish their drinks? But their cold eyes weren't on her. They were on Megan. One of the men grabbed her roughly by the arm. "You'll need to come with us, Ms. Myers."

How was it they just knew her name? Susan wondered and realized they probably could read it off their tracking bracelets.

"I haven't done anything wrong." Megan insisted, tugging, but the large man with the scary dead eyes only strengthened his grip. "Ow," she whined. "You're hurting me. Stop it."

"Has she been upsetting you, Mrs. Monroe?" one of the other officers asked her softly. "You look a bit pale, even for one of you."

Susan shook her head, but unable to speak as tears formed in the corner of her eyes. She wanted to say something, but her heart was pounding so fast she felt almost faint. After a moment she cleared her throat. "We were just having floats and…you know how women get at their time of the month."

Megan's eyes narrowed. "Susan!"

Susan gulped back her fear, her betrayal, and glanced at her feet.

"We'll take care of her." The officer forced Megan to her feet and her chair tumbled backwards. Everyone watched as he forced her arms behind her back.

"Let me go! Susan, tell them I'm all right. Tell them I'm not upset."

But she was upset. So upset. And Susan couldn't will herself to speak. She didn't want to be dragged away too.

Megan's eyes widened. "Susan!"

"You have no rights, you damn dragon." The officer reached for the handle of his electric rod.

Susan whipped her head toward the window of the sofa jerk, but could hear her friend scream. To keep her from sobbing, she bit her lip. The reflection in the glass showed everything. The electrical shock morphed Megan's skin from human peach to a glowing blue. Large wings flapped beneath her clothes. The charge of the weapon flowed through her limbs, lighting up her dragon skeleton. Back arched and talons splayed, her flailing body assaulted the ground below.

Megan's form changed and a stoned look crept over her face. Her expression was still; her eyes were sunken with fatigue. It took two officers to force her to walk toward the paddy wagon and another to shove her into the back.

Susan couldn't do anything. She was too afraid to speak, move, or even think how much she would miss her friend. Around her, everyone went back to what they were doing; like a TV show interrupted, life in New Haven 56 now resumed its regular programming. Barely an eye blinked out of place. But for Susan it wasn't so easy.

She wondered: If the police could know where they were at all times, what kept them from reading their minds, too?

Chapter Four

May 17th, Wednesday Morning
The Reynolds Home: 340 Gumdrop Avenue

"Have you seen my navy socks?" Travis asked his wife. He pulled open the usual drawer, but it lay barren.

"Your socks?" Alice shot him a look of exasperation, crossing her arms. "We are in the middle of an important discussion and you want me to tell you about your socks?"

"I can't go to work in bare toes, Al." Travis sighed, lifting the bedspread to look beneath it. With a creak in his back, he stretched down and pulled out a linty pair. A hearty shake caused a lint snowfall. "These will do."

Alice's eyes penetrated through him amid her silence. Couldn't she just stop judging him so things could go back to how they used to be?

"Are you through putting on your *socks*?" She said the word with disgust.

"I have two feet. One to go." Travis cringed. He didn't know why he said these things, why he egged her on, but he did. Day after day.

"Well, far be it for me to let your toes go naked while I...I go stark raving mad!" Her toes dug into the carpet, clawing at the floor underneath.

Huffing, her cheeks turning bright red. Her lips were pulled into a tight line and that vein on the side of her head pulsated as it always did when she was angry. Travis tried to kiss her cheek, but she reared back. Damn woman. He was trying to offer her the olive branch she wanted. Why did he keep trying if all Alice did was pull away?

"I want out." She whispered, her manic eyes searching his. "I don't want out next year, or next month. I want out now."

Travis shook his head, rubbing her arms. "Honey, I'm the chief of the New Haven police. I can't just—"

"Your *job?*" She hissed. "Is it more important than me, your daughter? Travis, we've been strung up in this damn bubble for over ten years. Barely get word from my parents. Wendy is forced to *socialize* and go to school with those *things*. I want to see the ocean. I want to see a real skyline. I want to be around real people again without wondering if they're going to puncture me and liquefy my organs!"

Travis sighed. "You know they don't do that anymore."

"That's not the point of this discussion and you know it! I'm sick and tired of being sick and tired of this place. Can't we just go?" Alice touched his arm. It made his skin tingle like those early days when they dated, when everything was new. "Anywhere. New York, Mexico. I'll even go to the Canada Territory if that's what you want. We're missing the best years of our life. Please."

Travis took her face in his hands. His chin quivered and when their eyes connected he saw love behind her rigid expression. Her lips puckered and he wanted nothing more than to kiss them. "Soon."

Alice pushed him away. "You've been saying that for years. Year after year. When Wendy turned, twelve, and then sixteen. She's going to graduate high school this year and if we're not careful, we'll never see her again."

Travis stroked her arms even as she turned her head away. "This job is important. You know that. But honey, it's not as important as you."

"You say it, but I just don't believe you. Haven't," her voice shuddered, "in a long time." Gulping back tears, Alice left, like she always did. Travis knew better than to chase after her. Instead his eyes cast around the room, glancing at all the memories that were there; the wedding photos, the bed where they used to make love.

It would happen again. Every few years Alice went through a bout of cabin fever, from being stuck in New Haven 52 and now 56. It always passed, but this time it was just a little bit worse than usual. *Worse than usual.* But there was work to be done and despite what he said, Travis wasn't sure he'd ever be ready to leave.

He didn't think so. It was his calling, his passion. Shapeshifters were monsters, but they were people too. He couldn't turn his back on them.

Travis slipped on his black jacket with the emblem for the police office on the back. Holstering his weapon, he sauntered down the stairs in time to hear the front door slam.

His home was the spitting image of the other two bedroom homes in New Haven, and there was nothing miraculous in his kitchen except for his daughter.

Wendy sat at the counter, perched on a barstool while she ate some cereal and was bent over some schoolbooks. There was a small dribble of milk on her notebook cover as she scribbled down some last-minute assignment. Travis watched her as he poured his own coffee. Always a pretty girl, she had dark hair and accented green eyes. Her smile always lit up his heart, but these days those smiles were few and far between.

Among the mutants, she stuck out in her tight jeans and loose sweaters. There was a time where she wore nice clothes, nearly as nice as a shifter, but that stopped months ago. Travis didn't understand why, but thought his fights with her mother might be part of it.

He placed his dark mug on the counter and leaned across to look at his daughter. Slowly she looked up and broke out into a wide grin. "Hi, Daddy," she said with a slight laugh to her voice. It made him feel like a fool for worrying. She'd come to him if something were really wrong.

"Need a ride to school?"

"No, thanks," Wendy smirked. "Being the chief of police's daughter makes you a big enough outcast."

"I'm not out to hurt them, you know," Travis said. "Just need to make sure they all live by the same rules. Same standards."

"And as long as they stay within those bounds, everyone will be fine," Wendy recited from memory, from old pep talks. His girl always paid attention and she'd always be his girl even after she was done being a schoolgirl. He wanted to tell her that. He wanted her to always know, but Travis knew teenage girls didn't need their dads smothering them.

"Still scares them, though."

Travis nodded and stood up straight with a sigh. "Guess that can't be changed. I'll clean your bowl if you need to head along."

"Thanks, Daddy." She packed up her backpack. When she spoke again her voice was quiet and unsteady. "Everything okay with you and Mom?"

"Sure." Even for a police officer he was surprised how effortlessly the lie came. "Just a few spats. Nothing to worry about."

"Really?" Her eyes searched him. They were trusting.

"Really," Travis said with a warm smile. He wasn't sure at first if she bought it, but the broad grin that broke across her face proved she did. She threw her arms around his neck and kissed his cheek. A feeling of warmth and love only Wendy could make him feel, flowed through him.

He squeezed her for just a moment, kissing the top of her head. "Now head off, munchkin. Don't be late."

Wendy waved goodbye and Travis watched her go. Then frowned. She appeared to him to be gaining weight, but she hardly ate any of her breakfast. Travis hoped his girl wasn't sick, but it wasn't exactly a subject you could broach with your daughter. Any suggestion that she was gaining weight might cause an immediate purchase of diet pills.

***

Travis arrived at the police Outpost just past ten in the morning. One of the perks in being the chief of police was being able to arrive later every once in a while. From time to time he allowed himself the luxury. He picked up a cup of coffee from the donut shop on the corner of Main Street. The service people had been so afraid of him that they tried to give it to him on the house, but he left behind a few Haven bills and coins anyway.

He knew the mutants needed the money and he got no joy with watching them suffer and struggle. Sure, the New Haven system had its detractors, its critics, but Travis wasn't an organization. He was just a person trying to do a job the best he knew how, and that meant making sure the dragon shifters lived their lives out in harmony, away from prying eyes.

The Outpost was just beyond the inner gates of New Haven 56. While the city was the perfect small town from a 1950s postcard, the Outpost was clinical and functional. There were several brick rectangle buildings with multiple floors in the complex. Each one had its purpose and Travis headed toward the largest. His office was on the ground floor.

At the steel door, he swiped his badge to unlock it and headed inside. A receptionist in a simple navy uniform gave him a slight distracted glance as she typed at her computer terminal. Travis walked down a narrow hallway and swiped his badge at another steel door.

It gave him access to the surveillance and intelligence operations. Those rooms were lined with flat panel screens that projected images from every corner of town. Travis joined two officers who sat, unblinking, as they studied the screens.

"Anything?"

"Everything's quiet today, Chief." Thompson was a good officer who never let Travis down, which was why he saw to it that the man followed him from Outpost to Outpost.

Travis nodded. "Keep up the good work," he grunted, and continued on his way. The room across the hall was intelligence. Several officers listened to phone calls and private conversations picked up on the grid. While everything was recorded, only certain words would trigger red flags.

His interest piqued, he pulled open the door to the room. Patience wasn't his strong suit, but he waited for the officer to take his headset off. "Chief, we picked up Lawrence Stark's name being used twice in the same home. Once in the kitchen, once on the phone."

"Name?" Travis asked.

Marc glanced down at his screen. "Jeff and Susan Monroe."

"Put a tail on them." Travis sipped his coffee and continued on. The door behind him latched with a metallic boom.

His office was small, with no windows and barely enough space for his desk and computer station. Travis didn't mind much. He spent few hours in there, and more out with his men or patrolling the town. His chair was comfortable as he stretched in it and sipped the remainder of his coffee.

When it was empty, he chucked it across the room. It landed softly into the wire wastepaper basket. Travis grinned.

If the world had been different, maybe he would have gone on to be an NBA star.

Oh, well. The world, for all its changes, still wasn't a bad place to be. Travis kind of enjoyed it and truth be told, didn't mind the shifters half as much as he pretended.

***

Travis was on the docking bay inspecting ration food deliveries when his walkie-talkie crackled. "Go, Nancy."

"Ms. Seers and her men are here."

He cursed under his breath. "They weren't due for another oh-two-hundred."

"I know, Chief." Nancy's voice strained. "But they showed up early and they have papers signed by justice."

"Okay, okay," Travis glanced at his watch. If they timed this wrong… "I'll be there. Send Walt down here to finish the inspections."

"Yes, Chief."

"Over and out." Travis sighed and handed his clipboard to the truck driver. "You're cleared. Drive on through to the gates toward the city."

The driver snorted. "Good luck."

"I'm gonna need it," Travis muttered.

***

The waiting area for visitors in Outpost was pleasant, but stark of windows and ambiance. Travis kept it that way for a reason.

If you made people too comfortable they'd want to stay, and the type of people that visited the New Haven police weren't the type he wanted to hang out all day. Most days he wished they'd just let him get back to his damn job.

Rebecca wasn't any ugly woman. Quite the contrary. The skirt she wore hugged her shapely hips and her hair was soft, parted to the side. Her face was pleasant, almost always smiling, and if the circumstances of their relationship were different…well, he'd have a lot to confess to his wife for. She stood, along with two men in pressed suits, as he reached for a handshake.

The visitor pass pinned to her label jutted left and right. "Chief Reynolds, I hope we didn't come at a bad time."

"Of course not." Both of them were lying, but there was no harm in a few pleasantries. "I trust you had a good journey this time."

"Tip top," Rebecca admitted. "We have a list of shifters we'd like to visit on this trip. Shouldn't take more than half a day, if your escorts would be so kind."

The man to the left, the one who was always shifty and studying Travis as if he didn't approve of the chief, handed him a list of names. Travis studied it. "Hmpf. I'll see to it, if you'll wait here."

Her face twitched. "So soon? Usually you make us wait hours and act like bringing us sandwiches breaks some unconstitutional law."

"Just trying to cooperate."

"What would make this time so different?" Travis waved his hand, but Rebecca smiled smugly. "Ahh, the Justice

Department talked to you, didn't they? Maybe finally threatened to take away your badge if you didn't cooperate with the court's decisions." She clasped her hands in front of her. "Must feel real good, to be taken down a few notches."

Travis wagged his finger at her. "Now, you wait here, Rebecca. I do a good job of running this police force. The damn shapeshifters, they live a better life in here than most Americans do out there. You know that. I just need to make sure everything is orderly."

Rebecca expelled a gasp. "I don't know that for a fact, do I? Some barely have enough food to make it from month to month and most rarely get any say in what type of jobs they have. There is no room for growth. Their rights—"

"—were stripped decades ago by your precious justice system. If you don't like what you see, don't blame me. I just enforce what they tell me to."

Her cheeks reddened, and Travis fed off it. Rebecca continued, "I, and the rest of the Dragons Rights and Protection Commission, am working on changing that. If I see that one of them is mistreated under your watch, I'll make sure the Senate and Congress hear about this."

"They're not convened right now."

"I'll make them," Rebecca said hotly, her nose flaring.

Travis raised his eyebrows and shook his head. "Look, it's probably good that a lady like you is around to make sure the police don't take liberties, but you're not going to change anything. Americans will never be in favor of shifters being reintroduced into society. This is the best answer we've got.

The alternative is to just exterminate them like the pests they are."

His words were harsh, harsher than he meant. Travis didn't usually speak about the shifters that way, but definitely felt there was truth in his words. It made him uncomfortable as he tried to swallow it back as he read the disgust on Rebecca's face.

"I'll get you an escort." Travis said and left the waiting room. He glanced at the list once the door closed behind him. One of the last names on the list was familiar, from that morning. Why did Rebecca want to meet with Jake Monroe?

Travis stopped an officer in the hall. "See if you can pull any tapes or security information on a Jake Monroe. Then, escort Rebecca and her staff on her interviews and inspection."

"Yes, Chief." The officer nodded. "Sir, patrol is already en route with an upriser."

They really were becoming more frequent, weren't they? Travis sighed. Just what he needed, more headaches. "Keep Rebecca away from the conditioning barrack, no matter what happens."

Chapter Five

New Haven High
100 School Way

    As soon as the yellow bus came to a stop, Wendy hopped off and pulled her earbuds free. She listened to music on her iPod so she didn't have to socialize. As she stepped off the bus with the other New Haven police kids, she cradled her books in front of her stomach.
    And searched the area.
    Throwing a glance over her shoulder, she looked for her friends Marsha and Steven. They spent their early childhood together in New Haven 52 until their parents were transferred together to the newest colony, New Haven 56. Wendy didn't mind much growing up with the dragons. In fact, most days she didn't really understand why they were different than she was. They acted a little weird, like people in the television shows she always watched, but other than that they were nice.
    Finally, she saw her friends and gave them a wave. Her face lit up when she saw them hustling toward her and they met over by the stairs that led to the school. "Hey, guys."
    Steve nodded, but was too cool to remove his shades. Wendy wasn't sure where he was looking, but it definitely

wasn't at her. His hair was a dark tousled black. He always wore a black jacket and a cocked fedora on his head sat to the side. "You guys do the homework for science class?"

Marsha was a pretty blonde whose tight shirts and miniskirts made her stand out against the parade of Donna Reed poodle skirts. She gave Wendy a knowing look. "Who has time to do homework, right? We're graduating in less than a month! Soon we'll be out of mutant-ville and we can go anywhere we want! I'm so going to New York to be a fashion designer!"

Steve leaned back against the rail, a toothpick twirling in his mouth. "I think it actually might be harder than that, darlin'. But more power to you, I say. I'm heading to the coast to check out some babes. I can't wait to see what the real world is like. I hate being stuck in this damn prison."

Wendy shook her head at them. "I think you might not graduate if you don't do the homework."

"Please!" Marsha exasperated. "They can't make me repeat this late in the game. Besides, my dad works in surveillance. If they did that to me, I'm sure he'd find something nasty on them and then they'd be sorry."

Wendy's jaw dropped. "Marsha, your dad can't abuse his power like that."

"It's not abusing." Marsha rolled her eyes.

"It's in the job description." Steve laughed at his own joke. "Oh, c'mon. Don't be so uptight all the time. I know, I know, you're the chief of police's daughter." He flipped his shades down to make eye contact so that when he rolled his eyes, Wendy could see it.

Angry, Wendy glanced away. "Sometimes, Steve, you make me wonder why I hang out with you at all. I guess I just feel like I should since I've known you my entire life."

"We're stuck together," he agreed. "The three of us, but the sentence is about to be pardoned. In just a few short months we'll be able to pretend this never happened."

Marsha squealed with delight, hugging her books close to her chest. "I can't wait! Finally be able to go shopping at some real stores and just not take what they send us."

"You do already, baby," Steve said, then cast a glance at Wendy. "You on the other hand look to be about vying for the Frump of the Year award."

"Steven!" Marsha narrowed her eyes at him and walloped him on the back of the head.

Wendy's shoulders hunched. He always had a way of making her feel inadequate and self-conscious. With friends like him…

"Be nice, or I'll look the other way when the mutants skin you alive," Marsha snorted. Wendy's heart raced and when her eyes met Marsha's her friends eyes softened.

"It's all right. We all know he was born without a nice bone in his body. See you in class."

"See you later?"

Her stomach rolled. "Later." Wendy skipped up the steps, mingled in with the shifters, and stepped into the hollowly lit hallways. She headed toward her locker and tried to ignore all of the looks that the others gave her, even the teachers. Being the daughter of Travis Reynolds was like being God; everywhere she went, people parted for her to get out of her way. When she was little, Wendy thought it was great. What a power trip it had been.

Now it just made her feel like she stuck out, like everyone was watching her. It wasn't paranoia, Wendy thought as she glanced up at the video cameras in the corners of each hallway. People were watching her.

With a sigh, she stopped at her locker to get a book. When she slammed the door, Jake Monroe was there.

Wendy's heart skipped a beat as she looked into his eyes. They were haunted, trying to read her. She wanted to ask him to, but she couldn't. Not out loud. If anyone where to suspect what they were doing, she'd be expelled. And for Jake, it would probably be worse. "Hey," she said softly, trying to control the tremor in her voice.

His hey was more nonchalant, almost casual. She wondered how he managed to always seem so aloof and in control. Wasn't he nervous? Didn't he care? Course, he wasn't the one that had to carry it around, pretend everything was normal. Wendy was the one who had to wonder if her parents noticed, and she was running out of ways to hide it. "I know yesterday you had to go to the nurse, so I thought you might want to copy my notes."

"Sure, that's nice of you."

For a moment, Jake stood closer to her and the smell of his cologne hit her. It wasn't potent; it was light and airy, and reminded her of those nights in the field where no cameras could reach. He held out his notebook and Wendy took it, adding it to her stack.

"I'll give it back to you before third period." She smiled.

Jake did too, backing up a step. Their eyes met and her heart felt as if it were plummeting to her toes before racing back up. "Bye." He said quietly before he turned around and headed toward his group of friends, all on the football team and all wearing the same jacket.

"Bye." Wendy whispered, watching him and thought he was different than the rest. There was a seriousness, an intelligence there wasn't in the others. That's why he was special, that was why she liked him. When he was around, Wendy felt calm and she saw the effect he had on others.

She excused herself to the bathroom. Along the vanity stalls, several girls primped their perfect hairdos and reapplied their lipstick. They giggled loudly, talking with grand hand gestures about boys, bake sales, and their families. Wendy snuck past them, hoping to avoid being recognized, and rushed into one of the stalls. She placed her books down on the back of the toilet and flipped open Jake's notebook.

Each stroke was soft and elegant, as if prepared by an expert calligrapher, which was why her heart was soothed even as she read his note. To Wendy it felt as if he were there and folding her into his warm embrace.

Oakland field tonight at 8:45pm. Pack a bag. Xxoo

She smiled at the simple representation of kisses and hugs, but she couldn't let the note be found by anyone. Wendy flushed the toilet to mask the sound of her ripping the paper, then wrapped the pieces in toilet paper and flushed them down again. Then checked to make sure that no stray bits ended up on the floor.

As she did, Wendy was overcome with a wave of nerves and nausea. Bending over her, she gripped the toilet as her mouth opened. The loud buzz of the bell rang through the bathroom and was followed with the sounds of girls zipping up their makeup kits. The smell of hairspray wafted through the stall, worsening her nausea. The bell meant it was nine, which also meant her bout of sickness was right on time. As it had been for the last seven months.

Wendy groaned and her body temperature jumped as a spasm contracted in her stomach. It rolled up her body, clenching and releasing her throat, and a stream of vomit spilled from her mouth. She spat, tears streaming down her face as her body wretched like on an out-of-control rollercoaster.

Her left hand clutched at her stomach as the heaving subsided. It wasn't flat against her sweater.

Her belly was round.

***

She tried to pretend that nothing was wrong, but it was getting harder now she was nearly in her third trimester.

She was still sick as a dog. Her breasts ached and her lower back was in constant pain from the growing fetus. Most days, it took a constant effort not to waddle side to side. Lucky for her, her stomach wasn't that big yet, but it would be soon. In three months, she would have a baby.

It was getting harder to hide.

At first it sounded so foreign, so horrible, but now Wendy steeled herself to the fact that was going to be a mother to a shapeshifter. A dragon. A mutant grew inside of her.

How had it happened? Well, she knew how, but it wasn't possible. She was perfectly human, a normal teenage girl, and the only boy she had ever been with was a mutant dragon. All the stories she heard made it sound impossible. Shifters couldn't mate with humans. They weren't human anymore.

Wendy thought at first it would be like one of those TV movies from back in the old days when they still made movies. She, the teenage girl, would tell her boyfriend—for lack of a better word—that she was pregnant. He would suddenly turn harsh, angry, and look at her with cold eyes and say, well it can't be mine. Wendy probably even would have understood, given the circumstances, but he didn't. But Jake didn't do that.

Part of her wished that he did.

Was there some part of her that wasn't normal? Was she a freak? How could she be pregnant with a dragon kin? Wendy's eyes filled with tears as she thought about her mother finding out.

Her mother was always going on about how horrible their life was, how sorry she was that Wendy had to go to school with the shifters. If Mom found out, Wendy was sure they'd just get rid of her, push her out of New Haven for good. Even worse, maybe they'd make her abort it. Maybe that's what should have happened, maybe that would have been best for her life. But for some reason Wendy didn't want to.

Wendy bit her lip, studying her textbooks, and silent tears fell from her eyes. She lowered her head, to keep anyone from noticing how upset she was. They were supposed to be taking a test, but she hadn't even finished writing her name on top of the paper yet. What was she supposed to do? Take a stupid pop quiz like any of that would matter once everyone figured out what was growing inside of her?

Wendy was startled by a knock at the classroom door, peering up she saw two uniformed men with someone she recognized from her dad's office. They addressed her teacher. "We would like a word with Jake Monroe, please."

Her stomach tightened and a new feeling of panic rose in her throat. Jake collected his books and when he walked past her desk, they tried not to look at each other. Wendy glanced down, her pulse elevated and beads of sweat formed on her brow. It'll be okay, she told herself over and over. Everything will be fine. They just want a few words with him. He's not going away. He's not.

Angry, frightened hot tears clung to her eyes and her chest quivered under the pressure of her breath. Wendy hadn't realized anyone noticed, not until she found a hand on her shoulder. Unable to look up, she gripped her pencil in one hand and the edge of her desk in the other. There was the soft squeak of loafers as her teacher, Mr. Doubosh, squatted beside her. "Wendy, what's the matter? Would you like a pass to the school's nurse?"

She shook her head, unable to speak, but the rise of vomit in her throat was coming hard and fast. She gagged, put her hand over her mouth. Unable to control it any longer she bent quickly and vomited all over Mr. Doubosh's expensive shoes.

She saw the horror on the kids' faces, saw some break out in mocking smiles. Couldn't it all fade away? Couldn't this all be nothing but a bad dream?

***

Nurse Chapel was an older black woman with silver curls and a soft smile. When Wendy was sent down to see her, she made her lay down in a secluded area with a curtain drawn around her. In the dark, Wendy began to feel better and the cold compress against her neck was certainly helping. But when the nurse stuck her head in, she pretended to be asleep, curled on her side.

"Child, if you think this game is going to work on me, I'd like to inform you I've had two of my own, who went on to have two of their own. I'm familiar with all the tricks and gimmicks you kids can dish out."

Wendy scowled, but refused to move or roll over.

The nurse sighed. "Have it your way. I'm leaving a few hard candies on the counter here for you. It should help calm your nerves and your morning sickness."

Wendy's eyes fluttered open and her heart skipped a beat. She drew a quick breath and held it.

"That caught your attention, didn't it? You probably take me for an old shifters fool, don't you? I know there's little for humans to do in a place like this, but I'd at least think the chief of police's daughter would be a bit more careful."

She went on. "You've been here a lot in the recent months, Wendy. If you're having this tough a time, you should see a doctor. Have you told your parents yet?"

Wendy squeezed her eyes shut. *Please, just go away!*

"You're no child anymore. Eighteen and soon to be graduated. You know this is serious. You and your baby need prenatal care. I've put a call in to your mother. She's going to come pick you up and take you home."

"What!" Wendy screamed, rolling to face the nurse. She pushed herself up in a seated position and nearly toppled over as dizziness overcame her. The nurse braced her arm. "You told my mother! How could you? What about my right to privacy?"

"Child, no one in New Haven has a right to privacy. You know that. Besides, I didn't tell your mother. That's your job."

Wendy shook her head, new frightful tears in her eyes. This couldn't be happening. This was going to ruin everything! Her mouth hung open and she stared at the nurse. "You...stupid bitch." She whispered, sobbing with a hand over her face.

The nurse sighed. "I take no comfort in seeing you like this, but someone has to look out for you. I'll give you a moment to yourself, before your mother shows up." She patted Wendy's hand.

Wendy jerked it away. "Get out!" Her eyes raged with fire and drilled holes into the back of the woman's head as she left the room. Wendy thrashed, kicked her feet, and knew nothing would be the same every again.

Chapter Six

The East Coast
New Haven 56 Project

New Haven 56 was a quiet suburb of perfected Americana encapsulated inside a bright shining bubble of protective magic and light.

A zoo. An expensive zoo for monster mutants wearing dresses and fine pressed slacks.

Each New Haven was the mirror of the last, except for minor improvements. Each had its own Main Street, the ice cream parlor on Broadway, and the moving picture theater on Third. There were no skyscrapers, malls, or towering apartment buildings. Houses in New Haven 55 were the exact replicas of homes in New Haven 1, right down to the paint chips and the modern plush carpets.

The music and cars appeared transplanted from a period piece drama about Buddy Holly, jukeboxes, and sock hops. Why shifters preferred suburbia over large cities, and why this time period appealed to them, was unknown. But it kept them as docile as housebroken pets.

Jenna tinkered with her handheld phone, playing an old-fashioned game called First Person Shooter. Cute 2-D games

like that were long replaced by virtual 3-D reality, but Jenna was a sucker for the classics and liked cooperative play across the Internet best.

Glancing up for a moment, she saw there were still three cargo vans in front of them at New Haven 56's checkpoint. Jenna returned to her game and knew that once they cleared the bubble, Internet access would be restricted to local network only.

Shifters might have been allowed to live, but their movements and freedoms were restricted. A small price to pay for life, and not one she'd afford them if given the option.

Her team did good work though. They had their problems, but had been together for ten years. Before things went bad they were considered the highest-ranking investigation team in all of New Haven, running covert assignments across the U.S., some in Europe. What they did now was laughable and an embarrassment.

Only Jenna was to blame. Why they stuck with her after how she treated them was a mystery, but she was glad they did.

Dirk snapped his bubble gum while staring down at his phone. "Flank right. Frank right!" He signed. "Damn, Jen."

Jenna smirked. "Oops. Sorry about that grenade, but we got the flag."

Jameson glanced up to make sure traffic hadn't advanced before returning to his phone. "Even in a game she's ready to sacrifice you for the greater good of the team."

"Har-har."

Jenna sighed and stretched out her shoulders. "I hate being cooped up in this van. Oh, no offense, Jameson."

"It ain't the Ritz, I know."

"What is these days?" Dirk asked. "The shifters have it better than we do most of the time. They get all the squares, jobs where they earn fake money, and even drive-ins. They don't know how good they have it here."

"They still make the cracker," Jenna said.

Jameson gave a stilted laugh and rolled the van forward a few inches. "Perfect for my grandma's homemade chicken soup."

His grandma did make the best. "Do you think all the stories she told us are true? Was she really there the night it happened?"

"Can't see why she'd lie. You know she was a child actress before it hit."

Dirk snorted. "Just be glad she wasn't a few years older or we'd be having this conversation with an unfertilized egg."

Jenna chuckled. Her ears picked up movement from the back of the van. She leaned backwards and banged her fist against the wall. "Be still in there or I'll make you, you get me!"

"I just wish they'd put the movie industry back together already. I'm tired of re-runs."

"If only the virus hit before the Hannah Montana show."

"It might have hit *because* of the Hannah Montana show." Dirk corrected.

Jenna fought against the urge to laugh. "Well I hear webisodes across the net are making a comeback. They're a breath of fresh air over those Bollywood productions we're forced to watch."

"Hey," Jameson said with offense. "Those are good. The girls are hot. Besides we don't have much choice. They're the only place left with an entertainment industry."

"We kinda lucked out though. Look what happen to Japan."

Jenna nodded, remembering stories she read how electronics used to be made there. Now it was nothing but a graveyard. Their obsession with plastic surgery did them in. Europe fared better and now former third world countries were racing to succeed Japan. Death and despair were always good motivators.

In front of them were several armed guards in matching black uniforms. The van rolled through the blue-hued magical bubble that kept the shifters imprisoned as much as it protected them from the humans that wanted to kill them. Jameson rolled down his window and stuck his badge outside for the officer to see.

"Officer Rick Jameson," he said. "We're bringing in seven captures. Radioed ahead about four hours ago."

Frank took the ID and compared it to the list on his clipboard. Some officers would use their PDA or cell phone to store the list, but Frank was older and didn't rely on technology as a golden rule. His flashlight shined on the pad and through the constant stream of light a soft trickle of rain could be seen. "You guys been busy." He handed his badge back to Jameson and peeked around the corner of his rolled down window. His long mustache flapped when he talked.

He shined his light into Dirk's face first and then Jenna's. "Just want to make sure you have no stowaways."

"Why would I do that?" Jenna asked dryly.

"Wouldn't be the first time you did something I couldn't understand." Frank gave them a grin and then waved them on. "Checkpoint C." He slapped a piece of paper in Jameson's hand before stepping back. A gate opened to allow them passage.

The van crawled over each speed bump. Surrounded on each side were the official buildings, and like all official buildings, they were uninspired rectangles. They weren't exactly unsavory, but they were dark, dank and felt more like army barracks rather than the quaint small-town life beyond. Jenna preferred it here; this, at least, was real.

Jameson pulled the van up beside a large brick building with several flights of stairs. They stopped inside a yellow grid that lit up when the engine was cut. Jumping out of the van, Jenna went to the back, made sure her gloves were secure, and threw the door open. "Welcome to your new home."

Each of them was still in their monster form, unable to return to human form while in restraints. She made sure not to make eye contact. "One false move and this grid will fry you. I got you in here so your bounty is mine. It doesn't matter to me if you head in there crispy or raw." Jenna yanked their chains free and pulled them from the van.

"What's all this 'I' business she's always going on about?" Jameson asked.

Dirk somehow always ended up with an easier load than they did and wrestled with two. "There's no I in team, Jenna."

She snorted, pulling on her chains hard and it forced the shifters onto their knees. "There's no whiny-ass bastards either and I'm stuck with the two of you."

Jameson grinned. "She likes us."

"She really really does!" Dirk grinned back, maniacal and crazy.

Jenna, despite her best attempts, gave a short burst of laughter. Footsteps moving toward them caused her to pause and lengthen her posture to a rigid sort. Several officers approached and were led by the chief of New Haven 56 security, Travis Reynolds.

He was a good guy and ran a tight ship. His feelings for the shifters might not have been as hardened as her own, but his experiences were different. He was a few years older with silver around his temples, always with a friendly smile. Travis shared it with her now.

She returned it, always feeling warmer in his presence.

"Nice load you have there. I was beginning to wonder if you were ever coming back." As Travis spoke, the officers with him took the reins of the shifters and lead them away toward the entrance to the building. There they would be tagged and kept in isolation until their wings were clipped and they were assigned homes and jobs. The indoctrination period took a solid three weeks of work.

"Took a while to fill the van this time," Jenna explained.

"It's beginning to seem like we're running out of shifters to hunt," Dirk said.

Travis nodded in agreement. "I think we have most of them now. Everything else is just going to be slim pickings. Might be time for an assignment change for you three."

Jenna couldn't imagine doing anything else. "We can talk about that later. Right now, there are a few steaks with our name on it."

Jameson rubbed his hands together in anticipation. "Want to join us?"

Travis shook his head. "Appreciate the offer, but have some things going on at home these days. Maybe soon. Welcome home, Jenna."

"Always nice to be back," she said dryly. "What's going on at home?"

Dirk and Jameson grimaced. "Tact isn't exactly her strong suit."

"Don't worry; it's nothing about the job." Travis grinned, heading back toward the building. "Now get out of here before I find something for you to do that *is* work-related!"

The men sprang into action, but Jenna watched after her boss. What coul be wrong with his family? He wasn't the type to offer flip information for no reason—maybe there was a reason he wanted her to know. In either case, Jenna was going to find out.

Chapter Eight

The drive through the checkpoint brought them to a series of gates and an underground tunnel. When they emerged, they were dumped far from the city square. The tunnel behind them sealed with a blue force field and on either, side stood two police officers dressed as security guards. It was night, so the streets were quiet. There were a few cars traveling the road, but nothing that constituted as heavy traffic.

They drove through the grid streets lined with evenly spaced trees and perfectly coordinated flowers. The air that blew in smelled sweet, like the smell of honeysuckle and freshly picked blueberries. Jenna took a deep breath, with her eyes closed, and despite her reservations it did feel like coming home.

Ascending a steep hill, the lights from the residential homes brightened into view, well-placed crickets chirped and Jameson had to swerve to avoid crushing a red tricycle with streamers beneath the wheels of the van.

Jenna saw a family sitting on a porch drinking lemonade, while others flew kites with two small children. Shifters were not allowed to have more than two. Anyone who didn't comply was "ostracized" long enough to abort and be retrained.

Taking a hard right, they came to a short street lined with family-friendly restaurants. To the left was Dusty's pub. It helped that they had the best steaks and monster-sized potato wedges money could buy. It was expensive—as was anything with real red meat in New Haven—but it was their favorite place to unwind after a job.

The pub was dully lit and brown booths littered the perimeter of the smoky bar area. Deer heads and other hunting memorabilia hung around the tables. A portly bartender poured foamy beverages into giant steins and slid them down the bar. Fallen peanut shells littered the counter as people hunched over their drinks and kept to themselves. Every once in a while they darted glances back at the round booth in the corner.

In that booth, Jenna studied the menu even though it hadn't changed in over five years. Around them all the booths were empty while the stools at the bar were overcrowded. "It's nice the way they give us privacy. I think I'm going to have the twelve-ounce."

"With a nice toasted baked." Jameson grinned and flipped his menu closed. He snapped his fingers. "We're ready to order over here. Service! Where's our service?"

Dirk grimaced. "You could at least be a little courteous to them. We don't want them to spit into our food."

Jameson made a face. "We're ready to order, *please*."

Jenna sipped her water and nearly spat it back out. It tasted so sparkling fresh that it couldn't be natural; she worried about what chemicals might be wetting her palate. She glanced up as Jeff Monroe, the owner and operator, stepped forward. Clean-cut, short hair, perfect polo shirt. Just like everyone else in their little Stepford town.

"Good evening. Tonight for specials—"

"We don't need the specials," Dirk said.

Jeff spoke louder, as if he didn't hear him. "For specials, we have a delicate pounded chicken in a cream glaze with mushrooms. It is quite succulent, and I highly recommend it."

After they ordered, Jenna handed him her menu. "Why is it you always recommend the specials and not the house items?"

Jeff organized the menus in his hand and then stuck them neatly under his arm. "We just try to push the specials, Officer Morgan. There's no conspiracy."

Jenna grinned. "My reputation does precede me. Do you wait on all the humans that come in here, or just us?"

"I'm betting it's just us," Dirk said.

"Just you." Jeff's words held no humor.

"I'll count us lucky then." Jenna added. "You either like to humor your staff because they refuse to wait on us, or you like skirting with danger. Which is it?"

Dirk and Jameson exchanged glances. "Next she's going to whip out her knife to clean under her fingernails." Jameson said.

Jeff decided not to answer, which Jenna thought was probably self-preservation kicking in. "I'll bring your drinks right over. Oh, would you like some bread while you wait?"

Jameson grinned, glancing at his watch briefly. "Please."

Jenna's eyes followed Jeff as he returned to the kitchen while Dirk leaned back in the booth and flicked his arm over the rest. His fingers grazed Jenna's shoulder. She tensed and scooted over a smidge to get away from him.

"Why do you keep glancing at your watch?" Dirk asked, toothpick twirling at the corner of his mouth.

"Places to go, people to do." Jameson laughed.

"Who is it this time?" Jenna asked. "Not that little bookworm at the library."

"Again." Dirk added. "You know, if you keep this up, you're going to run out of humans in this town to date and then what are you going to do? Double back?"

Jenna snorted.

"She's a doctor actually. Fairlane Jennings."

"The one that runs the tests?" Jenna asked, interest piqued.

"You know it. I only roll with the best. It's why I tolerate you guys."

Jenna laughed as their beers were sat on the table. She turned to thank Jeff for his service and met his penetrating eyes. For a moment she thought she saw something in them, recognition. Like he saw something in her he knew, understood.

Like he knew that Jenna Morgan had dragon shifter blood running through her veins.

Only paranoia, nobody knows.

Across the way, Dirk smiled at her. Jenna nervously returned it and brought the bottle to her lips.

Chapter Seven

The Monroe family gathered around the kitchen table for a traditional dinner of chicken, roasted potatoes, and Brussel sprouts covered in melted cheese as quiet music played on the radio. Chatter was light and playful while the children avoided eating their greens. Jeff leaned back in his chair, wiping the corner of his mouth with his napkin. "How was school, Marie? Jake?"

Susan picked up her glass of liquefied cow organs and sipped. It was chilled, perfect, but nothing tasted good on her palate. Nothing was the same since she watched Megan get carted away.

It was like Megan was a disease, contagious, and now Susan was just supposed to go on like nothing happened? Like her best friend never existed? It was so easy to forget that New Haven was a cage. A well-guarded steel cage, and if they stepped out of line…

Her hand visibly shook the glass and the vibrant red juice sloshed around inside the crystal goblet. Susan lowered it back to the tablecloth and beneath it squeezed her hands together. Jeff met her eyes from across the way and Marie sighed dramatically.

"Did you guys even hear me?"

"You made the honor roll, big whoop. You make it every year." Jake rolled his eyes while rolling his brussels sprouts.

"Eat your vegetables," Susan said softly.

"Mom, it doesn't matter how much cheese you put on them. They're still brussels sprouts."

"Listen to your mother and eat your greens." Jeff said. "She went to much trouble to pick up those extra rations today and I won't have you wasting them."

Jake sighed. "Fine, but in a few months, I'll be an adult and then I can eat what I want."

"Well, thank God." Marie said, crossing her arms. "Then maybe some of us will get to eat a bit more without the garburator here chomping it all up!"

"Have you thought on what type of job you're going to apply for after graduation?" Jeff asked. "I could always use the help at the restaurant if you want to apply. Maybe chef or prep cook?"

Jake paused in the cutting of his chicken for just a moment. "I thought maybe television repair man."

Marie snorted and rolled her eyes. "Golly gee, Jake, you think you have the intelligence for that?"

"Yeah, I do," Jake said defensively. "I can do it if I want to. Right, Mom?"

Susan's head snapped over to her son. "Pardon me, what?" Her eyes were moist and she watched in horror as both her children's faces fell. "You know, I'm going to put on the coffee and get dessert ready." She slid her chair back and stood. "Hand me your plates if you're done."

She took each of them and didn't comment like she normally would on the uneaten bits of food. She scraped the remains into the garbage basket and started loading the dishwasher.

"Kids, why don't you go put on *Laverne and Shirley*? We'll serve dessert in there in a minute." The wooden chairs slid against the floor. Susan's dishes clanked together in the dishwasher as she latched the door shut and picked up the wet sponge in the sink.

She nearly dissolved into a fit of tears as Jeff's strong arms wrapped around her back, and his head rested against hers.

Sobs lodged in her throat, and the sponge slipped from her hand back into the porcelain blue bowl. "I," her voice was unsure, squeaking, "can't. I can't do this, Jeff."

"Yes, you can," he whispered. The warm kiss from his lips on the back of her neck used to be enough to pull her back from the brink, but not now. Eyes squeezed, she counted to ten, pictured sheep, children parading through town in perfect dresses, and mouthed *you are human, you are not a mutant.*

You are not a dragon.

Susan shook her head and Jeff spun her toward him. He took her face in his hands and gave her a long, slow, kiss. "Baby, look at me." He repeated it more forcefully. "Look at me."

Her head lifted and his, intense gaze strengthened her. "They just took her," Susan whispered, "she's gone. Just like that."

"Because of what she did. What she said. Sue, I can't have that happen to you." Jeff's lip trembled and the fear on his face was so palpable, Susan felt it. "You have to pull it together. Let's have some pie before I have to head back to the restaurant tonight. All right?"

Susan nodded, fast and erratic. Her fingers probed her wet cheeks, making sure they were dry. "I must look a mess."

"Beautiful as always." Jeff kissed her, whispering his love for her against her cheek. "Why don't you run upstairs and freshen up a little and I'll cut the pie."

Susan stared at him like he had two heads. "You? Do you even know where we keep the pie server?"

Jeff chuckled, breaking out a toothy grin. "You could show me. How's that for a start?"

She nodded and her curls bounced along with her. Susan opened a drawer and showed him. "Try not to crack the crust too badly, dear."

"And you," Jeff kissed her chin delicately, "go upstairs and take care of yourself. This family, we need you, honey."

She was so thankful for him, to be loved so completely. Susan gazed at him to tell him that and stroked back his hair delicately. After one more brief kiss she excused herself upstairs, her heels sinking into the plush lined stairs. Up on the second floor, Susan used the common bathroom to pat her face dry and put on a new coat of lipstick. She thought she heard something in the hall.

Susan pushed the door open and stood in the intersection between the three bedrooms. "Marie, is that you?"

The bedroom door opened just enough for Jake to stick his head out. "Just me, Mom. Packing for practice."

"Why they have these late-night practices is beyond me."

"Eight-thirty isn't exactly late."

"I guess not, you're right. Well, I hope you win the championship this year. What a way to go out." With a faraway smile she thought about what that game would be like, how proud she'd be of Jake. She could even smell the popcorn and hot dogs to go along with it. When she dropped the fantasy, Susan saw Jake was staring at her like a dope. "What's the matter? Is your mom so uncool that you must gawk at her?"

"No, Mom. You're swell. Real swell. I guess sometimes I just forget to tell you." Out of nowhere, Jake hugged her. Susan gasped in surprise and squeezed him back, really leaning into the hug.

A fine boy, maybe he would be okay in the end. Maybe they all would.

Chapter Nine

"You're blaming this on me?" Travis asked his manic wife as she paced the living room. She was on autopilot, in a complete frenzy, and it was driving him mad. Almost even more so than knowing his little girl—Travis couldn't even complete the thought.

"Yes!" Expelling a big breath, Alice slapped her thighs with her open palms. "She didn't come to us because how we're always fighting."

"Oh, right, because I fight with myself."

She sighed. "You're the one who refuses to listen or give me any wiggle room."

"I have a job. You knew that when we got married."

"And you said after a few years you'd try something else. Go into the private sector. Instead I've spent the best years of my life in a bubble!"

Travis wiped the spit away from his mouth. "We were happy, weren't we? We raised Wendy. You had her. You had your job—"

"Teaching kindergarten to a bunch of mutants? It isn't even real education, Travis. It's conditioning them to behave like *us*."

"That only lasts for a few years. If you were that unhappy you could have taught third grade, elementary, high school. I could have gotten you anything you wanted."

"Right I could have anything I wanted because you decreed it? Well, no thank you." Alice turned her head, and upturned her nose.

"So you'd rather be miserable?" He grabbed her by the shoulders. "And you want to bring us with you, is that it? Damn it, Alice." Travis glanced away and fought the urge to charge out of the house for good.

She laughed and tears clung to her lashes. "That's how you see me, is it? A bitter angry woman out to push my misery on everyone else."

The anger tumbled out of him. "Aren't you? That's why Wendy's upstairs crying her eyes out right now, isn't it? We should be supporting her right now, not arguing about this like it's a problem that needs to be taken care of."

"She's crying because she ruined her life. Not me, not me." Alice insisted, waving her finger. "I'll be stuck in this house for another eighteen years raising another baby while you run along—"

"You don't know that," Travis whispered. "She's eighteen, maybe she wants this baby. Maybe they'll get married, but you didn't even ask, did you? All you care about is how it's going to affect you. Me, me, me. It's all you've ever cared about, admit it. I was the husband on your arm. Wendy was the possession to dress up and prance around like a porcelain doll. None of this fits into your plan."

Alice's eyes blinked out of control. Her quick sharp of breath said Travis stepped over the line. "You think I'm selfish? Me? When you're the one that let us live among those *things* for your job?"

Travis opened his mouth, but his eyes fell to Wendy charging down the stairs. Her hair was wild. Her face swam with tears as she pushed right past them. Travis grabbed her hand, squeezed her fingers, and begged her to stop. "Honey, where are you going?"

"Out!" She nearly screamed. "Away from all this fighting!"

Alice glared at him. "I told you—"

"Stop it!" Wendy screamed, grabbing at her hair. "I can't listen to you talk to Dad like that. Or talk about the shifters like that. They're not things, they're not monsters." Her teeth gnashed and her eyes were frenzied. Travis sucked in his breath and wondered for the first time who the father was. "Just leave me alone!"

She pulled away from her father and when he refused to let go, Wendy pushed him. "I'm sorry, Daddy." Wendy's voice shook. "I'm sorry, but I have to go."

Something in her voice stilled him and Travis let her slip through his fingers. Wendy opened the front door and ran down the brick steps, leaving her parents to stare after her.

The door swung back and latched. Travis was not usually an emotional man, but tears stung in his eyes. He had the feeling that he might never see her again.

"How could you just let her go?" Alice demanded. "She needs to be back here. We have things we have to discuss and hammer out. Go after her!"

Travis shook his head, defeated. "What she decides is her decision. She's not a baby anymore, Al. We should support her, but this isn't our call."

Alice fumed, biting her lip. "And you have no problem with this? Her storming out of here in the middle of the night?"

"If I was her, I'd want to be out of this house too."

Infuriated, she raised her hand to slap him. Travis took a deep breath, steeling himself for the assault when he picked up a stench. His nose tingled and he smelled the familiar twang of gas.

Somewhere in the house, something snapped. Alice stared at him questioning, lowering her hand. In the back hall, a squeak and the sound of footsteps made her gasp, spin around. Her voice was that of a little girl, unsure and afraid. "Should I call the police?"

"I am the police. Just stay here." Travis placed a hand on the butt of his revolver and crept down the hall. The darkness led him to the entrance to the basement. The stars were darkened and only the faint light from the moonlight allowed him to see an orange glow at the bottom. He stopped to peer down, one hand on the door frame and a foot hovering above the next step. Hands braced his back.

Why could she never do anything that he asked, even when it came to a break in? Suppressing a sigh, Travis saw that the orange glow was growing. It wasn't light. It was fire and now it was racing up the steps to meet them. It crackled, coming to life with a roar of a lion charging its prey.

Travis pushed Alice back and slammed the door hard. Pivoting, he grabbed his wife's arm and charged her out of the hall. "Run!" He said the words, but they were drowned out by the whoosh of a fireball.

He threw them both down. The fireball grew like a fiery sky above them, and the heat melted his shirt. "Alice!" he screamed, but his vision was claimed by smoke. It snaked its way down his throat, choking him off from air.

Her scream came and Travis held his breath, desperate to find his lovely bride. "Baby!" Beneath him the floor groaned and as it buckled, as the foundation crumbled, Travis desperately felt at the carpet, looking for Alice's hand.

***

Red and orange flame shot up and out as smoke smothered the base of the home, blowing out the grass and trees like a saucer-shaped UFO landed on the property. The roof collapsed on itself like a house of cards. The mailbox snapped and rocketed across the street, bouncing up on the sidewalk and smashing the front bay window of the Waters' home. It corked their dog, Sparky, right in the snout.

He yipped, running in a circle around the living room. Mr. Waters cleaned his glasses as he ogled at the sight across the street. "Marge." his voice cracked like an old chimney. "I think you best get the police on the phone right away."

They gathered on the sidewalk. Others from nearby streets walked by, some in slippers and their bathrobes, clutching the hands of their children. Silent horror and unspoken dread descended on the group. Sirens beckoned closer and the shifters feared they were too late if anyone were home. What would this do to the community? Who would the police think was responsible for this?

Before the fire engines arrived, the dragon shifters went to their houses, safe, and latched the doors shut. Like it would make any difference if the humans wanted in.

If the humans wanted in, they came in.

Chapter Ten

Wendy arrived at the empty Oakland field where the baseball games took place. Jittery, she glanced over her shoulder to make sure no one was there, that Dad hadn't put a tail on her. Or that he wasn't across the street in the family sedan. No one was there and Wendy was worried that Jake had changed his mind. Maybe he would just rebuke her and the baby. Who could blame him, right? It wasn't his problem, it was hers. She was the one stuck with it.

Tears in her eyes, she gasped a half sob when she saw someone step out from behind the trees. Laying back in the shadows, Wendy could make out the rustling of the branches and the sound of soft steps. Rushing towards him, she wanted to drop her bag, but her fingers were clenched so tight they wouldn't respond. When she was close enough to make out Jake's features, the worry in his face and the pure joy in his eyes, she sobbed. Wendy stopped in her tracks and just cried.

"Wendy." His voice was soft and consoling, but she had held it in for so long that she just couldn't stop crying. Jake's soft hands wiped the tears away from her cheeks. Then with rushed breath, they kissed, clinging to each other's bodies and Wendy thought she must be dreaming.

Clutching his flesh between her fingers, her eyes clenched tight. "I'm so scared. I'm so scared." Her teeth chattered, but not from cold. The fear gripped inside her belly and her limbs shook. So weak, her legs wobbled.

Jake held her close, his arms tight around her, as if sensing her need. "Me too, me too, but we're not alone. We have each other. I've been so worried about you." Jake sighed, kissing her again. She relished in his touch, in his lips, and the soft scent of his cologne. She thought she might die if they got caught, if she might never be able to feel him around her again. "Are you okay?" He rushed on, kissing her cheek and then just held her. He just held her.

Wendy was sorry she doubted him, but they hadn't had a chance to talk in weeks, almost a month. Through their notes their plan came together, but it felt like this day might never come. Now she felt stronger being with him. She knew they were young, but they could make it work, couldn't they? Couldn't this work?

"I'm okay," she said with much more confidence than she actually felt. "I've been sick, real sick, but I think," her voice trailed off, haunted, "it's been moving. That must mean he's okay, right?"

She always talked about the baby as if she knew it was a him. Wendy didn't know why, but that felt right and natural. Jake placed both his hands on her rounded belly, beneath the baggy fabric of her sweatshirt. His was a look of wonder and amazement, laced with fear. "We'll find out soon. I promise. I promise I'll take care of you, Wendy. No matter what happens. Okay? I'm just, sorry I did this to you." He gave a little shrug, looking meek and apologetic.

She shook her head with the threat of fresh tears. "We did it together. It was stupid, but I can't, can't wish him away. Does that make me an idiot?"

"No," Jake said with confidence, draping his arms around her. "No. But it makes me realize how special you are to me. I know I have a lot of growing up to do, this isn't going to be easy, but—"

"We'll be together," Wendy said with a big rosy smile.

Jake repeated the words with a deep calm and it settled her like it always did. He was special, Wendy thought to herself. No one calmed her like he did.

She rested her head on his shoulder as they made their way through the park. Jake retrieved a hidden bag beneath a bench and handed it to Wendy. "Right where she said it would be."

They made their way over to a black unmarked van next to the concession stand. Every step, Wendy said a prayer. When they approached, the back doors opened and a police officer pulled them in.

He was George Stanton and Wendy recognized him from the few times she visited her dad at the outpost. She was so grateful he saw things their way and was overcome with a gratitude she couldn't voice. Instead, she looked to Rebecca Seers, who was smiling broadly. "It's finally, finally nice to be able to talk with you, Wendy." Her hand was offered in a warm handshake.

Wendy crushed her in a hug instead. "Thank you. For everything you've done."

Rebecca patted her back with a slight smile. "Easy, girl. We don't have a lot of time to get you out of here." She glanced to George.

He took it as permission to continue. Lifting Jake's arm gently he inspected his security bracelet before placing a device against it. In a moment the bracelet beeped and unhooked from around the boy's wrist. "No one will be looking for him on the grid at least until his parents report him missing."

"We have a few hours or maybe until tomorrow morning." Rebecca sighed. "We have to make tracks and will be passing through a checkpoint. You two will hide back here under some blankets. Cliché, I know, but I can get us through the checkpoint. Just trust me."

Wendy nodded. She did trust her. Rebecca believed in the innocence of shifters. She was maybe the only one who really did. If anyone would help her hide, it was her. "Okay."

Jake squeezed her hand. "We'll be fine."

"We'll drive clear through until morning." Rebecca handed them their blankets and prepared to sit up front with her two associates. "Our facility has a doctor. He knows you're coming and he's going to make sure you're tip top."

Wendy often worried that the baby wasn't developing right. But now, hearing someone else say it made her heart clench.

Rebecca offered a friendly smile, but her eyes darted to Wendy's belly. "I'm sure you are. Now, no more worries."

She had a friendly face and voice. Wendy thought this was how moms were really supposed to be; it was what she wanted to be to her baby. She just hoped she wouldn't screw it up. What did she know about being a mother? Worry first, she though, about seeing him born. "Thanks, Ms. Seers."

"Oh please, call me Becky." Rebecca and George exited the van. She latched the doors shut before getting in the front of the van, taking the passenger seat. George, with his part done, headed toward his unmarked squad car.

Her associate pulled away from the lot. Rebecca spoke with a calm confidence. "They'll be fine. He's keeping her calm."

"If the checkpoint guards don't buy this?"

Rebecca took a breath and she spoke through gritted teeth. "Do what you need to get us away. We need that baby."

***

The checkpoint was a ten-minute drive away, but beneath the blanket, it felt to Wendy like hours. Every bump and turn dragged forever. Since she couldn't see where they were going, what they were doing, it made the fear fester. Her eyes became accustomed to the darkness and she could make out Jake beneath the blanket. Gazing at him made everything feel better. They were really going to be together, like a real couple, where they didn't need to be afraid anymore. He just needed to pretend to be normal, human, and he was. He so was.

When they came to a stop and she heard voices—Rebecca's and a stern male—Wendy felt vomit rise in her throat. She swallowed it back, like scorching lava running down the length of her throat. It wasn't nearly as bad as the fear they would get caught. What would happen to her baby then or to poor Jake? He squeezed her hand, must have seen the fear in eyes. His own seemed to say, *it'll be all right. Just stay calm.*

But it was so hard and the rush of panic was taking her. Wendy tried to even her breathing. A fresh burst of cold air rushed towards her as the back door opened and the inspection continued. Her heart skipped and she was sure they were going to get caught. Jake's eyes were wide, horribly afraid, and they gripped each other's hands tightly under their blanket. Their eyes locked and the look of love he gave her spoke volumes. It was worth it, it was all worth it if he would just keep looking at her like that.

"As you can see, officer," Rebecca said, "everything is in order."

"Uh-huh. We don't trust you much, Ms. Seers."

"Well, I don't trust you either, so we're even, and we do have a working partnership. I wouldn't want to put into my report that you were uncooperative, would I?"

"Ma'am, I never said I wasn't cooperating."

"Then we can be on our way?"

Paper ripped from a spiral binding. Next was the sound of paper smacking into someone's hand. "Yup. Just drive safe. We're supposed to get rain tonight."

Some pleasantries were traded. Wendy could almost breathe again as the tightening in her chest abated. She almost could, but for her worry that something would change at the last minute. He would double back on instinct, his police-officer gut saying to check under the blankets.

But the passenger door slammed, the engine came to life and they rolled forward.

Relieved, Wendy closed her eyes thanking God over and over. So relieved, so relaxed for the first time it felt in weeks, she almost fell asleep until Rebecca spoke. "Come on out, you two. I've got some snacks if you're hungry."

Wendy and Jake moved behind them in bucket seats. Wendy was hungry again and grateful for the crackers, fruit, and milk. Jake, though, wasn't speaking. His eyes were trained on the road. The side was illuminated by bright lights and as they pulled onto the highway the horizon was awake with shimmering skyscrapers. Wendy saw them before on day passes, on trips to her relatives on the holidays. To her it was different, but she had seen it before.

Jake had seen it only in photos, and in movies that were made before the plague came. Now his mouth had fallen open, his skin was pale, and he appeared mystified as he glanced around out at the windows at the passing cars and rolled down his window to take a deep breath of fresh air.

"Welcome to the world, Jake." Rebecca said with a smile.
"It's so … big."

Wendy laughed slightly, nearly spitting out her milk. "It is big. We're going to drive across two states."

"Wow," Jake nearly laughed. "I want to see it all. Oh, what's that?" He pointed out the window.

"McDonalds. That's what they call their golden arches," Rebecca explained.

"Oh, like a rainbow?"

"They sell cheeseburgers," Wendy said.

Clarity lit up his face. "I like cheeseburgers."

"Take a small detour," Rebecca ordered her driver.

"Ma'am, we don't know how long we have to make our getaway," he argued.

"The boy has lived eighteen years and never had a McDonald's cheeseburger and fries. If he's going to live among us, we need to start corrupting him as quickly as possible." Rebecca glanced back at Wendy and gave her a wink.

Wendy felt good; better than she had in a long time. Deep inside her, she felt the strong kick of her baby. Rather than being repulsed or afraid, she felt happy. Whatever would happen next, she was sure that Rebecca would make sure they were safe.

Chapter Eleven

Jenna's head swayed back. Her hands clamped onto Dirk's pecs and squeezed with enough strength to cause him to yelp, short of air. Her hips ground against his, driving him further into her. His rough hands traveled up the length of her body, passing over her abs and her bare breasts, sweat mutant along the nubs of her nipples. Her mouth fell open, her breath erratic as her senses heightened.

Dirk's eyes closed and he moaned, with that look on his face she liked so much but couldn't admit. His hands slipped beneath her sweat-laden red curls, forcing her head down so he could kiss her. Their lips met and his tongue slipped against hers. The urgency drove her on further.

A moan she didn't mean escaped her lips, and her eyes squeezed tight. She grabbed both his wrists, holding them against the mattress slightly above his head and drove her body further into his. Their pelvises moved in time, Jenna using her upper body to keep him pinned, and their kisses tapered off. With a devious snarl, she bit his neck and throttled her intensity.

Dirk's eyes fluttered open with surprise. Jenna gave a little laugh, dangerous and not kindhearted. Her head rolled against his chest and she sought to finish it. Pleasure rippled through her body with each thrust, and their breathing fell in time as if the sex were something they did often. She felt in that moment that they were one, that she wanted nothing more than this. But she tried to force it out of her mind and only feel the pleasure.

Just feel the pleasure.

Her body trembled in an uncontrollable spasm. Slowing her movements down, she pushed herself up to look into Dirk's eyes. His eyes were closed as he grabbed her ass, rocking her forward to kiss her again. A small smile played across her lips at his sweet expression, the beauty of his face. She couldn't help but think, *I love you.*

Jenna slipped her arm out to brace her body on the headboard. It stopped her head from slipping down too far and Dirk's eyes opened with more than surprise, but a bit of anger. She slipped off him and grabbed for her jeans. "Want some more wine?"

Dirk pushed himself up on his elbows to look up at her. "No." His voice was quiet, but angry. Jenna heard it enough times to recognize it even before he did.

She slipped a slinky top over her bare breasts. It compacted them against her body in a way she knew drove him crazy. "I have a frozen pizza if you're hungry."

"I'm not hungry, Jenna." He flopped down onto the mattress, one arm tucked behind his head. "How long are we going to do this?"

Jenna sat on the other side of the bed, lighting a smoke. She took a deep inhale. "I thought you liked doing this. You're the one who came looking for a booty call." Truth be told, she expected him to, and if he hadn't, she'd be disappointed.

"I don't want just a booty call. If I wanted that—"

"You'd knock on the door of a mutant?" Jenna smirked. Another mutant because he didn't know she was a shapeshifter. She barely knew herself when she was set to wed him.

Then everything fell apart. She was a criminal. Working for the very people who'd throw her into captivity.

Dirk looked hurt. It made her heart pulse with pain.

"So what, you want to cuddle? I thought we were beyond that."

Jenna could feel Dirk shifting on his side. She jumped when his fingers stroked her arm. "I want more than just this. You know how I feel about you."

"Yeah." Jenna said simply, but she was afraid the emotion might be evident anyway. She took a long drag of her cigarette and tapped the ashes into her empty wine glass.

"You used to feel the same, but ever since you got back— Listen, you've been back for almost a year and you still…don't seem like you."

"Maybe this is me. Maybe you just refuse to see it, just like you always do." Jenna turned her head slightly to glance at him.

Dirk gave a labored sigh, "Maybe talking about it would help. You ever think about that, Jen? For seven months you were just gone. No one heard anything from you and then boom, you were on the news for what, executing mutants in the field? I thought you were in trouble, maybe even dead. And after us taking shit for what you did, Travis put you in charge of the squad again, and you didn't offer any explanations. Not to me or Jameson. For all I know, Travis doesn't even know why you went apeshit."

He knows, Jenna thought, closing her eyes for a moment. "So, you're upset that I came back and displaced your leadership, is that it?"

"Right, because I've been living with a grudge against you for the last year. That's why I waited to have this conversation buck naked in your bed."

Jenna tried to suppress a smile, but was having trouble even pretending to be angry. "Dirk, let's not do this, okay?"

Dirk sighed and his eyebrows rose to the ceiling. Jenna fumbled with her cigarette pack, but couldn't work the lid well enough to flip it open. *Stupid fingers.*

"Excuse me if I thought it was time we have a meaningful conversation. I know these nights mean more to you than you say. I feel it when we're together. I'm just not sure why you keep me at a distance?" He sat up and stroked her hair back.

Jenna tensed, aware at how close she was to spilling everything. "I can't offer you what you want. This is all I have to give you right now, so you need to accept it."

"Just like I had to accept you were gone, then you were back. No questions? No answers? Just this is the way it is?"

"Pretty much, yeah."

"And if I don't?" Dirk asked with a defiant edge to his voice.

Jenna shifted to look at him. She needed him to see her eyes when she spoke. "Then it's over, even this."

"Maybe it should be over if it's never going to amount to more. Maybe I'm tired of being your damn sex toy."

It wasn't what she thought he'd say. Jenna dropped her eyes, avoiding his gaze. "Maybe then you should go." Her voice was even, without a tremor.

Dirk's tongue clucked along inside his cheek. He threw the sheet off and Jenna stared out the window again as she listened to him get dressed. She managed to get another cigarette lit and watched the smoke slowly drifting up from the glowing amber of her butt until Dirk stepped into her line of sight. Jenna studied him and he studied her.

"I don't get you." His chest rose with a deep breath. The rippled muscles of his chest still glinted with sweat, drawing her eye to every curve.

She studied him and exhaled a long puff of smoke. "Thanks for the bulletin, but I already knew that."

"Right, because you have me all figured out. You know what I'm feeling and thinking better than I do."

It was accurate, but Jenna didn't say anything.

"That's because I'm accessible to you. I let you in. You shut me out a long time ago, Jen. I don't know why I try so hard to get back in."

"Other than the great sex?" Jenna asked.

Dirk grabbed his shirt from the floor with a quick flourish and it snapped in the air. "You're a real pig for a woman."

"So are you," she said sourly.

Dirk shouted at her, his teeth exposed, but his words were drowned out by a high-pitched rolling thunder. Their attention went to the window and Jenna watched as the night sky glowed like amber. Flames and smoke rose up through some trees and the perches of low roofed homes. It soared, growing higher and wider, before settling down into a burning heap.

Jenna stood without realizing she did it and took a final drag on her cigarette. She grabbed her collapsed jacket from the floor. "Have Jameson pick us up." She snuffed the filter into her wine glass and then they tore through her loft for the street.

****

The van was outside in less than five minutes. Jenna took the front seat, while Dirk was regulated to the back. She turned to Jameson who was dressed in a t-shirt with a giant iron emblem on the front. The guy was nothing if not dedicated to his hobby. "What's going on?"

Jameson's jaw was tight with a quick glance at her. "It's," he stuttered, "Travis."

Jenna couldn't hide her surprise and for a moment, the van spun in a way that meant it was only in her mind. It meant just like other shapeshifters, she was dangerously close to shifting.

Couldn't happen. She wouldn't let it. She couldn't lose control.

She rubbed her forehead and felt the shift of weight behind her thanks to Dirk leaning forward into the front. He spoke while she couldn't.

Dirk leaned in. "That explosion wasn't far enough away to be the outpost."

Jameson was speeding and he didn't let up as he took a sharp right, gripping the wheel. Jenna had to lean a hand on the dashboard to keep herself in her seat. "They targeted his home?" She asked.

"Yeah, we don't know yet how bad it is."

"Get us there in one piece, Jameson, but get us there yesterday."

Dirk's hand was on the back of her seat to steady himself, but she wished it wasn't so close to her exposed flesh. "Who would do this? He's the chief of police, for God's sake. Shifters?"

Jenna didn't know, "We'll find out." If it was mutants, if they hurt him or his family, she'd make sure they all paid for it. She'd burn the place to the ground if she needed to.

****

She opened the door to the van before it came to a stop. Across the street, firefighters worked on putting the flames out while squads of police officers were forming a grid around the entrance to the street. The Reynolds home was reduced to a pit of burning ash, and the path that led to the front door was streaked black.

Jenna hopped out of the van and moved toward an officer before she even realized it. Her body was on autopilot and her mind played back memories of Travis, meeting him for the first time, all the confidences they shared, and how in some ways he had been more like an older brother than a boss.

George, an officer she knew only in passing through Outpost, was glum as he watched the scene.

This was bad. Real bad.

Jenna saw no way for any of them to get into the building before the flames were put out. Even then, it was going to be more of a dig operation to remove the bodies than a rescue mission. Jenna hung onto hope that they weren't home when it happened. "Was he in there?"

Startled, George's head snapped to attention. "Jenna, hey." He cleared his throat.

"Was he in there?" Her tongue thrashed against her lips.

"No confirmation yet, but there's no evidence to say that he wasn't. Car is still in the driveway."

Jenna turned her attention to the melted, disjointed piece of metal sitting among the fragments of the house. "Suspects?" Her voice sounded hollow, flat.

"Who do you think?"

Jenna understood the gut reaction, but this didn't look like an arson to her. "Do you really think they have the right materials to level his place like this? Fire maybe, but that was an explosion."

"We won't know that for sure unless we can get in there. If there's enough there left for us to gather evidence from."

Behind her, Jenna heard the footsteps of her crew. They were silent, out of respect for Travis. He was a good leader, a fair boss, and on occasion a drinking buddy. They were with him only a few hours ago. If only he had taken them up on the offer for steaks and drinks. Now Jenna may never find out what the trouble was he was having at home, but maybe it didn't matter.

Or maybe now it mattered more than anything.

"We should start canvassing the area. Talk to the shifters across the street. See what they heard."

"Right," Dirk said dryly, "because they're going to want to talk to us. They won't tell us anything. They'll stick together just like they always do."

"We have officers for that, Jenna," George said. "Not that I'm not grateful for the offer."

"Your officers are busy. We can bang on a few doors. It's what we're good at."

"Besides," Jameson said without a sense of humor, "a lot of these guys know us. They might be just scared enough to answer."

George nodded. "Just stick to protocol. Inside Haven we have to keep everything aboveboard. No crazy antics."

Jenna would have riled him up if under different circumstances. This time she just nodded and stepped away. The diminishing flames danced behind her. Jenna stepped off the curb and then paused, glancing at the homes. All the lights were off and everything felt quiet. They were probably shuddering behind their curtains.

She glanced to each of her crew. "Three houses, three of us. Should we arm wrestle for them?"

"Why don't we just go in order of importance?" Dirk asked. "Me, Jameson, you." He stormed off across the street and Jenna watched him go.

Jameson gave her a pointed look. "Have you considered taking up yoga as a relaxation technique instead?"

Glowering, she shoved him toward the direction of the middle house before trudging along to hers. The window was shattered and Jenna's senses heightened. She knocked on the door, a hand on the holster of her gun. When there was no answer, she knocked hard "Police! Open up or I will take down this door!"

Jenna waited, took a deep breath, and kicked in the door. According to police procedure, she didn't need to issue the warning, but had to stop short of hurting the shifters unless they made an offensive move against her. She stepped inside the house and it smelled like coffee and apple pie.

Taking a step into the living room she put her hand on top of the old television unit. It was one of those refurbished models where it looked more like a cabinet or a dresser than a flat panel monitor. The top was still warm.

Glancing around she saw a mailbox beside a recliner; there was the window-smashing culprit. Jenna relaxed her hand that hovered above her weapon. "Hear me out," she bellowed loudly. "Show yourselves in ten and answer a few basic questions. Force me to come find you and we'll do it in Outpost."

Jenna knew that most shifters conveniently forgot about the place's existence, but with a reminder they'd shudder in fear at just the mention of the place. "One…two…" Her voice trailed off as upstairs a dog whined and then the floorboards squeaked above her. Glancing at the ceiling, she listened and waited for the residents of the home to show themselves.

They turned out to be two old end-stage-of-their-lives shifters, which meant they were probably older than Jenna's great-grandmother. They looked innocent enough in their matching slippers and robes. Hell, Jenna thought the husband had more hair than his wife. Both of them were wearing glasses large enough to magnify their pupils. "Oh look, Geoff, we have a guest. How nice."

"Would you like some tea or coffee?" His voice rasped, like he needed a glass of water to clear something out of his throat. "It's late and it might keep you up, but we have decaf."

"And cookies," his wife smiled. "Fresh-baked this morning."

Jenna resisted the urge to sigh, slam them against the wall, and aim her pistol at their heads. "I just have a few questions, so cut the homemaker crap. I'm Officer Morgan. I'm sure you know who lived," she caught herself, going pale, "lives across the street."

Geoff exchanged glances with his wife. "We know, but we'd really like to do this over tea—"

"Did you see anything shortly after eight P.M.? Noises? Anything?"

"Well we were watching *Wheel of Fortune*. It was a new episode and Vanna looked just so pretty!"

Jenna was getting tired of their act. They had to realize that a new episode of anything they watched hadn't been made in nearly one hundred years. She kept her anger in check by biting on the inside of her cheek. "Go on."

"There was an explosion across the street. Mailbox came straight through our window and corked little Sparky right in the head!" Geoff laughed. "So we went outside to see what was going on, after we called the police."

"*You* called the police?"

He nodded. "Yes, I just said that. Are your ears okay, child?"

"Fine," Jenna huffed. "Did you see anything outside?"

His wife shrugged. "People. Neighbors from streets over. We all heard it, felt it. We were worried." Her face was cast down, far off. Jenna realized she was sad. Maybe she shouldn't have felt bad for her, but she was beginning to.

"Did you see anyone sneaking away from the house? Anyone strange that didn't blend in with anyone else?"

She shook her head, hands gripping each other in front of her. Jenna didn't believe her. "What are you afraid of?" She asked the elderly woman.

Her eyes grew large. "Me? Nothing. It's just not often that a police officer bangs down your door so late. It has me, kind of afraid, don't you know?"

Jenna thought that was probably true. "Law is law. I have every right to go where I want and I want to be here. I want you to answer my questions. Honestly. If not, better grab your coat."

Geoff put his arm around his wife's trembling shoulders. "Now, Martha. Just tell her what you told me before we came back inside."

His wife's nod was slight enough to almost escape Jenna's interest. "Two dark men. They were already away from our street. On the corner."

"Dark men? Dark how?" Jenna asked.

"Their clothing was dark. I couldn't see their faces, like they wore masks."

Dragon shifters could see better at night than most could during the day. If Martha hadn't seen their faces, there was good reason for it. "Did you see which way they went?"

Martha was quiet as she considered this. "They got into a black van. I didn't see where it went. We all retreated home. Back into our houses."

"Why?" Jenna demanded.

"We didn't want to be outside when the police showed," Geoff whispered.

She could understand that and didn't need a further explanation. If she was going to solve this thing fast, she needed to get outside and find that van. Jenna turned from them. She didn't thank them or apologize for breaking down the door; it was just the way it was. Outside she crossed the street, with no sign of her crew yet, and saw the flames were out. Now they were working on removing the wreckage, looking for the bodies of Travis and his family.

Jenna felt manic. She crossed her arms and paced, her face drawn into a narrow pout. Dirk came across the street with Jameson at his side. Jenna couldn't read Dirk's face while she listened to their reports. They almost matched hers exactly, except the absence of the mailbox and *Wheel of Fortune*; theirs were watching *Jeopardy*.

"Mine saw the black figures too," she said.

"What's this mean?" Jameson asked. "Except that again I'm going to be disqualified tomorrow from my Xtreme Ironing League."

Jenna ignored his humor. "What they're talking about goes outside the scope of mutant mischief. They went stealth, they wanted to remain hidden."

"That explosion couldn't have been just arson," Dirk agreed, but his tone was distant. He stood to the side, his arms crossed and his body angled away from her.

"We need to get to the Outpost and review the security footage. Maybe we can see someone going in or that van driving away," Jenna said.

"Shouldn't we report what we found to George?" Dirk asked.

Jenna silenced both her partners with a single glance. "They're too busy. They have things to do here. We're," she thought about an appropriate term, "freelance." Jenna took out her phone and scrolled through the alerts from the main office. "Outpost is still in lockdown. No one is leaving or coming in."

"If we're lucky, maybe they're stuck inside here with us," Dirk said.

"If we're lucky," Jameson echoed. "Who wants to be stuck in a town with organ-sucking fiends and two murderous exploding bastards?"

"Welcome to New Haven," Jenna said dryly. "As horrible as shifters are, we need to find the guys responsible for this. Travis dedicated his life to brining order to this place. Let's see that we keep it. And I call shotgun."

Dirk sighed with frustration.

"Where's the part where we go in guns blaring?" Jameson asked.

"Not this time," Jenna said as they strolled over to their van.

"Damn." Dirk said.

****

They road in silence toward the Outpost entrance. The atmosphere was tense, and not just because of Travis. When Jenna tried to make eye contact with Dirk in the mirror, his eyes turned away. So much for a good working relationship. Guess she screwed that too.

Screwing him had been way more fun than this.

When they got to Outpost the guards blocked the entrance. They waved their arms and shook their heads to get them to stop.

Jenna's brow furrowed. She slid from the van and jogged over to them. "What's the meaning of this?"

"No one gets in. Laurel's orders."

Laurel, the Chief's second-in-command.

Jenna's blood pressure skyrocketed, and her face filled in to match her hair. "Do you know what happened? You know what we're looking into?"

"Laurel warned us you'd try to play that card. Look, Morgan, we're all in knots over the chief and his family, but you're not welcome here tonight. And if Laurel gets her way, you won't be welcome tomorrow either."

Jenna sucked on her bottom lip and her face cringed with anger. The only thing on her mind was avenging the chief. "I'll give her tonight, but tomorrow I'm coming back. I'm just as much as part of this force as the next person."

"To the chief, maybe. But not to the rest of us. We'll never forget what you did, Jenna." The officer turned away, ending the conversation.

Jenna wasn't one to regret her choices, but right then she did.

Chapter Twelve

By eight-thirty, news about the fire at Chief Reynolds' home reached every corner of New Haven 56. Susan and Jeff had a few friends plus their new neighbors over for blueberry crumble cake served with coffee. It kept their nerves in check and passed the time.

Almost too quickly.

Susan glanced at her watch. It was nearly ten. Where was Jake already? Once the dishes were stowed out of sight in the dishwasher, she stepped into the living room.

Marie was in her pajamas and curled up on the rug close to the television watching an episode of *Barney Miller*. Normally Susan wouldn't let her watch such gritty television, but after the crazy night she thought they all deserved a little peace to do what they wanted. On the porch, she found Jeff sitting on the railing and stargazing.

Stepping beside him, she caught his eye and they held hands. "It's quiet," she said.

Jeff nodded. "It's nice to just have a few minutes of peace before bed, you know? The new neighbors are nice." His voice was strained, trying to keep the worry out of his voice, but Susan could see it in his eyes.

"We should have a neighborhood barbecue soon. A little meet-and-greet." She gave a laugh, but her body was rigid.

Afraid. Dark times were coming with the chief dead.

He kissed the back of her hand. "You've always been the only welcoming committee this place needs. I love your tender side."

"I'm all tender," she said with a slight laugh. "Do you think—do you think we'll be all right?"

Jeff slid off the railing and kissed her forehead. "We'll be fine, but we can't—can't talk about it, Susan."

She knew that, but her chest tightened anyway. "Jake isn't back yet. I'm worried."

"He's just being a boy. I'll have a talk with him tomorrow over breakfast." His arm went across her shoulder. "Join me in bed?"

A bashful blush crept across her cheeks. "Marie is still awake."

"We'll be quiet," he leaned over to bite her ear, and a shiver went down her spine.

Going back inside, Jeff slipped up the stairs while Susan went into the living room. She bent to stroke her daughter's hair and plant a kiss on her forehead. "Do me a favor and go up to bed after this episode. There's still school tomorrow, young lady."

"Yes, Mum." Marie rolled her eyes, but smiled.

Heading upstairs, Susan began to unbutton her blouse. For a moment she paused at her son's darkened bedroom. Something about it felt wrong, out of sorts. But she let it pass and stepped into the master bedroom where, in the dark, her husband waited to surprise her.

Chapter Thirteen

In the morning, Jenna learned that the surveillance officers were just a little bit touchy about letting just anyone get access to their vids. It frustrated her to no end so she stood there, arms crossed, and let Jameson handle the talking. He was using his smooth voice, the one reserved for politicians, and he kept his hands clasped together. As if somehow it made him look more honest than he actually was.

"We just need to play back the videos from eight P.M. in front of the Chief's house. I'm sure you want to catch the guys that did this just as much as we do. You can watch with us and when we find something, you can take all the credit."

Dirk shot him a glare. He liked nothing better than good cred.

After much haggling, and the promise of coffee, Jenna and her team were granted entrance into the surveillance room even though their clearance level shouldn't have allowed it.

Jenna hated combing through evidence, especially the kind that kept her in one place for more than twenty minutes. While her team watched and listened, she headed out into the hall. She swallowed three red capsules and took a sip of water from the fountain.

The hall was void of people so she opened the door to security. "Officer Andrews," she started and marched over to his station. It was a small desk with a mountain of paperwork and series of closed- captioned monitors. Jenna could see the front entrance to New Haven littered with vans and people quarantined inside.

Andrews was an okay guy and they got along fine. He stood when he saw her. "Hey, any word yet?"

"No," Jenna said softly and tried not to think about Travis. "Can I see the manifest on who managed to get out of New Haven? I'll need the list on who is stuck in the Outpost too."

Andrews raised his eyebrows. "Are you leading the investigation? I can't imagine Laurel handed you the reins."

"I was tight with the chief and his family. If you think I'm going to sit on the sidelines and let someone else handle this—"

Andrews snorted. "Someone else who was also tight with Travis? We're all loyal to him, Jen. You don't get to act like you're the only one."

Jenna knew that was true, but she didn't care. "I was the best investigator this force ever had."

His eyes narrowed. "Until you went nuts. They're never going to let you or your crew lead this investigation."

She took a deep breath to contain her anger because Jenna knew in her heart of hearts, he was right. "I couldn't take being in the city limits for that long. What can I say? Just let me see the damn papers."

Andrews's eyes turned away. "It goes against my better judgment."

She poked him in the chest. "Your judgment was always crap."

He synched his PDA with hers. In a minute, the records were scrolling on her phone. It looked like nothing out of the ordinary was going on in the quarantine. Except that just ten minutes before the explosion, Rebecca Seers and her van were cleared.

Jenna didn't trust her. Anyone who thought mutants should be given carte blanche to live in the United States, to do whatever they wanted, was dangerous. She wasn't sure if Rebecca would want to hurt the chief, couldn't think of how that would help her cause. But Jenna couldn't rule it out yet.

According to her PDA, the guard who let Rebecca through was named Jon Vicars. Jenna wasn't familiar with him, but knew his name. She would head out into quarantine and find him. On her way her earpiece chirped. "Yeah," Jenna said as she touched her ear.

From the slow breath on the other end, she knew it was Dirk. "We found something on the video. We saw the van. Jameson is working on getting access to some of the other vids to see where it went. They are probably somewhere still inside the city."

"Great," Jenna stopped moving and slid her back against the wall so two officers could move past her. "What's with the apprehension then? You sound like someone shot your dog."

"The van is near identical to ours. We're trying to get a shot with the license plate, but so far we're having no luck."

"Well, unless you think Jameson took the van to do something else than Xtreme Ironing, I think we don't have reason to worry."

"You know I do have other interests," Jameson chimed in. "There's yoga. The ability to go to my zen place with deep breathing. You should try it, Jen. It might help your anger issues."

She scowled. "I thought this was a private conversation."

"See? Case in point. Breathe with me, in and out. In—Hey!—"

"Thanks," Jenna said quietly.

"No problem," Dirk sighed. "Where are you headed?"

"Outside to talk with a guard. I'll let you know if I find anything."

"Me too," was all Dirk said, but Jenna knew there was more on his mind. There was more on hers too.

Slipping outside, she was hit with a blast of warm wind that smelled like bagels, red meat, and potatoes. Separately the smells were fine, but together they mixed in a way that turned her stomach.

The vehicles were still parked in a straight line, waiting to be let out of New Haven. Agitated, the drivers slammed their palms on their steering wheel, sipped coffee, or said derogatory things about the police force loud enough for everyone to hear. Jenna understood their frustration, but it couldn't be helped.

There were two guards at the front gate. One tall, one short, both were trim. "Jon Vicars?" Jenna asked and eyed them both. It was the tall one that raised his hand slightly. "I have a few questions for you. You signed off on Rebecca Seers' crew leaving New Haven ten minutes before the explosion."

"Everything was in order," Jon defended.

"I didn't say it wasn't." Her eyebrow cocked over her left eye. "Was something out of order?"

"Her paperwork was in order, same as usual. She was a bit hot under the collar. More than usual."

"How so?"

"I wanted to inspect her manifest, for the things in the back of her van. She said she'd mark me down as uncooperative, but I wasn't being that way. Well," his eyes rolled up as he thought, "not completely that way. I was just trying to do my job."

"And it made her jumpy," Jenna said. She wondered what this meant. The van she traveled in was a simple black, just like Jameson's.

Her ear buzzed again. "Thanks, officer." She turned her back and touched her lobe. "You find something?"

"It's more what we haven't found," Dirk was tense. She could practically see his shoulders hunch. "You better get back in here."

***

Dirk faced off with Officer Dawson, in charge of surveillance. Both of them faced Jenna as she entered the room. "All right, what's going on?" She glanced down and saw Dirk's hands clenched. When she inspected Jameson, she saw he didn't look much better, which bothered her more.

"There are surveillance vids missing," Dirk said hotly, shooting a glare over at Dawson. "And this guy can't find them."

"They should be stored on the local server," Jameson explained, "but they're not there."

"We're running a diagnostic," Dawson swallowed. "We're checking the backup drives. The cloud."

"I know I'm not a technical whiz, but are we saying someone deleted the vids?" Jenna asked, sweeping their faces for answers.

"Oh, somebody deleted them all right," Dirk said. "We saw the van turn right onto Main Street. We pulled another vid that showed them turning left onto Chocolate Circle and then, every vid after that is gone. For every connecting street that might lead to a getaway."

"Someone, here. In this office. Deleted the escape root vids?" Jenna's blood pressure was beginning to rise. She felt faint and put a hand down on the table to steady herself.

"We can use the lack of vids to tell us where they went. If we know a certain street was deleted, it's probably safe to assume they took that root," Jameson said.

"Helpful, but not the point." Jenna's eyes flashed with anger. "We're saying someone in this office *helped* these guys blow up Travis' home. That's what we're saying."

Dawson broke eye contact, his cheeks red. Dirk stared him down. "Yup, right under their noses."

"Why?" Jenna demanded. Was this why they kept her out of Outpost last night? Was someone busy, covering their tracks? She knew there was no answer. Not yet. "For all we know, you did it," she accused Dawson.

He blinked, startled. "Excuse me? I let you in here and now you're accusing me—"

"Yeah, I am." Her eyes went wild, wide, and her mouth opened wide. "You were alone when we got here. You have access to the vids. And you have the clearance to servers. Local. Main. I don't think we can trust you." Jenna said and leaned on the table, peering into Dawson's face.

"What should we do with him?" Dirk asked.

"Uh, guys? Don't you think we might be jumping the gun a little? We technically shouldn't even be here," Jameson said.

"Damn right you shouldn't be here." The voice was low, smoldering, and Jenna didn't need to turn around to know it belonged to Laurel. She did anyway so they could make eye contact. "What is the meaning of this, *Officer Morgan*?"

Jenna took a deep breath, felt smug, but was pretty sure she looked even smugger. "We've been tracking the bomber and someone has erased the vids to the escape route. Someone in this office. You've got a leak, Commander."

Laurel's face didn't change for a second. She looked as indignant as ever. "You shouldn't even be here. Just the fact you and your crew had access to the equipment compromises this investigation. *Nobody trusts you*, Jenna."

She knew there was an *anymore* tacked on to the end of that sentence. "Travis did."

"And now he's dead," Laurel's voice softened when she said it. "They're moving the bodies into the Outpost now."

Jenna nodded slowly, blinking her eyes. She could feel Dirk's penetrating stare on her, but ignored it. "Thanks for breaking the news to us gently."

Laurel's nose flared "Like it was broken easily for the officers that pulled what was left of him from the rubble? Everyone loved Travis. You are no different." Laurel took a deep breath to compose herself.

"Look, I understand why you want to help, but I can't let you. I think you know that." She turned her head to speak to two officers that came in behind her. "Escort them out of Outpost and back into New Haven." Her attention turned back to Jenna. "Return to your van at once, or I will have you thrown into a holding cell."

Jenna wanted to scream, claw her eyes out, and tell her she couldn't do that. Travis was more than her boss, more than her friend, and she wasn't going to sit idly by and just let the investigation continue without her. "Yes, *Ma'am*."

She pushed past her, the other officers and everyone else that got in her way. Jameson and Dirk chased after her, but she didn't stop until she back inside the van. A moment later her two partners took their seats and watched her with suspicion. "We're just going to do this? Give in without a fight?" Dirk asked.

"It's not like you," Jameson agreed. "Normally I would cheer you on for your anger management, but the Chief was the man. He dug us, even when he shouldn't have."

"We can do more investigations in there more than we can do in here. We'll never get anywhere with Laurel breathing down our necks."

Dirk gave her a grin. It made her heart skip a beat before it normalized again. "Should've known you were up to something."

Jameson started the engine when two police officers waved them on through the gate back into New Haven 56. "Should we get some hash browns or should we just got on with it?"

"What do you think?" Jenna sneered.

*****

Jameson was a bachelor, but lived in a stylish modern pad. Nothing seemed to go together. He had a fine Italian leather sofa, but a surfing board hung on his wall. There were trophies and medals for his Xtreme ironing skills next to fine art that looked like it belonged in a museum. The television was always on, and was balanced on top of a well-worn ironing board.

Jenna sat on the sofa sipping her coffee while the men took chairs on the opposite sides of a coffee table. Jameson was hunched over, working on one of his many cell phone computer contraptions. She was pretty good with technology, but mostly used it to game or for fun. "Okay, I used the alert system we usually use to spy on the Outpost. Man, they're gonna kill me if they ever figure this out."

"It'll be an honorable death at least," Jenna offered.

Dirk put his feet on the coffee table, but slowly pulled them back when Jameson glared at him. "Would you do that at my dear old mother's? Have some respect for the glass top,

Dirk." Jameson shook his head. "Okay, well, here's a bit of news. There were two body bags brought in. Not three. Bulletin says the daughter's body wasn't recovered."

Jenna and Dirk shared a look. "She wasn't in the house?"

"Or her body wasn't recovered yet. My money's on she wasn't home."

"Or," Jenna said, "she was kidnapped by whoever did this. She got in the way and she saw something she shouldn't, so they snatched her."

"The force will be all over this," Dirk said. "APB already out on her?"

Jameson nodded. "Officers are looking for her all over New Haven."

"They'll check all the regular places," Jenna said. "Her friends, hot spots, probably school. But if she's with whoever did this, she won't be so easy to track. Not if someone on the inside is helping. There's something about this I really don't like."

"Which part?" Jameson asked.

"The part where someone on the force deleted the vids and helped kill the chief and kidnap his daughter."

"Oh, that part."

"What do we do?" Dirk asked. "What's our first step?"

Jenna rubbed her face. Did they focus on finding the girl? Or focus on finding out why the chief was murdered? "Jameson, can you pull down everything Travis did yesterday? Everything that shows his schedule? I gotta believe that if someone killed him, it was for a big reason. Just to kill the chief—just, can you do it?"

"Yeah, you know I can. It'll take me a few minutes." Jameson's eyes moved across multiple screens at once as his fingers flew.

"Look for anything out of the ordinary. See when the call to 911 came in. If anyone flagged it, tried to hide it, anything. Mind if I raid your fridge? Just need something to take the edge off."

Jameson shook his head, but his eyes didn't leave his cell phone. "Go for it. Have whatever you like except for the green substance in the fridge. I'm not sure what it is. I think I'm growing my own ecosystem."

Jenna's nose wrinkled before heading off into the kitchen. It was small, but had all of the necessary component; except for edible looking food, she thought sourly. Peering inside the fridge she saw it was mostly bare and the green substance in a small container did scare her. Luckily, she found a box of crackers by the stove. They were soft rather than crunchy, but at least they would calm her stomach. Jenna crammed a handful in her mouth and chugged some water after them.

Her mind floated back to Travis, the last time she was at his house and had dinner. Alice was never Jenna's biggest fan, but she didn't have a lot of those. Still, they tolerated each other, and she really liked Wendy. A sweet, innocent girl. She didn't deserve what was happening to her, if indeed she was kidnapped. Hopefully they would find her at a friend's house, unaware of what happened

Jenna braced the counter, feeling the sting of tears in her eyes. She hated crying. Travis believed in her before anyone else did and even when he shouldn't. She didn't care what

Laurel said, she'd find who murdered him. So worked up, Jenna didn't hear the footsteps until it was too late to compose herself and felt the warm touch of Dirk's hand on her shoulder.

"I bet you're loving this," she said coolly.

The lines on his face were drawn in sadness. "No, I'm really not."

"Sorry. That was—I was out of line. You just always show up when I'm vulnerable." Jenna wiped her hands on her jeans, trying to give them some distance, but she was already backed into the kitchen counter and there wasn't much she could do other than to meld with the wooden top.

"I know when you're hurting. We all are, but I know he was special to you."

"Still is," Jenna's jaw was firm, defiant. "He's been dead only a few hours and already he's so past tense. The mutants here," she shook her head, "none of them will ever know how much the job meant to him. Sometimes I think he was a crackpot, caring so much."

"I know."

"They're monsters. They'd eat us if we turned the other way. But instead they're in here, pretending to be us. Like they're so normal, family, friends, flying friggin' kites with their families. He gave up the chance to do all that to protect them, make sure they were safe. They'll never know what he gave up. For *them*."

Because he saw humanity in the dragon shifters, but Jenna didn't. She felt how savage the blood was that ravaged through her veins.

Shifters were dangerous, just as she was.

"I *know,* Jen." Dirk put his arm around her shoulders. Despite everything that was left unsaid, Jenna leaned against him. Her hands curled into tight fists, bundles of pent-up emotion and her head lay on his shoulder. It was wrong, but familiar.

Dirk kissed the top of her head and it felt nice, too nice. Pushing him away was the right thing to do, but Jenna only wanted to keep him close. Wasn't fair to her, wasn't fair to him, but there she was, letting it linger on.

Allowing Dirk to love a shapeshifter. So weak, Jenna was disgusted with herself. "About earlier—"

"Forget it," Jenna stretched away, breaking the embrace. "We have more important things to worry about than us right now."

Dirk gave a slight nod that barely registered as movement. "If you'd feel better to talk about it now, get it out in the open—"

"I really wouldn't," Jenna said. She picked up her coffee from the counter and headed toward the living room. Hoped it would serve as a message.

She heard Jameson bellow from the living room. "I found something!"

Jenna stepped from the kitchen and into the living room. "What do you have?"

"A 911 call came in at 8:15. George, stationed two blocks from the chief's house, was the first to radio in that he was approaching the scene, but get this. He didn't get there until 8:23."

Jenna raised her eyebrows. She picked a mug off the table and sipped it. It was bitter and cold, but also wet, which was something her mouth was missing right about then. "We have to expect that when the news came in, he drove faster than a bat out of hell, so why'd it take so long?"

"He was two minutes away, tops." Dirk said.

"We find George. We find out what he was doing for those extra five minutes." Jenna threw her attention to Jameson. "Can you still pry and spy from the road?"

He nodded. "Someone else will have to drive."

Jenna picked up the van's keys and tossed them to Dirk. "I have the back. Gentlemen, just in case, make sure you're packing. If George is up to no good, he might suspect someone is on their way."

Chapter Fourteen

Mutant Rights and Protection Agency
Alexandria, Virginia

Wendy awoke early that morning with a stretch. She begged for sleep to stay around awhile longer and refused to open her eyes. Slowly she became aware of her surroundings; her pillow was soft and the goose down comforter snug around her body was warm. She felt like she was home, secure and safe. Under the covers, she stretched her hand out and felt the heat of another body beside her. Her fingertips stroked his leg, feeling the small hairs on his flesh rise up. Finally she allowed her eyes to flutter open, smiling slightly at the sleeping face of Jake.

There was so much excitement and happiness the night before. Everyone she met at the Dragon Rights headquarters was so excited and after a long meet-and-greet, Wendy went to bed exhausted. For the first time, she fell asleep in Jake's arms.

It was just like she dreamed, just like she always thought it would be. She was sad for leaving her parents, but one day she'd be able to tell them. She really believed that. And maybe one day, with the help of her baby, Jake and all those like him would be accepted. Wendy hoped so. Wouldn't it be cool if it were their child that brought the world together?

The thoughts warmed her heart as she glanced around at their living quarters. It was comfortable and clean, if a bit on the sterile side. Wendy was looking forward to having her own place, doing with it what she wanted, buying her own things, finding a sense of style and making it feel like home. This place wasn't home, but would do while Rebecca and her staff made sure her baby was okay.

Thinking about him, Wendy slid a hand across her belly, warmly patting it. Somehow now that she was out of New Haven, it felt bigger, but she didn't care. It was her baby and out in the world. It would be okay to admit it.

Leaning up, she kissed Jake's lips and watched him smile in his sleep. She did it again, feeling his arms tightening around her. They kissed some more and she enjoyed his morning's breath, his warm body pressed up against hers. Falling into a deep embrace, she nuzzled her nose against his neck, sighing contently.

There would be trouble, rough decisions in the future, but for now she was so happy to be with him and in his arms.

"Morning," he finally said with a smile, his eyes slowly blinking open.

"Sleep okay?" Wendy asked, even though she knew he had.

Jake kissed the side of her head, his nose nuzzling her hair. "Perfect. It's nice to wake up with you. Think they serve breakfast in this place?"

"I think they'll do anything we want. They act like we're Adam and Eve."

"More like you're Eve and I'm the forbidden fruit." Jake slid his hand across her abdomen. "Are you feeling all right?" His eyes turned dark, concerned. It made Wendy smile to see how much he really did care for her. She wished it were something her dad could have seen. One day, she hoped he would.

"A little queasy, but I'm okay. A little nervous. Today is the big day." Wendy sat up, both hands on her belly. "The first time we get to see him. I hope he's all right." The edge of fear was in her voice and no matter how much she tried, she couldn't keep it out.

Jake understood, wrapping his arms around her. "And if he's not, will you regret everything? Being with me?"

"Not on your life," Wendy whispered, leaning on his shoulder.

"He'll be fine. You'll see," Jake said and it sounded perfunctorily, like something you said because you had to.

****

Wendy felt like a slab of meat in the butcher's case.

The doctors she met were nice, but as she lay on the table with her extended belly exposed she felt on display. They talked amongst themselves rather than to her or Jake, and she just wanted to scream, *Is my baby okay?*

Instead she blinked her eyes, searching their faces while gripping Jake's hand hard. He wore the pensive look of concentration, his eyes searching the monitor at the lumps and swirls that Wendy was pretty sure was her baby. But was he okay? Would he be okay?

"Gentlemen." Rebecca Seers broke Wendy's thoughts effortlessly and with a slight smile. "I believe you've lost your manners."

The doctors barely stammered, their eyes glazed over as they turned her attention toward her.

Rebecca placed a hand warmly on Wendy's shoulder and gave it a squeeze. "She is dying to know about the condition of her baby. Can't you tell? The poor girl is nearly in tears."

One doctor, short and with the perpetual smell of mint blushed profusely. "I apologize, Ms. Seers and Wendy." He smiled, offering his hand to Jake. "You're going to have a son and so far, he looks just fine. Just fine!"

Jake broke out into a broad grin and Wendy's heart pounded so fast that she wasn't sure her chest could contain the racing beats. "Oh, Jake," she cracked out, and the two teenagers embraced hard. Sniffling, Wendy glanced back at the monitor. "Is that really him?"

The doctor nodded, pointing to the screen. "There's the nose and over here, the feet."

"He's all right?" Jake asked apprehensively. "He's...is he going to be like me?" There was fear in his face and Wendy felt sorry for how apologetic he was. He shouldn't be; he was wonderful. She loved him despite their differences and didn't care if he was human or mutant. He was Jake and that was enough for her. It was like her dad always taught her. Shifters could do well if that's what they wanted and Jake did. He was raised by good parents.

How they must be missing him now. It made Wendy sad and she was sorry, but they had no choice. They had to be together and protect their baby. Rebecca would make sure they were safe.

"Every test and everything we've done shows that he's human. I'm sure there will be a few shifter traits, however—"

Rebecca cut him off by warmly placing her hand on Jake's shoulder. "This is proof that you, and the other shifters, are human. You were infected, but you are no different than me. No different than Wendy, and you deserve life and the liberties that go along with that." She smiled warmly at them. "With your help and this baby, maybe we can find a cure from your aliments and liberty will be right around the corner."

Wendy smiled kindly at the doctor, who wiped the cold gel from her belly and helped her sit up. She pulled down her shirt. "What now?"

Rebecca glanced over her shoulder, but there was no one else but them in the small room. It was the first time Wendy saw a trace of apprehension in the woman's face and it scared her. She was the leader of a great activist group; what did Rebecca Seers have to be afraid of?

"There's a small fishing community not far from here. Away from the prying eyes of the media and anyone else that might look for you. Jake, you need to be taught to blend, to hide among humans. We can't get caught. And sooner or later, someone is going to come looking for Wendy."

Jake nodded. "I can do it. If you teach me, I can do whatever you tell me."

Rebecca smiled at him. "I know. Only my key staff here knows who the both of you really are. We'll move you after lunch. Staff is already there getting the cabin ready for you."

"You're not coming with us?" Wendy asked. Jake helped her down off the examination table and draped an arm across her shoulder. Wendy delicately touched his fingertips.

"Someone else will be, someone that I trust my life with. I have to be here to keep up pretenses, but we will talk as often as you want to." Her smile was warm, reassuring. "Jake, you'll need to learn to take care of Wendy and your child. We're going to arrange for a job for you, but we'll get you everything you needed to get started."

"If they find us—" Jake's voice trailed off, rubbing Wendy's shoulder.

"You'll be protected. You have my word." Rebecca touched each of their cheeks in turn. "Now, go enjoy some lunch maybe out under the trees. Relax."

She was relieved, glad and happy. Hand in hand, Wendy and Jake left the examination room. From behind the closed door, Wendy thought she heard one of the doctors say, "We need to talk."

She must have misheard, Wendy thought as she rubbed her belly where she felt the baby kick. If there were something wrong, Rebecca would tell her. The woman was more than just their friend. She was their savior.

Chapter Fifteen

"He never came home."

The words left Susan's mouth, but it didn't feel real. This wasn't like Jake at all. He always came home on time and never stayed out all night. It was supposed to be impossible. If an underage mutant was out past curfew—ten p.m.—the police were supposed to be notified. They would pick them up and return them home. That was how things were done, but no one came. No one called.

Her son was missing.

Jeff glanced around Jake's room and Susan could see that he was disturbed by what he saw: the perfectly made bed, the folded clothes over the back of his chair. Jake was always a good boy. He always did his chores before he went to practice. He always did what his mom asked of him. "Maybe he—" Jeff broke off, "I just don't know, Susan. Did the phone ring at all in the middle of the night?"

"No, I would have noticed. I sat up half the night waiting for him." Susan had dark circles under her eyes that concealer wouldn't begin to cover. She looked puffy, certainly not her best. "Should we call the police?"

Jeff sighed, bending to peek beneath their son's bed. "With everything that's going on, I don't think this is the best time to call them."

"Our son is missing," Susan said intently, quietly. "And you're worried about how that will look?"

"I'm worried about the rest of my family. Marie, you," Jeff rubbed her arms. "He can't go anywhere or hurt anyone. He'll be back and he'll have some explaining to do."

"I just want him home safe," Susan whispered, hands over her mouth. There were thick tears in her eyes and fear netted in her chest. "He can say anything he wants if he'd just come home."

"Oh, honey." Jeff hugged her. "Please, try not to panic."

"What if he's hurt somewhere? What if he can't come home?"

"You know as well as I do, if he was in distress the police would be notified. They'd go to him. They'd call us." Jake's tone was still soft, even. It made Susan want to scream at him. Couldn't he get emotional, just once?

"With everything that's going on? How do we know that? How?" Susan's voice broke off. "I just got him more eggs yesterday. I promised him I'd make them for him. How come he's not here?"

"Do you want me to keep the restaurant closed today?" Jeff rubbed her arms, making eye contact. "I can stay with you."

Susan shook her head, her chin quivered. "You go. We both shouldn't go crazy." Besides, she knew that if Dusty's didn't open, the police would get suspicious. Maybe even think somehow they were involved in what happened to Travis Reynolds.

"I'll swing by his school, all right? Talk to a few of his friends. See if they know anything, okay?"

Relief flooded her eyes. "Oh, please. Call me, after you talk to them."

"I will, honey, I will." Jeff kissed her forehead. "Try to relax. Go about your day as normal as possible, for me. I can't live without you, hon." Jeff gave her a smile; it gave her strength. Then he was gone.

After a moment of looking inside her son's closets, she went downstairs. Marie was sitting on the sofa with her notebook cradled to her chest. Her eyes were wide and she was staring off at the wall. The look on her face said she didn't really see it, didn't really see anything. "Marie?" Her mother bent over and stroked her hair back.

"I don't mean it, you know," her daughter whispered. "When I tease him, I don't mean it."

"He knows. Don't look so sad, he'll be back." Susan kissed her daughter's cheeks. "I bet you'll see him at school or he'll be here when you get back. You have a test today, don't you?"

Marie nodded. "Math. I hate math."

"You better hop to it then. Off to school. Tonight I'm making your favorite."

"Jake's favorite too," Marie reminded her. She stood up and grabbed her lunchbox off the floor. "Bye, Mom." Her eyes were haunted, moist, as she headed out the door.

Susan sighed, wringing her hands together. She hurried into the kitchen and picked up the phone. She dialed the number for the school and paced the floor back and forth.

Finally the switchboard operator answered. "New Haven High. How can I direct your call?"

She paused and took a deep breath. "I need to speak to Coach Walters please. This is Mrs. Jeff Monroe."

"One moment please." A beep resonated across the phone and then Susan was placed on hold. Light music from Barry Manilow played and she found her nerves calmed by it. Toward the end, she began to hum lightly along. Finally a gruff, but pleasant voice answered. "Mrs. Monroe, nice to speak with you again."

"Coach," Susan tried to get control of her rising panic, "I was wondering if everything went all right last night. At the practice."

"Ma'am?" the coach asked, as if he hadn't heard her.

"Last night's practice? Jake," Susan twirled the phone's cord around her finger, unable to believe she was really saying it out loud, "didn't come home last night."

"Oh Mrs. Monroe, that is horrible, horrible news. I'm sorry to be the one to tell you this, but there was no practice last night. Jake, well, he quit the team last Friday."

"Wh—Pardon?" Susan's legs were rubber. She thought she might slide right down to the floor. "He quit?"

"Yes, ma'am. He said it was interfering with his studies. I know he's always struggled, but he's a bright boy. Have you been in touch with the police?"

"Not yet," Susan said lifelessly. It felt like she was floating and when she glanced down at her arm, she saw it was beginning to shimmer. Her skin was turning blue. She was losing control of her form; the shock was too much for her.

"I recommend you do."

"I will. Thank you so much for your concern. I really need to go." Susan rattled on, hanging up the phone before Coach said good-bye. Behind her, she could hear wind gathering steam as her wings stretched. The transformation into a real mutant was nearly complete, and with that morph came the power of anger, hunger. Susan opened the door to the fridge and instead of a hand gripping the handle were tight claws, pointed and sharp.

Reaching inside, Susan pulled out a container of juice and jugged it back. Some dribbled down her chin and her tongue licked the corner of her lips to gather off stray moisture beads. With that done, her form morphed back into a human one. The rage she felt was under control, it was in check. Bliss overcame her and Susan's face tightened, as if she had applied too much acne cream. Her skin contracted, constricted and she felt a tingle stretching through every fiber of her skin. To be young and to be beautiful was a shifters' right, but it was also a dangerous curse.

She nearly dropped the container when the phone rang. Susan placed it down on the counter as she answered. "Good morning, Monroe residence."

"Well, there you are, my dear!"

Susan's heart felt like it stopped inside her chest. "Megan," she practically screamed into the receiver.

"That is my name, or so they tell me." Her tone was playful and filled with fun.

"I thought—I mean the police," Susan whispered, eyes darting around the kitchen, "the police took you."

"I know, I know! I was there, remember?" Megan laughed, her voice airy like she had not a care in the world. "I just needed to cool down. I'm sorry if I frightened you, but I'm all right. I'm home with my boys and have been dying, *dying* to talk to you. Now they're off to school, work and the like."

Susan squeezed her eyes shut and her shoulders quaked with a sob. "Oh, Megan—are you sure, sure you're all right?"

"Don't I sound all right, sugar puff? What's the matter? You sound like they canceled your favorite soap opera. It's not about John and Marlena again, is it? I missed yesterday's episode."

How could she be so casual? "Megan, I hope you're all right. Really I do, but it's about Jake." Susan's lips quivered. "It's about my son."

"You sound horrible. Should I head over? I could make a lemon Bundt cake."

"There's no time. He's—" Susan lowered her voice, as if someone it would make it better, "—he's missing. Last night, he didn't come home," she sobbed with a crack. Susan covered her mouth and tried to compose herself.

Megan gasped. "Oh dear, Susan! I'm too stunned for words. Do the police know? Have you called anyone?"

Susan shook her head, unable to speak. "I was afraid. Jeff thinks that with everything going on with the chief, they'll be suspicious. But, he's just a boy. What do I do? What?" The words charged from her mouth.

"Clean your face, darling. Clean your face and come meet me. There's someone I know who can help you."

It felt like Megan was the sun to her storm cloud, always able to help and pull back the veil of black. She always knew what to do. "Where? Who? I'll meet you right away."

"Thirty-Seven Acre Woods Road. There's a building. Go to the basement. It's safe to talk there. *Very safe.*"

Susan didn't understand how any place could be safe to talk. "Who can help me?"

"Lawrence Stark, darling."

Terror struck her heart. "No, no. I can't. What if the police see me? They might take me away. They might take me away too."

"Just like me? Don't I sound fine? The police were understanding, really, hon. But if you want your son, if you want help finding him, Lawrence can help you. He knows this city in ways no one else does. He's a smart industrious young man."

Megan did sound fine, happy. But earlier, she was so upset about how they were forced to live their lives. Susan didn't understand the sudden change. Maybe she could take this chance, maybe Lawrence could help her and she could keep it quiet. Jeff would never need to know. He'd worry so much if he knew she went to Lawrence Stark.

"Will you come, Susan?"

She thought about it, twisting the cord around her finger. "Yes, I'll come. I'll meet you there."

"Good." Megan's voice was smiling. "Good. You be a good girl and get ready. I have a quick errand to run and I'll meet you there in fifteen?"

"Okay. You're sure—you're sure about this?"

"Definitely, hon! Lawrence Stark is going to be the answer to all your prayers."

****

Acre Woods Avenue in a small cluster of streets in the far east of New Haven, where all the roads were named after Winnie the Pooh. Susan loved reading those stories and watching the cartoons so always wanted to live there. Except for the fact that the blue bubble that kept New Haven safe came down sharply around them. When you looked out your window you could see the bubble veering down despite the fact there was a tense collection of trees made to look like a forest. Really, it was like hanging a beautiful portrait on a steel beam. Underneath, the beam was still present.

Susan parked her car behind a cluster of others and checked her reflection. It wasn't that bad she thought and gave a quick powder to her nose. The address was a giant, steepled white church with marble stairs. The door was heavy as she pushed on the metal handle. Inside it smelled like coffee and disinfectant. Lights dimmed as the door slowly shut behind her, blocking out the sunlight. Its bottom dragged along the floor and screeched shut, like a vault.

She felt a bit trapped as she eyed the entryway. Along the left were mailboxes for the members of the church. Straight ahead around a bend she saw pews, but directly in front of her was a set of plush steps leaning downstairs into the basement. From that way she head the clinking of silverware and the light rumble of voices. Susan took a deep breath, death-gripped the railing, and slowly made her decent down.

She could barely see as the stairwell darkened. Her eyes blinked to adjust as she came to the bottom level. It was a small basement with chairs lined up ready for bible study. Along one wall, a table was set up with coffee and cookies. Susan recognized several of those gathered. Through the crowd, Megan stepped with a huge grin.

Susan felt better just seeing it and her heart opened up, welling with pain for her missing son. They gripped each other's arms. She felt like crying, leaning her head on her friend's shoulder.

Megan patted her head gently so not to disrupt her hair. "Now, now. It'll be okay, won't it? Nothing to be sad about, right? We're going to help you."

Susan wiped her tears away delicately. "Who are all these people? Is Lawrence here?"

Megan held a finger to her lips. "Not yet, dear. Sssh, not yet."

She didn't understand what was going on. Her eyes cast to Megan. Her friend's wrist had a bright red mark on it. What was that about? Did the police hurt her? Was it something else? Susan's chest heaved with anxiety and she wanted to run, to get out of there. It was stupid to come. Jeff would kill her if he found out. What if she were putting him and Marie in jeopardy just by going? Always listening to her crazy friend, he'd say. Getting pulled into one stupid scheme after another. Who did she they think they were? Lucy and Ethel?

Susan's eyes were attracted by a tall man. He was dressed in a simple black suit that matched his hair and his eyes were cool, like the mid-morning sky. The lines around his lips and eyes were severe and sunken. She felt afraid of him and again felt the instinct to run as he glanced at her. His hand swept across a device that looked like a radio. A low noise pulsed around the group as a beam of light traveled in a circle around the wall. When it completed its trajectory, the room lit up in a blue glow. Susan didn't understand what was going on, but Megan grabbed her hand and forced her to take a seat.

"It's safe to talk now," Megan whispered in her ear. "Lawrence made that device and it works because of how close we are to the bubble. It makes static cross their communication devices."

Susan couldn't believe it. Somewhere they could talk without fear that someone might listen in on them? How did she not know that Megan was in this deep with Lawrence and his followers? She was a fool to come here. Now everyone would see, it would get back to Jeff. *Susan, you dope, you should have just gone to the police.* Wasn't that what respected members of the community did? They relied on the authorities for this type of thing. She wanted to go, she wanted to bolt, but Megan gripped her hand to keep her still.

"No one leaves while Lawrence is speaking. No one."

Lawrence turned toward the crowd, his hands clasped together. "My friends, last night was the catalyst of change for us, the shifters of New Haven 56."

Intense silence filled the room as everyone waited for Lawrence to continue. Even Susan's heart stilled as she watched him. It was the first time she ever heard him speak, ever saw him up close. The fear of him, everything he stood for, was palpable. Her mouth was dry and her lips were chapped. She couldn't find the will to swallow.

"With the death of Travis Reynolds and his family, scrutiny will shift to us, my friends. It is time to unite, to stand up against them. It's like I have always said, there are far many more of us than there are of them."

Susan couldn't believe what she was hearing. As her eyes swept across the room she was more horrified. People here believed him. They wanted to rise up? What would that do? What of their agreement with the humans was voided?

"We have friends on the outside," he said as though he could read her mind and Susan wasn't sure that he couldn't. "Rebecca Seers and her crew work to grant us rights, privileges, so one day we can leave our prison. It will not be in our lifetime, friends. Not unless we rise up and do something about it. We should be in control of our own destiny, should we not? Travis was sympathetic to our cause. Now he's gone. It won't be long until we're next."

Susan twisted her purse strap tightly around her hand. What if he was right? Would they just be snuffed out if the people on the outside, the government and the country, decided they were too big a liability? She was a thinking, breathing, person with family, friends. Except she wasn't a person, was she? Susan, despite all the acting and show, was just a mutant.

It wasn't her fault. She didn't ask to be this. She didn't ask to be born this way. Susan was sorry, if she could change, she would. She just wanted to be normal.

Lawrence's eyes fell to her. He got down on bended knee in front of her and took her hand. "What is your name?"

"Susan," she whispered, not able to look up at him. She struggled with all her will to swallow and calm her frantic heart.

"Welcome, Susan," Lawrence and the crowd said in a soft monotone. "Why don't you tell me," he continued, his voice soft and insincere, "what has you so upset?"

"Everything you said. And, um," Susan's voice trailed off, "my son. He's missing. Hasn't been home since last night."

A quiet murmur rolled through the crowd, blanketing them in caustic anxiety. "You worry, don't you? If he was out past curfew, why didn't the police find him and bring him home?"

Susan nodded. "Yes." She blubbered, unable to control her tears. She felt hands from strangers placed on her shoulders and words of strength were whispered to her. It made her feel better, like she was with friends. Family.

"You fear the police have him?"

"No." Startled, she peered up at him. "Why would they? I'm worried he's hurt somewhere. Why would the police have him?"

"Do they really need a reason, Susan?" Lawrence stood back up, pacing the carpet and facing the crowd. He held his hands out like he was deep in prayer, cupping the air. "We have no rights. We have no say in when they come and what they do in our homes. If they wanted Jake Monroe, for whatever their reason, why not just snatch him? We must go on, pretend nothing has happened, or it might happen to us. If we make a scene, like our fellow friend, Megan, we could be next. Couldn't we, friends?

"That's why we must stand up, organize and be prepared. As a group, as an army. We can take them, seize control of this city."

How did he know her son's name? Susan was confused, conflicted and when she glanced over at Megan, and saw how intently her friend was listening, she felt betrayed. Lawrence couldn't help Jake. Her friend just wanted her to join the cause, become one of Lawrence's soldiers in a war they could not win. Susan didn't want to die, but she didn't want anything to change either. Couldn't they just live as they always did? Head down, Tupperware and pool parties, late-night snacks gathered in front of the television. Wasn't that what life was all about?

After the speech was over Susan fumbled with a paper cup and tried to pour herself some organ juice. But she was so upset that she splashed it all over her blouse. Sighing, she cleaned it up with a napkin. "Let me help you with that," Lawrence said. He took the cup from her without waiting for an answer and poured her some.

"Thanks," Susan said.

"You don't agree everything I said, do you?" He smiled curt, but kind. His eyes blinked fast as if lint debris had fallen inside.

"I like my life the way it is."

"Other than your son being missing," Lawrence reminded her. "Living in a box, with people watching you all the time, none of that bothers you? It'll be fun, converting you to one of us. You want to be here. If you didn't, you wouldn't have come."

Susan sipped her juice to calm her nerves, but it made her stomach rumble. With the feeling that she was going to be sick, she left the church and hoped never to return again.

Susan was disgusted with herself. She could not believe what she allowed to happen. If anyone found out she went to a meeting led by Lawrence Stark, she'd be done in. What if someone there told Jeff? Or they told someone and that someone told Jeff? He was a popular person in the community and it was her job not to make waves. *Don't rock the boat.* How many times had she heard him say that or her parents? It was practically a mutant motto. So upset by what she did, Susan's hands were clammy against the steering wheel. She was never so relieved to see her home, free of any parked cars in the driveway.

Thank goodness Jeff hadn't popped home for lunch like he sometimes did. What if he came home, what would she say? Susan had to put it out of her mind. She was going to make a nice lunch, prepare a big dinner, and call the police about Jake. Her brain must have left the building earlier, to let it be deceived by Megan.

The phone rang. Susan considered not answering it at all, but what if it was important? What if it was Jake? She grabbed the receiver in a flurry, nearly dropping it. "Jake?"

On the other side there was static. A muffled voice came over the receiver. "Mrs. Monroe, if you want to ever see your son again, you'll do exactly as we tell you."

Her heart galloped like a runaway horse. She spun, her back to the fridge. "What do you know about my son?" She held a hand to her cheek, her fingers clamped into her flesh in horror.

"We can have him returned to you safely, but only if you do as we say."

Susan's mind raced with thoughts and accusations, but she couldn't voice anything. She was frozen silent.

"Four p.m. in the park on Central Boulevard. A briefcase will be placed next to the water fountain. Take it. Open it in the privacy of your bathroom at exactly five-fifteen p.m. If you do not, we cannot guarantee your son's survival."

Susan wrote what he said down, but she couldn't believe what she was hearing. Tears stung her eyes. "How do I know you mean what you say?"

"Do not tell your husband. Tell no one. And Mrs. Monroe, change your shirt before you go out."

The line went dead. Slack-jawed, Susan stared at the red stain on her blouse.

How did he know? How did he see her? Were they watching her now? The phone slipped from her fingers. The receiver fell as if it were attached to a bungee cord, slapping against the wall. The vibration knocked throughout the spacious kitchen.

Chapter Sixteen

Jameson's elite tracking abilities led them to a coffee shop over by Main Street were the wait staff wore paper hats. Music inside was inspired by Buddy Holly and the hardest thing on the menu was rocky road ice cream. The tables were crammed with the beautiful shifters Jenna expected. Their chatter was hushed and their eyes moved erratically.

She walked among them like a sheriff among thieves, her steps purposeful, slow and her eyes studying each of their faces.

Her boots squeaked across the tile and the eyes of the shifters were on her. Until she tried to make eye contact. Then their eyes shifted away. They were wide, filled with horror, and seemed to beg *please don't let her look at me*. But Jenna looked at all of them, smirking and enjoying their discomfort.

One cowered in the corner, nursing his milkshake. He was clean-cut enough and Jenna smelled vulnerability on him. "Why is everyone sitting at the front?" she asked, not bothering with introductions.

His hands shook so that his milkshake sloshed out of his tall glass. He answered with his eyes squeezed shut. "Cop. There's a cop." His arm shot out straight as an arrow and his finger extended.

Jenna followed it with her eyes and saw him. Still in his uniform, he sat in a back booth by the window with an uneaten glazed donut on a sparkling plate. George kept flipping his fork in his hand over again. A nervous twitch Jenna suspected.

She signaled her team with a nod of her head and as they made their way toward him, Jenna scowled at the shifters. They parted for her as she moved past, hurrying with their coffee and snacks in hand. She slid in the seat beside George. Dirk and Jameson sat across from him.

So upset by whatever was bothering him, George jerked. He blinked at Jenna. She tried to hold eye contact, but he shifted away again before she got a read off him. "I'm surprised Laurel let you out of the Outpost. I heard what you guys tried to pull."

"You mean you heard we tracked down that someone was deleting surveillance vids?" Dirk asked.

Jenna suppressed a sigh. Dirk always did know how to make a point.

The coffee cup rattled in George's hand. "I didn't know that. I just heard you were trying to hijack the operation."

"We're just looking into a few things and need a few answers. I think you can provide that for us, George." Jenna used her smooth talking voice. The same one she sometimes used to pick up guys who were not named Dirk.

"I'm not in charge of the investigation. I don't know what you expect me to be able to tell you." George rubbed his neck.

"Maybe why you're sweating a pint of water might be good. It's a bit cool in here," Dirk said.

Jenna nodded her head toward Jameson. Happily, he puffed up his chest and studied his cell phone. "Want to explain to us why it took you over ten minutes to go two blocks after it was reported that something was wrong at the chief's house?"

George glanced between them, leaning back against the booth. He wiped his hands together. "Wait a second, are you guys interrogating me? You think I deleted the vids? I don't even have that kind of access."

"No, we were curious about the state of traffic congestion in New Haven," Dirk said with heavy sarcasm.

"No one said anything about you deleting the vids," Jenna said, "unless, of course, you're confessing."

"Damn it, Jenna. You can't just go around accusing people." George's fists clenched and his eyes squeezed shut.

She softened her voice to edge him into trusting her. "Then, just tell us what's going on. Were you really two blocks away? Maybe you fell asleep. I don't know unless you tell me. And if you waste my time, while the chief's killer is still out there, I'm really going to be angry."

"You have no authority to ask me these questions." George's eyes narrowed in anger. "I did my job. I got to the chief as soon as I could."

"Are you sure?" Jenna asked. "We could make a formal complaint. We're not against paperwork, are we, fellas?"

"No," Jameson and Dirk said drily.

George rolled his shoulders in a way that showed Jenna he was agitated. She didn't get it. He was a cop. He should be able to hide his emotions better than he was. Unless, of course, he knew something so bad that it had him rattled. "What's it going to be?" She asked quietly, but with an edge in her voice that dared him.

"Look, it has nothing to do with the chief. Nothing to do with what happened last night." He fidgeted from side to side in his seat.

"Let us be the judge of that, okay?" Dirk asked.

"No," George sputtered. "You don't know what you're asking me."

"We could do it in the Outpost," Jenna offered and put her hand on his arm. "A little peace offering for Laurel. Maybe she'll let us into the investigation if I prove we're worthy."

"We're not worthy," Jameson snickered. "What? I love that movie, guys."

"You can't do that. Jenna, c'mon. Let this go," George said.

"You know you're talking to Jenna Morgan, right? She hasn't let anything go since the day her brother toppled over her Legos," Dirk said.

Jenna cast him a wry glower, but it seemed like his words worked. George was beginning to falter. "It's not what you think. I was doing someone a favor. She was in trouble, I was doing what I had to help her out."

"Who?" Jenna asked.

George shook his head. "I can't. Can't tell you."

"Were you helping a mutant?" Jameson asked with a lace of disgust. "Did you leave your post to help a dragon mutant shifter?"

"No," George shot him a look, but his eyes were frightened. He was indecisive, Jenna realized. He didn't know how to answer the question. She wasn't sure if she believed him anymore. "Look it's not like that—"

"You keep saying that," Jenna said, "so why don't you stop and just tell us what it is like."

"We won't tell anyone. As long as it has nothing to do with what happened to the chief last night." Dirk was smooth and comforting, and even Jenna believed him even though she knew what a gossip hound he was. If the information was good, it would spread like wildfire through the police station, thanks to fan-the-flames-Dirk.

George folded his napkin into a neat little triangle, with a bit of paper flapping over the side. "I was helping Rebecca Seers. This can't get out, Jenna. It'll cost me my job."

Jenna's chest tightened and the searing anger made her temples throb. "You better get explaining what you were helping *her* for."

George took a deep breath and Jenna could feel how rigid her teammates were on the other side of the table. "There's some support growing on the force for what Rebecca is trying to do. There was evidence inside New Haven that shifters aren't what we think. They're more human. I…I helped her get the evidence out. Out of New Haven."

His admission floored Jenna. Floored her. There was no evident. Dragon shifters weren't human. She ought to know.

"You helped her smuggle something out past Outpost?" Dirk asked, his jaw slack.

"You don't know, all right?" George was defensive. "You aren't here, spending time with these people. You don't see the brutality."

"They *deserve* it," Jameson said, his cheeks flushed. "Are you defending these monsters?"

Jenna's eyebrow twitched from anger and she felt that feeling of lightheadedness sweep over her. She reached for the pouch in her jacket to grab her pills that kept her from shifting from emotional peaks and crests caused by her personality. "What evidence?"

George opened his mouth to speak. Beside him, the window shattered behind the impact of a high-speed bullet. It pierced through his skull. He slumped over, his head rocking against Jenna's shoulder. His mouth fell open while his head opened up like a cracked pumpkin, depositing blood and brain tissue onto the left side of Jenna's face. She couldn't move, but inside her brain screamed with searing heat.

Shifters screamed, running from the diner. Dirk and Jameson fought against them as they ran into the street, searching for the shooter. Jenna carefully pushed George over and gently placed his head against the table. The side of his head was collapsed like a fallen cavern and she wondered what had he been in the process of telling her that warranted killing an officer in the middle of the day?

Travis's murderer was still in New Haven. Whatever reasons they had for killing the chief, they were now in the process of tying up loose ends. Desperation and horror washed over Jenna. She popped two small pills into her mouth and swallowed them back dry.

****

Jenna had never frozen up in the line of duty before, and she didn't like it.

Inside the women's restroom, she scrubbed her face to remove all traces of George's blood from her skin. Her cheek was reddened from the abrasive towel, but other than that she looked good. There was no evidence of anything except for the brain matter splattered against the shoulder of her black jacket.

She brushed it into the toilet and flushed before noticing the particles left on her fingers. Jenna glanced at it in horror, felt a gurgle in her belly. She wiped her hands on some paper towel already in the wastebasket before hurrying outside.

Police were already on the scene, quarantining shifters and taking statements. Jenna's eyes fell on an officer as he forced a waiter to the ground. The waiter's paper hat tumbled to the ground as he screamed and his face flinched with pain. The officer raised his baton high overhead, disgust on his face. Jenna looked away, knowing emotions were running high. She had to do what she did best. Piece this together.

Before New Haven tore itself apart.

Jenna walked across the street toward a hardware store. Dirk and Jameson were out front. "Shooter was positioned on the roof of this building, best I can tell," Jameson said. "He took George out before heading down this back alley."

"We lost him when he got into the back of a van," Dirk said grimly.

"Same van?" Jenna asked.

Jameson nodded. "Maybe we're looking in the wrong place, Jen. Maybe this is the work of mutants."

"And they got a sniper gun, explosives where?" Jenna was aware her voice was a bit too high-pitched. She knew why mutants were locked up, but Jenna's gut spoke loudly to her that it wasn't them pulling the trigger. But maybe they were the reason. Maybe they were why Travis was killed and that idea made her hate them even more.

"Rebecca smuggled them in with the help of George." Jameson said.

"Except you're forgetting they just killed him," Dirk reminded him. "Why kill someone that's on your side?"

"Because they're damn-ass crazy?" Jameson asked.

Jenna sighed. "We're losing track. We go where the evidence leads us. Right now our biggest lead is dead so we have to look into what he told us. Little as it was. The fact that Rebecca Seers was up to something on the same night the chief was killed can't be a coincidence. It's connected. We just have to find out how."

"We need to talk to her," Dirk said with resolve. "Too bad we can't call out while we're in here."

"And we can't get out until the quarantine is lifted."

"So, what do we do?" Jameson asked. "Drive around until we spot a van just like our van?"

"Check town activity reports," Jenna ordered. "See if anything weird or unusual is going on outside the norm."

Jameson nodded, reached for his cell phone, and headed toward their vehicle. Jenna took the moment to cross her arms and study the scene. It should have been loud and disorderly, but it wasn't. The shifters were perfectly under control as the police kept them bunched together for questioning and searches. If they were anywhere else but a New Haven colony, the scene would be playing out differently. Much differently.

Her head turned when she realized Dirk was studying her. A breeze swept across his face, dancing hair across his forehead, and Jenna restrained herself from setting it right. "Staring?"

"Just wondering if you're all right."

"Because my reaction inside the shop was slow?"

"Slower than usual. Course it's not every day someone is executed like that in New Haven. Not a police officer anyway." A toothpick twirled against his lips that Jenna hadn't realized he had.

Was she losing time again?

"Thanks for defending me to yourself. It's appreciated." Jenna walked away, feeling his eyes penetrating through the back of her head. It was one thing to feel vulnerable with Dirk inside the safety of an apartment, but it was another thing while they were on duty. Laurel might have thought she was off the case, but to Jenna, nothing was further from the truth. She wouldn't stop until she found out what was going on. The brain splatter across her shoulder of a good officer was just added incentive.

When she approached the van, the look on Jameson's face as he sat in the driver's seat put her on alert. "What'd you find?"

He barely glanced up, his thumbs moving across the transparent surface of his phone. "Mutant killed herself this morning at her job. Few hours ago."

Jenna's eyebrow corked. She heard Dirk's footsteps behind her approaching. "That's unusual. Him?"

"Her," Jameson corrected. "Everyone that knew her said she was healthy and happy."

"Anything on her in the Outpost? Was she seeing one of the therapists? Maybe her indoctrination was slipping."

"That's the thing, Jen," Jameson sighed. Uneasy his face was cast down and his skin was pale. "When I try to bring up her profile to see if there are any vids on her, I'm blocked. It says I don't have the proper credentials to access her."

Dirk and Jenna exchanged a glance. "Can you hack in?"

"With the equipment I have here? Not in under a few hours." Jameson sighed. "I placed a few calls to some buds. At least I thought they were. They're stonewalling me, Jen. I tried to find out if they have a lead on Travis's kid or what happened with George." He shook his head. "They acted like I was the plague."

Something big was going on. Bigger than they realized. She remained thoughtful, calm, but thought that the goodwill she received from the force might be over now, with Travis dead. Who knew how long it would be before she lost her job? She couldn't worry about that now, despite how tough things were in the real world. No matter what happened, Jenna had to see this through.

"All right then. We do it the old-fashioned way. We head to her work and see what we can find out." She hopped in the van, getting herself situated while Dirk did the same. "Where'd she work?"

"Haven High School."

Chapter Seventeen

The halls of Haven High were clean even by mutant standards. The air had a hint of lemon and the tile floors were waxed and buffed to a perfect shine. Perfect place for a murder, Jenna thought to herself as she led her team toward the nurse's room.

Already her mind was convinced that whoever this lady was, she hadn't committed suicide.

Mutant suicide rates were the lowest they had been in over ten years and New Haven 56 never had one. What a coincidence it would be to happen this week of all weeks.

There was a mutant outside the nurse's office. He was nervous, appeared to be on guard. Dressed in a nice suit with fair hair swept back, Jenna guessed he was the principal of the school.

Putting the shifters in jobs of authority made her nervous, but at a school she supposed it made sense. As she approached him, her phone chirped a warning. It was her mutant warning device. When in close quarters to plummeting blood pressure, it beeped. She had to be close enough and the mutant needed to be tagged for it to work. This guy was close to a stress rampage.

"I'm here to relieve you, mutant," Jenna crossed her wrists in front of her body. Behind her, Jameson and Dirk followed suit. "Why don't you head to your office, do a little yoga, and have a nice tall glass of cow juice?"

He blinked his eyes rapidly. "I didn't think the police was ever coming. They told me when I called to stay with the body, that there was trouble downtown, but I didn't think it would take this long." The color faded from his cheeks and were dangerously close to shimmering himself into a scaled, chubby dragon.

"Just relax and take a deep breath," Jameson said from behind her. He stepped up and put a hand on the man's shoulder. "We don't need an incident and you're fine. We're fine. Everything is rosy here. Your life is perfect, right, man?" He grinned, slapping the man on the back.

When the principal expelled a big breath of air, pink returning to his delicate features, Jenna relaxed and moved her hand from the butt of her gun. Jameson moved the man away down the hall to a bench while Dirk opened the door to the nurse's office and stepped inside.

Jenna wasn't sure what state they would find the body in, but was surprised to see it looked fine. The nurse looked like she just simply fell asleep at her desk, still in her uniform.

Her head was rolled back, her mouth set in a small smile. She was heavyset, but her skin appeared perfect, without discoloration or even a patch of blotchiness. Her soft brown curls were pinned back to her head in a way that made her look far too young to be a practicing nurse. Jenna wondered how old she really was. There was no way to tell until the mutant disease ravaged your body to the point it started falling apart after decades, maybe a century, of pristine beauty.

Dirk slipped on a pair of latex gloves and inspected the body. Jenna, already wearing her black gloves, poked around her desk. Nothing appeared out of place. Even her day planner was still there. Flipping it open, it looked like the nurse had a full week of social engagements. Certainly not what you expected from someone so depressed she would kill herself.

Dirk lifted the nurse's hand slowly and called Jenna's name. She saw there was a syringe clamped in her meaty hand. "Death by injection."

"See if you can find out what it is," Jenna ordered. "See if it is something she'd stock in here."

"Got it," Dirk said as he worked to lessen her grip. Their van had top-of-the-line equipment; it would be able to identify the compound, if there was enough left in the needle.

Footsteps behind her told Jameson had returned. "Old coot's going to be okay."

Dirk cast him a look. "Sounds like you like him."

Jameson snorted. "He's a shifter. I have no disillusions about what he is, but he's still a coot."

Jenna suppressed a smile. "See if you can sync up with her phone." She nodded her head toward the phone on the desk. "See what she was up to. Who she met, what she was doing. E-mails, text messages, phone calls."

"Can do," Jameson took out one of his phones and took a seat in a waiting armchair.

"Hurry," Jenna pressed. "We don't know how long we have before the police show up and escort us out."

"You're always big on the pressure. You ever notice that? One big pressure cooker. Maybe if you joined me on some Xtreme Ironing or a pumpkin flinging competition—" Jameson stopped as she threw darts at him with her eyes. She adored Jameson, but she didn't need to be told she was a stress maker.

Dirk delicately held the syringe in his hand. "I'm going to run this out to the van and run some tests." He paused, waiting for Jenna to say something. Probably give her approval or throw him warm gooey eyes, but she did neither. With a slight sigh, he pushed past her and hurried through the hall.

"You don't always have to be so hard on him," Jameson said without looking up. "It doesn't matter what a bitch you are, he'll never get over it."

For a moment she forgot to breathe, and her heart felt juiced. Jenna crossed her arms. "Did I ask for your commentary?"

"You didn't not ask for it either. Besides," Jameson's blue eyes pierced through her, "you weren't here. You weren't the one who saw what happened after you left him at the altar. Not sure why you're the angry one." Quietly, he went back to his phone and Jenna couldn't stop a slight tremor in her hand.

She focused on searching the desk and tried not to think about that wedding dress, the house they wanted to buy, and all the other conversation they had before everything changed. Before she found out the truth. She couldn't expect Dirk to understand all that. Her voice was a hushed whisper. "And what happened?"

Jameson's fingers didn't pause as they keyed in entry after entry on his phone. "Not my place to tell. Her phone's wiped. Someone knew what they were doing. I guess that takes suicide off the table."

"The school has a server room. All messages, incoming and outgoing, are stored there. If we're lucky, they didn't think to wipe that. Or didn't have time."

On his feet before she finished, Jameson gave her a quick glance before leaving the room. Jenna almost wished he stayed there so she wouldn't have to be alone with her thoughts. Sure, she knew she hurt Dirk. Those nights in the real world when she was hunting shifters, going off grid and breaking new constitutional law, gave her a lot of time to think. Most of them she thought of him. Her mind played out all the what-if scenarios; what happened after she left, how he handled it, but to hear about it from a third party... Jenna thought her crew forgave her for the things she did, but maybe Jameson couldn't forgive her for what she did to his best friend.

She wasn't sure she did either.

A name caught Jenna's eye as it swept through yesterday's appointments. Most people were there for the normal stomachaches, fevers, or sports injuries, but right next to *vomiting* was the name Wendy Reynolds. The chief's daughter saw the nurse the day of the chief's death and her disappearance.

Now with the nurse dead … was it possible that everything that was going on wasn't about the chief, but about Wendy?

Fearful for the girl, Jenna's stomach tightened. She closed the book, not wanting anyone else to make the connection before she had a chance to investigate, and turned around as Dirk entered the room.

His swagger was back. Whatever he felt for her earlier that day was back in check, like it often was. "Check it out, Jen. I finished the test. Hyped-up medicine designed to raise blood pressure. Potent stuff too. If it was you or me, we'd probably implode."

"But mutants' hearts would be unable to take it. They'd simply drift to sleep."

"And the heart would just shut down." Dirk said.

Jenna was quiet as the gears of her mind spun. "Medicine like that? Would a school nurse keep it?"

Dirk shook his head. "It was experimental. Never released to the public. It was thought it could stop a mutant on a rampage, but it never worked. It only killed the test subjects."

Jenna thought back. "The initiative to stop a mutant on a rampage was abandoned almost twenty years ago."

"Yup. Want to guess who was put in charge to safeguard it's formula?"

"I'm guessing from that smirk that I'll never guess. Or at the least, you want to tell me."

"New Haven Council. The group we have all of this, and by this I mean all five New Havens, to thank for."

Jenna raised her eyebrows. "The implications of that are huge. What the hell is going on here?"

Dirk gave a slight shake of his head. "If they got their hands on it, these guys are more than just dangerous, they're professionals."

"I think we already figured that out," Jenna took a breath, "Wendy was here the morning of her disappearance."

"Man, all the strings are coming together."

"Yeah," Jenna diverted her eyes away from Dirk, but could still feel his eyes on her body like he undressed her in his mind. Not like he needed to. He knew exactly where everything was.

"Something on your mind?" Dirk asked quietly.

She hated the way he did that. "Last night. I was overly harsh. Just, sorry." Jenna gave a little pout and kicked her foot at some imaginary dust.

Dirk was wearing his angelic wide-eyed expression. "You? I'm not sure if I'm more shocked by the apology or the fact you recognize when you're overly harsh."

"Didn't always used to be like that," Jenna admitted, even though she didn't know why. *Stop it, Jenna. You do not need this right now.*

But she did. Part of her really did.

"No. Didn't. I miss that girl, but this one isn't so bad either. She defrosts a mean pizza."

Jenna grinned, turning her head to cast it away. It didn't work and she felt Dirk take her hand. Apparently when you gave a man an inch, he really did take a mile. "If I hurt you, it wasn't my intent. And I am, you know, *sorry*." When did that word get so hard to say, anyway? It was a small two-syllable word, so why was she always choking on it?

"Last night was—you're not talking about last night, are you?" Dirk sighed, loud and frustrated. "You pick now of all days, at a murder scene, to talk about *that?*"

"Well if that's how you're going to be, I take it back. I'm not sorry." Apparently it was easier to un-apologize. It actually almost felt *good*, which was part of the problem. Why did it feel so good to always be a jerk?

Was she just a bitch? Or was it because she was part dragon?

"You can't take it back."

"Yes, I can," Jenna said with defiance, turning her nose up.

"Nope, you can't. Sorry." Dirk's voice trailed off. "So, since you brought it up. Why'd you do it? Why'd you leave without even," he struggled and gave a hard blink of his eyes, "talking to me?"

Jenna, stunned that he asked, didn't have a lie prepared. Her eyes were moist with stinging tears, but luckily, her ear chirped at that moment. Dirk's head tilted in a way that told her he heard it too. Jameson's voice came next. "Jen, ask me if I found anything."

She sighed. "Have you found anything, Jameson?"

"Totally glad you asked me that. Two things. Which thing you want first?"

"Uh, how about the first thing." Jenna rolled her eyes and Dirk chuckled.

"Our dead nurse called Alice at work. Told her something was wrong with Wendy and to come pick her up. This was not long after the beginning of the school day. I guess our missing-in-action girl vomited in her classroom with a Jon Voight type."

Jon Voight, Jenna thought fondly. If only he didn't get turned into a mutant and then killed by snipers. He was trying to eat starlets, for better or worse. Jenna bet they only tasted like crunchy bones, anyway. "What happened second?"

"Rebecca Seers was here in the morning. Vids and logs show she came in and talked one student in the guidance office. Per regulation, any mutant speaking to her—well, surveillance was cut."

"Right." Jenna said curtly.

"She was here to talk to…Jake Monroe. Mutant kid. On the football team. Don't get why she'd want to talk to him."

"Good work, Jameson," Dirk said.

Jameson snorted. "All my work is good."

"I think we need to do two things. Talk to Wendy's teacher and see what happened. I gotta believe that this thread has something to do with Wendy. Find this Jake Monroe and see what Rebecca wanted."

"If we get caught asking him that, it's a big violation," Dirk said. "If Rebecca isn't up to no good and she finds out we breached her organization's right to privacy—"

"There's no right to privacy inside New Haven. You know that." Jenna walked out of the office and started down the hall. Now if only she could find this teacher's classroom. Pulling out her phone, she used her police clearance to pull up a blueprint of the school with an overlay of mutant assignments. She found the one she was looking for by the time Dirk nipped at her heels.

"I'm just saying we need to be careful. I want answers, same as you do."

"I know," Jenna said and cast him a long look. They turned down the hall and she stopped at the door. She decided to play low-key, and opened it slowly and stuck her head inside. The teacher did look a little bit on the older side.

He paused in the middle of his lecture, leaning up against his desk. All eyes were on Jenna. "May I help you?" he asked.

"New Haven Police. I need you to step outside for a few words." Jenna held the door open and wore her menacing you-don't-have-a-choice scowl. She waited for Mr. Doubosh to follow. She searched the records and found his first name was Frank.

Frank's complexion was practically green. "I'm not sure how I can—"

"I'll be asking you a few questions. Try not to lie to me," Jenna said. Dirk shifted with discomfort beside her, never a big fan of her interrogation manner.

"All," he stuttered, "all right."

"Wendy Reynolds. She was in your class yesterday. Had a little incident. Care to tell me about that?"

Frank was clearly confused. "Not much to tell. She wasn't looking all that well, poor girl. I thought it might be spoiled milk. She threw up all over my shoes. I sent her to the nurse."

"Embarrassing," Dirk commented.

Frank gave a nod. "She was crying, but I think that started before she was ill. Yes, I think maybe she was crying right before Ms. Seers came to my door."

Needless to say, Jenna's interest was piqued. "Ms. Seers came to you? Why?"

"She wanted to speak to one of my students, which is too bad because he really could use the extra practice on his work. If he wants to be a television repairman, he really needs to attend to his studies more. It's not an easy job," Frank explained.

"Is he in your class now? Jake Monroe?" Jenna asked.

"He's in my first period class, but he missed it." Frank's eyes clouded over. "He's absent and—well, his father was in earlier. Very upset."

"Is the boy all right?" Dirk asked.

"No one knows. He hasn't been seen by his parents since last night."

Jenna felt her blood pressure plummet and her skin suddenly felt very dry. Her mind reeled as if she was given another important piece to the puzzle. Dizzier than she realized, Dirk grabbed her arm to stabilize her. "Easy, Jen."

"May I…may I return to my class?" Frank asked quietly.

Jenna nodded. "Go." She stared at the floor, her mind whirling, trying to figure out exactly what was going on. How were these two teenagers caught up in the middle of the chief's murder?

"There's no way a mutant can go missing," Dirk said.

"But he still is, isn't he? Somehow the alerts weren't triggered."

"More corruption? Are you all right? I've never seen you look so pale." Dirk's eyes were laced with concern.

"Just upset, I guess. Haven't eaten."

"We should stop and get something then."

Jenna shook her head. "No time. We have to head to the Monroe residence. I want to learn more about this kid. Jameson," she said into her communication link.

"I know what you want. But there's something wrong. There's no Jake Monroe in New Haven's system. It's like—it's like he's been erased, Jen."

Jenna swore to herself. "Can you see who's been accessing his family files? Maybe do a back trace and find some residue in the system? Backup systems maybe? Anything?" She knew she was grasping at straws, but Jameson would know what steps to take.

"Have I ever ironed while hanging upside down from a tree?"

The answer to that question was a resounding yes.

****

"We'd like to ask you a few questions," Jenna asked Susan Monroe. Dirk joined her while Jameson stayed in the van so he could continue his analysis. It was nearly dinnertime and Jenna felt crankier each minute that went by. If she didn't get food soon, she might implode.

Or explode. She wasn't sure which idea scared her more.

The Monroe home was quaint, like stepping into a Donna Reed re-run, but there was something about Susan that Jenna didn't like.

The way Susan paced the living room while gripping her hands didn't sit well with her. She knew something or was familiar with Jenna's handiwork; it was always hard to tell which it was. "What kind of questions?" Susan asked. Her voice was even, flat, but nothing else about her was.

"About your son," Dirk started. "There are a few things we need to know about him."

"What time did he go missing last night?" Jenna asked abruptly which got a penetrating glower from Dirk.

In her ear there was a sigh from Jameson. "Took you only ninety seconds this time. Techno-color me impressed, Jen."

Susan stammered. "My son? How did you—"

"Just answer the question. I don't have a lot of patience."

Susan blinked. "He went out last night to football practice at eight. Except—"

"Except?" Jenna prodded.

Her shoulders rounded and she stared at the floor. "I talked to the coach and there wasn't any practice, but I'm sure it was just a misunderstanding."

Jenna blinked and her posture went rigid. She wanted nothing more than to take the woman "downtown."

"A misunderstanding that has your son missing for twenty hours? Why haven't you reported it to the police, Ms. Monroe?"

Susan glanced between Jenna and Dirk. "I thought with everything going on, I shouldn't worry the police. I know," her voice trailed off. Her eyes were haunted, tragic. "I know my son isn't as important as the Chief."

"You've got that right," Jenna said snidely. "But the law is the law. All shifters need to be in by curfew. He wasn't. You knew. I'd drag him in for less and since I can't, maybe I'll drag in you."

Susan's eyelashes fluttered about. "Please, I don't know anything. I just want my son to be all right. Please. Can't you understand that?"

"Yeah, I can," Dirk was kind, placing his hand on her shoulder, but it made the mutant flinch.

"None of that explains why you didn't report him missing. That's what any good mother would do, isn't it? Any good law-abiding mutant. Just proves to me you have something to hide."

Jenna's glare provided too much for Susan. Her eyes fell to the floor; her shoulders hunched. "He'll come home. I know he will."

"Weren't you surprised when the police didn't show up here asking about your son? Aren't you aware that the Outpost would be notified if he didn't return home?" Dirk asked.

"Yes, yes I was. I thought with the Chief…well, you're here now, so I guess that's all that matters. I need to start a roast. Is it all right? Can you please go?" She was itching to get away, her feet inching toward the kitchen.

For a woman who was worried about her son she certainly didn't want to spend a lot of time talking about him. Her blood pressure did appear to be in check, though, and Jenna had no other questions. They allowed Susan to get back to her duties and then saw themselves out. Dirk yanked the door closed behind them hard. "Well, that was a waste of time."

"Depends on your point of view. I think we just proved that Susan Monroe knows her son is off-grid and is too afraid to tell us."

"Why?" Dirk asked.

"Damned if I know, but we're going to find out."

Chapter:

Jameson's coffee table was littered with half-empty containers of Chinese takeout and each team member nursed a cold bottle of beer. Sure, they were on duty, but it was a tough day, Jenna reflected. "Now that I'm a stuffed turkey, let's go over everything we know."

Dirk placed his chopsticks down on the table and slurped in one final strand of Lo Mein noodle. "We know George helped Rebecca Seers with something, and now he's dead."

Jameson picked up the thread. "We know George is the one who deleted records of Jake Monroe from Outpost's database. Who knows if he's done this before. Can't ask him since he's dead."

Jenna gave him a look. "Have a little respect for a fellow officer."

He gawked at her. "You are lecturing *me* about respect?"

"The nurse called Alice Reynolds about Wendy. We only have part of the clip since the rest were deleted, but she was concerned for her health."

"Why would someone want to delete that?" Jenna asked. "Let's not forget the compound that the New Haven Initiative is supposed to be keeping under lock and key. I think we all know what that means."

Dirk glanced at her with his penetrating stare that usually meant he didn't agree with her or wanted to sleep with her. Jenna was going with the former this time though. "You really think the HI would kill the chief?"

"That or someone stole it from them, but I'm guessing someone in the HI is dirty."

"Hold the phone, guys," Jameson said while he did exactly that. He glanced up with a look that was half little boy getting to ride the big boy's roller coaster and finding it was out of order. "Wendy, Travis's kid, bought a pregnancy test."

Jenna and Dirk exchanged glances. "How is it everyone missed this?"

Jameson shook his head, his eyes going wide and a bit of spit appearing in the corner of his mouth. All were signs that he was on the verge of becoming overexcited. "Human purchases and activities are recorded, but they aren't actively monitored because of the Human Privacy Act. It's only there in case of a problem. Plus, she being the chief's daughter, I'm betting most people looked the other way when she did things. She probably told the clerk it was for her mother." Jameson giggled. "Yup, that's exactly what she did. If you want, I can play the wav file for you."

"It's okay, we believe you." Jenna smirked. "So Wendy, pregnant, is vomiting in class. Morning sickness, could be. She's upset around the same time Rebecca Seers pulls Jake Monroe out of class. Now they're both missing."

"You look pale again," Dirk said.

"Different reasons," Jenna tried not to sound haunted, but wasn't successful. "What if Wendy and Jake were a couple?"

Jameson fumbled his phone. "A human dating a mutant? The chief's daughter?" His jaw went slack and his face turned three shades of green.

"And now she's pregnant. With a mutant?" Dirk asked.

"Half mutant," Jenna pointed out.

Jameson shook his head. "That's disgusting. Might as well be pregnant with a pit bull, except those make good pets."

Jenna scowled at him, her hands clenching into tight fists. "It's an idea."

"One that isn't possible," Dirk reminded her. "You know mutants aren't human. They can't mate with us. Sure, they might look like we do, but they're monsters. It was proved years ago. We've all seen the reports and autopsy vids."

Jenna tucked her hair behind her ears and avoided his gaze. "It's an idea and one that fits all the pieces."

"Yuck," Dirk's tone was distracted. "Might as well get knocked up with a zombie."

Jenna shot him a dirty look and felt that pang of heartbreak. If he knew the truth, he wouldn't want to be with her. If he knew the truth, he'd lock her up like the animal she was.

Monster. Killer.

So far Jenna had proved half those things right.

"Except why Travis was killed." Jameson was thoughtful. "Unless he wanted Wendy to get rid of it and the shifters struck back. They killed him before he could kill it."

That didn't much sound like the Chief to Jenna. He was gentle and kind for an officer. Certainly, he loved Wendy more than anything and she couldn't see him killing his own grandchild. Besides, Jenna could remember all those talks they had in private. He was the one that always made her feel better. He was the one who talked her down from killing shifters. They weren't just cockroaches to the chief. If Wendy wanted her baby, nothing would have convinced him otherwise and he would have loved the baby without a second thought.

"I think we're getting sidetracked."

Jameson scowled at her. "Since when have you become a mutant lover?"

"I'm not," Jenna said heatedly, her cheeks turning red. "Don't call me that again, Jameson. You know how I feel about them."

"Do I?" He leaned forward with sinister eyes. "Every time I suggest we look at them, you steer the conversation away."

"Because they don't have the means or the supplies."

"Guys," Dirk started, "c'mon. We're tired and upset. This is no time to start fighting."

"Maybe it is," Jameson said. "Maybe it's time we get out into the open where Jenna was for those two years. She just comes back. We accept her. But maybe she's not stable enough to run this crew. Maybe her judgment is still impaired from when she went loco."

Jenna grabbed her gun off the table and lunged for Jameson. She throttled him, pushing him back into his recliner with the full force of her body. Before he could react, her forearm pinned his head back right against his Adam's apple while her other hand released the safety and put the butt of her gun against his temple. "My judgment impaired? No, I'm as sane as ever. When I blow your head off it'll because I *meant* to do it. Are we clear?"

"Jenna, you don't want to hurt Jameson. Back. Off." Dirk spoke with his soft dentist voice.

She relaxed, even though the muscles in her arms trembled slightly. Jenna lowered her gun and her arm, slowly backing off of him. "What I said stands."

Jameson didn't say anything, just stared at her. Jenna wasn't sure what he really wanted to say. She knew what she'd want to say: Jenna went mental again. Jenna was unable to control her impulses. Never was able to. It was her birthright, so said her mother, but she just wanted to dig a hole and bury herself in it. Instead, she picked up her empty beer bottle and took it into the kitchen.

Angry with herself, she stashed it on the counter with the others. She'd find a way to make it up to Jameson. Maybe buy him tickets to a show or something. He loved shows. Right, Jenna thought to herself, like a few tickets is enough to forget your boss held a gun to your head for no reason. No good reason anyway.

She wasn't alone long. Jenna turned at the sound of the kitchen door swinging shut right into the disapproving eyes of Dirk, but they were more than that. They were sad, worried, afraid. "What the hell was that all about?"

Jenna sighed. "I don't need this from you right now." She rubbed her neck.

"You're wound so tight you nearly killed Jameson. I think this is exactly what you need."

"I wouldn't have," Jenna said softly, not really sure.

"Right. Just like you didn't exterminate all those shifters."

"When am I going to be able to stop paying for that?" Jenna asked bitterly. "When?"

Dirk shrugged. "I don't know. Maybe you'll always pay for it."

"Maybe one day everyone will see I was right."

"Then why get so upset at Jameson? If you think they're really monsters too, why'd you pull that stunt?"

"This is a crime. It's not justice to blame the mutants if they didn't do a damn thing. If they didn't kill the chief, then I don't want a lynch mob. Innocence is innocence."

Dirk smiled. "Guess underneath that tough exterior you're really still a cop."

"Try to be. Some days are easier than others."

Dirk rubbed her arms and it made her arms tingle. Part of her wanted to pull away, but she didn't. She closed her eyes and when Dirk's lips brushed up against hers, she pulled away. "As much as I don't want to, I think we should all take the rest of the night off. Get some sleep. We're going to need to recharge if we're going to follow this thing through."

Jenna moved away from his dumbfounded expression and stopped in the living room. "Good work today, Jameson. Find Wendy's friends. We'll interview them in the morning. For now, let's call it a night."

Jameson's eyes shone with accusations and spite, but he only nodded and went back to his work. Jenna climbed the stairs to the guest room. When she stepped inside, she locked the door.

Chapter Eighteen

New Haven Initiative
New York City

Things were easier when the dragon shapeshifters were nothing but monsters.

Humans were on the run. They hid in buildings, stayed together in great numbers, and never went out at night when the ever watchful shifters would swoop out of trees or down from bridges in the hunt for their next meal.

Then it was simple. Black and white. The humans were good and the mutants were evil and needed to be stopped. Together, with the acting military, they finally corralled enough of them to bring order to the country. Just like that, the shifters began to change. Now Alstair Humpreys wished he kept that bit of news to himself. Still wet behind the ears, he brought this news to his superiors who brought it toward Congress. He should have kept his mouth shut; he should have let them all be exterminated.

The world would change again if that baby was born. If Alistar, head of the New Haven Initiative, didn't find a way to stop it.

Another shot of whiskey was followed by another glance at the photo on his mahogany desk, finely crafted and meant for an important man. Not one that went around killing his friends, those that served him all their lives. Travis and his family deserved respect, honor and accommodations. Instead his daughter, the girl in the photo, fell in love with the wrong boy and as often was the case, created life before she was ready. The world wasn't ready.

Alistar wasn't ready.

But she wasn't dead. She and her baby still lived and where they were, Alistar didn't know. He did know that Travis, a good man from what he read, was dead, that he deserved better than what he got. Though Alistar thought they all deserved better than this.

A knock came from the far side of the room at his office door. Alistar glanced up. The room was dark and furnished in marble and leather, with only a faint glow along the walls. The light was just enough to illuminate portraits of beautiful women he never got to meet, posed on animal-skin rugs from way back in the 1950s when glamour was everything. Before glamour became such an obsession that it doomed the human race.

Outside a horn honked, followed by the screech of tires. New York, the city that never slept. It reminded Alistar on why he issued the orders he did and why he had to sacrifice one family for the greater good. He just didn't like it very much.

The knock came again, only louder.

Alistar pushed back his big leather chair and stood. Dressed in his best tuxedo and white shirt, his black tie was loose around his neck. For a moment he took a step toward the full-length glass-paneled windows lining the back wall of his office. Outside, rain spattered the streets. Between the skyscrapers he called home and work were small lights of traffic. Cars with families, children and loved ones. How could he expect these good, moral people to cohabitate with monsters?

Monsters that needed their organs to live and stay beautiful and forever young? He didn't care if shifters could breed with humans. It meant nothing, and he would be damned if he would repeat the same mistake he made nearly fifty years ago.

A woman's heels clicked against the marble floors behind him. "Alistar, didn't you hear me knocking?"

"I heard." He drank the rest of his whiskey, turning the crystal glass in his hand.

"Well, everyone is waiting for you, dear. It is your birthday party."

"Feels more like my funeral." He admitted and turned to his wife. Mary. A simple name for a simple woman, but he loved her. Her figure wasn't as perfect as it was when they first met, but the fancy dress did her justice. Her face sagged and needed far more than the light makeup and the lip gloss she wore to hide the signs of age, but this was life after the fall of the beauty industry. They were still getting a handle on what was safe and what wasn't.

Her smile still took his breath away. "Getting old isn't a crime. Oh, you haven't even done your tie yet."

Alistar stood patiently as he had hundreds of times. "It must be a crime. Getting old. Otherwise we wouldn't have turned ourselves into monsters to avoid it."

She gave him an unkind glance. "When do you think you can stop talking about work? Anytime soon?"

"Maybe when I'm dead."

Mary laughed through closed lips and it whistled around them. "Maybe we'll all get lucky and you'll get Alzheimer's."

"Even if I did, I'd never forget how beautiful you are." He placed a playful kiss on her lips.

Mary rolled her eyes at him with a smile. "Oh, please. I know you didn't marry me for my looks."

Alistar took her hand. "I married you because I love you. Now help this old man down the stairs."

She led him out of the office. His walk was hobbled and his back hunched over, but Mary's eyes were filled with love, and it did not go unnoticed by him. Or by the guests that he met one floor down. The room was lined with windows, overlooking the New York skyscrapers. It was filled with balloons, flowing confetti, and a towering cake of butter cream frosting layered with white cake.

Alistar smiled and clapped his hands together as he stepped off the stairs to address his friends, and colleagues amid the shouts of happy birthday. It was all drowned away by the popping of champagne bottles and the clinking of glasses.

He had only one birthday wish.

Middle of the night and his phone was ringing.

It took Alistar a moment to grab his cell phone and put it to his ear. Beside him Mary moved slightly, but still slumbered. Alistar wanted to keep it that way so he spoke low, in a soft gruft voice. "Better be important."

As fast as his old knees would take him, he hurried to the adjourning bathroom and wedged the door shut. He listened to awhile, coughing into his fist. "You found a way in. Find a damn one out. I'm not paying you to sit there in your van and damn complain. Uh-huh. Hasn't been lifted yet, has it? Shut up. I'll take care of it, but be ready to move. Too many people already know about this and I'll be damned if it turns into a PR nightmare!"

Alistar ended the call before quickly bringing up his contact list. His eyes squinted. He could barely see and left his damn bifocals back on the nightstand. "Laurel, what the hell am I paying you for? Lift the damn quarantine already." More listening, which just wore out his patience. He was tired of listening to everyone all the time. "I don't care how you do it, just get it over with. We're not done. We still need to get our hands on that girl."

Alistar ended the call and longed for the days cell phones were flip phones. Slamming your flip phone closed was a lot more satisfying then gliding your hand across a screen. That and his damn hands were starting to shake. One of these days he was going to try to add a contact and end up ordering a damn pizza.

He laughed at his little joke, quietly opened the door and stared into his wife's menacing frown. Her arms were crossed and that was exactly how she appeared; cross. "Mary," Alistar cleared his throat and wiped sweat from his forehead. What had she heard exactly?

"Don't Mary me," she huffed. "Look at you conducting business in the bathroom at three in the morning. I swear, Alistar, we are going on vacation and I am taking that phone of yours away. Now let's go back to bed."

Alistar took his wife's offered hand and followed her back to their sprawling king-sized bed. He dodged a bullet and for that he would go quietly to sleep.

Chapter Nineteen

The water in the tub ran a constant stream of white noise, filling the basin with the sweet smell of lavender bubbles collecting around the tap. They danced back and forth, growing and multiplying in size as the prism of colors shined under the soft glow of the overhead lights.

Susan sat curled up on the plush purple area rug around the toilet, her legs tucked underneath her. On top of the seat was a brown briefcase, the one she was sent to retrieve, but she was afraid to open it. She didn't want to see what was inside.

But she needed to. Needed to save her son. Needed to see Jake again.

Susan remembered when he was little, remembered the quiet times where he gathered his arms around her waist and gave her a hug. On his first day of school, when other kids cried, Jake went with great courage into his kindergarten class. Susan saw him glance back at her, but she never told him. Instead she only told him what a brave boy he had been. So brave, her little boy. If he was in trouble now, if someone had him, Susan could not turn her back.

She couldn't tell Jeff. Her love for him never wavered, but he was too by-the-book. Jeff would never allow her to do anything but go to the police, but she wanted to, especially when he asked questions. Have you called the police yet, he asked. Has Jake called? Susan didn't want to lie, but God she did. She did like it was second nature to her. Was it really a lie? The police did stop by and they did file a report, Susan assumed. Was it really a lie?

Startled, she snorted as someone banged against the bathroom door. "Honey," Jeff's voice called out, "are you okay in there?"

"Just taking a bath to unwind," Susan's voice sounded so hollow. She couldn't believe she was lying to him, again. "I'll be out in a little while." Her voice rose unnaturally high and chirped as if she sang a song.

"Okay, hon. Want me to get you anything?"

She felt so much guilt. Eyes squeezed she answered, "No. I'm all right," her voice cracked.

"The neighbors are coming over. I think Marie could use some company. We'll be downstairs when you're ready."

"There's pie." Susan couldn't believe she was thinking about pie at a time like this. "In the fridge from last night. You can serve that with coffee." Was Jeff even thinking? How could he invite people over without refreshments? What would the neighbors think of them if they let them go hungry and thirsty?

"Thanks. I'll take care of it."

Susan counted to ten as his steps carried him away. When she could no longer hear his footsteps, she leaned over and turned the water off. The bubbles were now level with the basin and threatened to spill over onto the mosaic tile floor.

Susan sighed, turning her attention back to the briefcase. It was like Pandora's Box. Once she opened it, there was no turning back. She just had to remember her son, being kept God knew where. Was he restrained? Was he in danger? Maybe he was crying, maybe he was hurt.

Glancing at her watch, Susan saw it was nearly 5:14 P.M. As the minute hand closed the circle and began to make another pass, she slowly depressed the buttons on the briefcase. The latches sprung open with a snap. With a shaking hand, Susan lifted the lid as if it was fragile and inspected inside.

Susan squeezed her eyes shut and covered her mouth with her hand to keep herself from crying aloud. With shaking hands she pushed the gun out of the way with her fingertips, she didn't even want to touch it. Underneath it, she saw a photograph of a man. A familiar man, Susan mused as she picked it up. It fluttered like an injured bird in her shaky grasp. Lawrence Stark.

Beneath that was a yellow envelope. Thick and long. Across it in neat print was the word *instructions*. What was it they wanted her to do? My God, they didn't…Did they really? How could she keep this from everyone? Why would this bring her son home?

****

"We just have a few questions for you daughter," Jenna's tone was relaxed and her body stance matched as she stood inside the Brist home. The father's name was Clark and his daughter was Marsha. By all accounts, she was Wendy's best friend. If anyone knew anything, Jenna bet her life that Marsha did.

Clark worked at Outpost, but only as a data analyzer. He shifted, left and right, wiping spit away from the corner of his mouth. "She doesn't know anything about the Chief."

"She was friends with Wendy. I'll keep the questions strictly to that, deal?" Jenna gave him a level stare, but Clark shook his head.

"No deal. I don't want you talking to her. There must be someone else that can talk to her."

Jenna's blood boiled. "I'm here to do a job. This isn't about my past. This is about the Chief's family and I'll be damned if I'm going to let a squint like you stand in my way." Jenna stepped forward, her nose in his face and her boots pushed right up against his. "Deal, or we do this at Outpost, Brist. And then I really start to wonder what the hell you're hiding."

She couldn't get into Outpost, but she would bet on her mother's life that Clark wasn't going to call her bluff. His eyes blinked afraid, and their focus drifted away. He backed up, his head down with a nod. "She's in her room. Upstairs and to the left."

Jenna acknowledged his answer by heading toward the stairs. Dirk followed behind and she heard Jameson offer some words of consolation to Clark. His footsteps charged up the stairs at them and Jenna knocked on Marsha's door. When she entered, the teen girl jumped off her bed, startled.

Marsha was a normal teen with long hair and a taste for short skirts. Her eyes were distant and afraid as she tugged free her ear buds. She threw them onto the messy bed. "Who are you?"

"We're with the police," Jenna said. "We need to ask you a few questions. Please feel free to sit."

Marsha's eyes traveled to each of their faces before she perched herself on the edge of her mattress. "About what happened to Wendy's dad?"

"Yeah. Care to tell me what you know?"

Marsha's hair fell in front of her eyes as she hunched over like she might be sick. "I don't know anything." Her voice trembled and filled with doubt.

Doubt, that was good. Jenna could exploit that.

"Sure you do," Jenna patted Marsha's hand and sat beside her on the bed. "You were Wendy's best friend. If anyone knew anything, it's you. We're not here to get you in trouble or Wendy, but we need to find her."

Marsha's eyes peeked through the blinds of her hair and Jenna saw thick tears and fear. The girl wanted to tell and Jenna just needed to push her a little further.

"She's missing, and I'm sure you know that. She wasn't home when the Chief— She wasn't home, and thank God for that, but we need to find her. I think you know where she went."

Marsha's eyes widened and she snapped up to her feet, pacing over to the window. Her hands cradled her crossed arms. "I don't know what you're talking about."

Jenna smiled at her. "Sure you do. You know exactly what I'm talking about because you helped her. Didn't you? You know how she got out. You know where she was headed.

If I'm going to help her, you need to tell me everything you know."

"I won't get in trouble?" Marsha asked, her voice shaking.

Jenna shook her head. "I promise. It won't leave this room."

"I—" Marsha covered her face and sobbed. "I hid a bag in the park. I got it ready for Wendy. Clothes, supplies. I hid it under the park bench so she could get it before she left."

"Left for what?"

"The outside," Marsha's lip quivered. "She was running away to have that stupid baby. I told her it was stupid. Tell her parents and they could just get rid of it, right? It was one of them." Marsha's nose crinkled. "But she loved it and wanted to keep it."

So Marsha hated the idea of Wendy having a shifter baby, but helped her anyway. She was loyal. "How far along is she?"

Marsha shook her head. "Six months? All I know is she's friggin' sick all the time, puking her guts out and complaining she feels like she's coming apart. And she was getting really big. I dunno why no one noticed."

People saw what they wanted. No one wanted to see what Wendy was going through so didn't. "Do you know where she was headed?"

Marsha nodded. "They were going to meet Seers and get smuggled out. She was taking her to the compound, to keep them safe until the baby's born."

"They?" Jenna's senses heightening as fear rippled through her body. Behind her she heard the floor creak as her crew shifted.

"Yeah," Marsha shrugged. "Wendy and Jake. Probably going to buy a house now or something. Big normal family. Except the baby's not really a baby, is it? It's a monster."

Jenna wiped her sweaty palms on her jeans. "Thanks, Marsha." She stood up and turned to face her crew. They stood with no movement in the doorway, but their faces were vampire pale. "Anyone else know other than you?"

"No, we were real careful. I was going to," her voice turned wistful, "going to tell people she spent the night here with me. To give her a head start."

Marsha's sobs followed heavy and with grief. Jenna left her to her pain, leaving the room and pulling the door shut.

"Seers smuggled an underage girl, a mutant, and half-breed freak out of New Haven. We have enough against her to bring her ass down." Jameson said.

Jenna's mouth was dry. "First we have to piece this information back to the HI. How'd they find out and why did they decide the best way to get rid of Wendy and her baby was to blow up the Chief?"

"Cover their tracks," Dirk said simply. "Small liability to get rid of such a big threat to our cause."

Jenna startled when he said that, but knew he was right. It was their cause to keep shifters locked up, because it was the right thing to do. But killing innocent people like the Chief and his family was not. "We need an outside line so Jameson can hack into the HI, and so I can call Seers and feel her out."

"Uh, guys," Jameson called as they excused themselves from the room. The skipped down the stairs and were out the door in a heartbeat. "There's an APB out for our arrest."

"What?" Jenna spat the words out with hurricane force and spun around. "For what? Asking questions? Doing their jobs?" The words on the screen blurred as tears stung her vision and her pulse raced so fast that her temples throbbed.

"What's it say?" Dirk asked, touching her shoulder, but she could barely feel it.

Her voice echoed hollowly in her ears. "It says we killed the Chief."

"They can't really think we would have anything to do with that." Dirk grabbed the phone and scrolled through as if he was looking for the punchline.

"We're about to find out," Jameson said.

Jenna blinked and heard sirens wailing. Cars pulled up on the curb and a moment later, Laurel was out of her squad vehicle and headed right for them.

"You know why I'm here. Let's make this easy for once."

Damn right, Jenna knew. She stormed up to her, jaw set tight. She swung a right hook into Laurel's jaw, grabbed her by the shoulders, and threw her onto the grass.

Jenna heard voices, but they barely registered. Her eyes were dark with fury as Laurel scampered back to the house. Jenna straddled her with her legs, bent down, and grabbed her by the scruff of her collar. "You think this will keep me sidelined?"

Laurel smile was smug as she wiped a trail of blood from her lips. "You make my job easy, Morgan." Her eyes danced with laughter and they trained somewhere behind Jenna.

Jenna didn't have to turn around to know who won, hearing several gun safeties released and she was sure they weren't aimed at the acting Chief of Police. She dropped Laurel, slowly raising her arms above her head, but her eyes never left the bitch's face.

"Sargent Jenna Morgan," Laurel's voice dripped with sweetness while her hand massaged her jaw, "you are under arrest."

Chapter Twenty

The smell of maple swept through the house while the oven held cinnamon-laced pancakes waiting for breakfast to be served. Upstairs, Susan sat at her vanity applying her makeup. She swept blush across her cheekbones and mascara to her lashes.

Her reflection looked perfect and serene. The blue of her eyes were steady and her shoulder length hair was pinned back elegantly, but, for the first time—maybe in her life—Susan hated it all. Inside, she was screaming uncontrollably. She wanted to cry, flail her arms, smash something. What was happening wasn't fair. Her family was a good and honest bunch so how had this happened to them? How?

She slipped her wedding ring off and left it on the vanity. What she was doing went against everything she and Jeff held dear. To wear it today when she went to Lawrence Stark's house would be a betrayal. She wouldn't taint it or her vows.

With a deep breath she and returning to the hallway. She smoothed her skirt and fluffed her hair, not knowing what else to do. Behind one door she heard the shower; behind the other, she heard sobbing. She knocked on her daughter's room. The door was shut tight despite the fact it was already eight AM.

She needed to get her off to school and Jeff off to work before she ran her…errands.

When there wasn't an answer, Susan squeezed her eyes shut and pushed the door open. "Marie? I made your favorite pancakes. Syrup warming on the stove." She sighed at the sight of her daughter dressed but sitting by the window, staring out at the family oak tree.

She smoothed her skirt before moving into the room. "Marie," she said, sitting beside her daughter and gave her a warm hug.

Marie sniffled against the collar of Marie's skirt. "I was looking at that old tire swing. Remember how he'd push me? It seems so long ago now. Oh gosh, Mom, what if he's hurt."

"He's not hurt. He'll be back tonight. Now head down and eat, but don't worry about your brother. Mom's got this."

Surprise flashed against her daughter's face. Marie's warm brown eyes were wide as she studied her mom. Susan would always love those eyes. "How?"

"Don't ask questions. Just know it's going to happen and we're all going to be fine." Susan took her daughter's chin in her hand and kissed both cheeks forcefully. "I love you to pieces, Marie. Now be a good girl and do what you're told."

Her daughter nodded and wore a smile, the first Susan saw on her since Jake went missing. The teen didn't ask any questions or say anything else while she picked up her book bag and headed for the kitchen.

Susan sat for a moment and tried not to cry. She forced the tears back and the thoughts of everything she was about to do from her mind. Smoothing her skirt, she returned to the hall and nearly bumped straight into Jeff. "Well, there you are," he said. "I knew you were somewhere since I smelled that wonderful breakfast you cooked." Jeff grabbed her by the waist and pulled her close.

She took a deep breath, taking in his aftershave and allowed her head to fall against his neck in a deep nuzzle. His arms were warm against her in a big bear hug. His kisses and love made her feel safe, comforted, but Susan knew she couldn't stay in it.

Not today. Terrified that Jeff would see through her, she fought back tears and an angry sob, her mouth frozen open against his neck while her hands gripped his shoulders.

"Any word?" Jeff finally asked.

She shook her head, kissing his neck. Her lashes swept tears away with a few blinks. "No, but the police are looking. I'm sure—he'll be fine." Susan forced a smile and prayed that Jeff would buy it.

"I'll drive around on my lunch break. I know his friends. I can talk to a few of them."

He did buy it and for a minute Susan wished he hadn't. Her lips felt dry. "That sounds like a good idea. I'm sure by tonight he'll be home for dinner and everything will be fine."

Jeff's eyes flickered across her face. "Are you sure you're okay? Honey?"

"Just not sleeping well. You head downstairs and have some food. There's juice in the fridge. Those new rations come in handy." Susan gave a laugh and slipped away from her husband, but clung to his fingers before heading into the master bedroom.

She sat on the woven bedspread and unfolded a piece of paper from her pocket. On it a phone number was written. Susan picked up the receiver of the old rotary phone and waited for dial tone.

"Lawrence Stark," a tired voice said on the other end.

"I need to see you. Today. Something's happened." Susan let out a slow breath so he wouldn't hear how nervous she was. "I hope you remember me. This is Susan."

"Well, Susan. Yes, I do remember you. It would be my pleasure to meet with you. Why don't you swing by my home when you have a chance? My wife just baked a nice coffee cake."

The color drained from her face. Wife. Children. Susan hadn't thought of that. Oh God, what was she—"Sounds lovely. If I'd like to have a word with you, alone."

"Oh, my interest is certainly piqued. Yes, I'll send everyone out to the park. Kids could use the exercise. Give me twenty minutes."

Susan hung up the phone and nearly vomited inside her mouth.

It was suicide.

Her car idling in the driveway of the Stark home, Susan stared into her purse at the black revolver that was nestled between tissues, lipstick and gum. She had to do it. She had no choice. Susan knew she couldn't tell Jeff or the police. For all she knew, the police were the ones who had Jake. In fact, she was pretty sure of it.

How would she get out of this alive? Susan didn't know. But she would forfeit her life if it meant that her son would be all right. Jake had so much life, so much to live for.

Maybe she'd be lucky. Maybe things weren't as bad as they seemed.

Susan snapped her purse closed before picking up the basket of muffins on the passenger seat and made her way up to the front door. The Stark home was one of the smallest she had ever seen. It made sense to her that he would be poor. He was stirring the pot, and the police would make sure he and his family suffered because of it. But maybe if they rewarded him, gave him the big pool Susan always dreamed of, maybe he would have kept his mouth shut.

Maybe now she wouldn't be on her way to kill him.

She rang the bell and stepped the side, peering in the small front windows when she heard the latch from inside open. Lawrence Stark smiled at her almost like a doctor would. "Susan, it's a pleasure. I have coffee on, please step inside."

"Thanks for having me over on such short notice." Susan followed him through the cramped living room and into the kitchen. It was small. The counters formed an L shape into a cozy dinning space. The sunlight gleamed down on the perfectly clean floors. On the fridge was the artwork of small children in vibrant watercolors.

On the table was a coffee carafe and small plates for snacks. The perfect host, Susan thought. How many times had she done the same thing?

And now she was being asked to…

"Please have a seat. Is this about your son?"

"Yes," Susan answered meekly. "I found him. I know a way to get him back."

"And you've come to me for help?" Lawrence smiled smugly. He turned his back and poured two cups of coffee. While he did that, Susan fumbled with the clasp of her purse. Her fingers shook so bad she almost couldn't get it open. She grabbed the gun, wrapping her fingers around the butt and pulled it out. She dropped her purse to the floor in the commotion and used both hands to steady it, while aiming at the back of Lawrence Stark's head.

Do it now, Do it before he sees! But she couldn't.

"One lump or…oh," Lawrence put his hands up as his eyes fixed on the barrel of the gun. "Well, I see. You had no intention of eating my wife's coffee cake, did you?"

Susan bit her lip. "How can you make jokes?"

He stirred sugar into his coffee. "I've expected they'd try to kill me eventually, but I didn't think they'd send you. Just shows how dangerous I've become to them and their way of life. I suppose I should beg you not to do it, for my wife and children, but the truth of the matter is, it doesn't matter. The movement is bigger than me so I am ready to die for it. It will carry on without me."

"You're giving speeches, even now?" Susan re-aimed her gun and pulled back the safety. It wasn't as hard as she thought. The muscles in her arms pulled taut. She fought her minds surging command not to shoot, but her heart's desire was to finish the job. The gun wavered in her hands.

"But I love my children, Susan. Just as you love yours." His voice begged with a soft tone. When he looked up, Susan saw the fear in his eyes. "What I do is for their future, for yours. You don't have to do this."

"Yes, I do. They have my son." Susan gritted her teeth. "They'll kill my son!" The color drained out of her again. She felt faint and knew if she didn't do it soon, she never would. Instead she would rip Lawrence's face off with her fangs. Once she tasted his blood, it would be over. *Really* over.

"And you think this will save him? You're a pawn. We're *all* pawns here. Nothing we do matters. All that matters is that we're locked up, like animals. We deserve more. We deserve better, but while we're locked up here, nothing will—"

His words were cut off by the bullet colliding with the side of his head. Susan squeezed her eyes shut as her face was splattered with his blood. She almost couldn't feel her finger depress the trigger. Susan could barely remember even telling herself to do it. She opened her eyes again as Lawrence's body slumped onto the kitchen floor. It convulsed and shook. Susan screamed and covered her mouth.

The phone rang.

Susan suspected it was for her. She rushed to the wall and put it to her ear, but she didn't say anything. The voice on the other end of the line was hushed, but almost sounded like a woman's.

"Wipe the gun clean and leave it by the body. Well done."

"What about my son? I want to see my son."

"You don't have much time. Better hurry." The line went dead.

Susan found a dishrag by the sink and did as she was told. She tiptoed past him and straight toward the front door. Glancing around, she saw the dead-end street was clear.

She drove home, hopeful that when she got there, Jake would be waiting. In her mind she played the scene out, how they would hug and he would promise never to lie again. But Susan would just be glad to see him. All she would do was hold him and be glad he was back, no matter what happened to her.

Angry sobs shook her back and forth. She could barely see the road all the way home and her body convulsed, but the way was clear of traffic and every light she got to turned green. Almost like someone wanted to make sure she got there in one piece.

No Jake.

Dinner was in the oven and the table was set, but Susan's mind was a mile away back at Lawrence Stark's home. The memory of what she did replayed itself on an infinite loop. Each time his body fell, Susan pressed her eyes closed and squeezing her fist around her blue handkerchief.

She dotted at her eyes, peering out the front door. When she heard sirens she hurried to the kitchen window to see over the neighbor's fence, but Susan couldn't make anything out. The sirens faded and she couldn't help wonder if they were looking for her.

Hours passed and her phone hadn't rung and no one had come. When was Susan going to see her boy again? The front door slammed and Susan quickened away from the window and hurried to the hall. "Jake?" She called breathless and with hopeful eyes.

Marie turned, her books cradled in her arms. "Is he here? Is he?" Her voice was rushed.

"No," Susan's heart wrenched and her daughter's face fell crestfallen. "But soon." She gave a brilliant smile. "Soon, I hope. I made his favorite for dinner. I'm sure he'll be here soon."

Marie's eyes gazed at her shoes, her shoulders concave around her small frame. Susan stroked her hair, rubbing it between her fingers. "Why don't you peel some carrots for me? I need them shredded for the salad."

Susan's mind fluttered about and only the ticking of the clock signaled the passage of time. If not for the kitchen timer, dinner would have burned to a crisp. She used her blue potholders to place it on the burner, and while it rested she called Marie to the table when the phone rang.

She grabbed at it, nearly tipping over a pot of gravy onto the floor. "Hello? Jake?"

"It's me, darling. Are you all right?"

Megan. Susan took a breath and closed her eyes. "Fine. Fine. I'm fine. Just about to sit down to dinner, so if you'll excuse me—"

"Too busy for a word of gossip? C'mon now, Susan Monroe. I'm sure you'll want to hear it if it concerns Lawrence Stark."

Bile rose in her throat and her heart plummeted to her toes. "Excuse me?"

"Dead." Megan's voice was flat as if speaking about the weather. "Dead as nails, done as dinner. He was shot, point blank, it seems. The entire town is in a fit. I'm surprised you hadn't heard yet."

"Well, with the Chief—" Susan mumbled, wiping a stray crumb from the counter.

"Yes, the Chief," Megan's voice cut through the air like a freshly sharpened blade. "I guess they were just biding their time to take him out. To find the right situation, the right person. I guess they've won, haven't they?"

Susan threw a glance over her shoulder to make sure the coast was still clear. "What do you mean, the right person? What are you trying to get at?"

"Me? I'm just making an observation. Are you sure you're all right, darling? What if I come over after dinner? We can talk, if you need to. I'll bring a crumb cake."

"I'm sick of crumb cakes and talking." Susan took a deep breath. "Just no, no Megan. I've had enough."

"Well, something has your mood set foul. Don't get mad at me, Susan. You were the one who asked to be taken to meet Lawrence Stark."

"That's not what happened. And you know it. That's not what happened!"

"It is," Megan hissed. "And that's exactly what I told them when they were here."

"Who?" Susan whispered, holding the receiver close to her mouth. "Who asked?"

"The police. Just a few minutes ago. I thought I should warn you before they get there." Megan sighed. "Did you really think they were ever going to see your son again?"

Susan's eyes were moist as the receiver went dead. "Megan?" She begged timidly, wondering if Megan was ever really her friend or maybe her friend never came back from her reconditioning. Maybe her friend was eradicated, wiped out in sessions designed to change her personality forever.

She placed the receiver back on its cradle with care before smoothing out all the imperfections on her skirt and stepped into the dining room. Susan's mouth opened to speak, but the sight of her family swelled pain in her chest. Her eyes focused on the empty seat beside Marie and a sob crept its way out of her mouth. Susan put her hand over her face and cried.

Jeff was at her side in a moment's breath. "Just calm down, Susan. We just need to eat dinner. I don't know about you, but those mashed potatoes look fluffy enough for an angel to ride to heaven on." His smile sickened to her. How happy he looked and how gleaming white his teeth shone. What a price they paid for their perfect lives.

Her eyes narrowed into slits and her tongue lashed at her teeth. "How can you be so normal? Our son is missing and you want to sit and have dinner?" Susan's hand rose to slap him, but she stopped in mid swing as horror crossed his face.

"I don't know what's gotten into you. We have to remain calm. We can't—"

"Make a scene? Have an emotion that isn't pleasant?" Susan attention fell to Marie, still seated at the table. Her fork was in her hand, but her eyes were frozen on her parents. "Marie, grab your coat. We're getting out of here."

Marie nodded and pushed her chair back as Jeff grabbed his wife's arm. "Have you lost your mind? Where are you going to go?"

"We have to get out of here. Now. You can come with us, but either way I'm going."

"Going where?" Jeff demanded.

Where could she go? There were no hotels, nowhere to hide out where the police couldn't find her. "I don't know. But I can't just stay here and wait for them to come and get me."

Jeff's eyes fogged over and his frown deepened. "Who? What the heck is going on, Susan?"

"Are we going to get Jake?" Marie's voice was laced with hope.

Susan wished she could have said yes when Jeff erupted like a long-dormant volcano. "Jake? You know something about Jake and you've kept it to yourself? Where he is?"

So finally he cared. Finally he showed some emotion.

The door rang and Susan was out of time.

Tears dripped from her eyes and she took a shake breath. "Out the back. Grab your car keys and we'll go out the back."

Jeff fumed, sucking on his bottom lip and his cheeks flushed with anger. "We're not going *anywhere* until you tell me what's going on. What you know and what you've been up to!"

Susan shook her head, backing toward the hall. His eyes looked at her with betrayal and that was exactly how she felt.

She heard voices outside. "Police! We're coming in due to your non-compliance."

Marie gasped and looked up at her father, her eyes brimmed with fear. "Daddy!"

Jeff yanked his daughter close and hugged her to his chest. Marie buried her face against his shirt, trembling in fear. His eyes were pinned to his wife and they held no love and devotion. He threw accusations though his clenched jaw. "What did you do, Susan Marie?"

Her mouth opened to respond, but only managed a squeak. As the front door splintered behind her, Susan grabbed the steak knife from the table and spun as two police officers burst inside. Guns were clipped to their belts; restraint harnesses were in their hands.

"Stay back," Susan warned, holding the knife out with a firm grasp of her hand. "I'm not going anywhere with you until I hear about my son!"

One officer stepped forward, his hands in the air. "Ms. Monroe, I think you know this will go badly for you. Why don't you put down the knife and just answer a few questions?"

"Mom," Marie begged behind her, "please."

Susan lowered the knife. "What about my son?" Her voice squeaked.

"We don't know anything about your son." He took the knife from her hand. "We're here to ask you about Lawrence Stark."

"Lawrence Stark?" Jeff asked.

The officer nodded. "He was murdered. The vids were tampered with, but we were lucky and caught some street surveillance of the car leaving the scene. Matches your license plate number, Ms. Monroe. We're going to need you to come down to the station for some questioning."

Marie cried out, covered her mouth with her hand. Her knees collapsed and Jeff caught her, holding her to his chest. The image was pure anguish to Susan felt like a bullet tore through her to see her daughter so distraught.

"I just want to see my son." Susan's voice cracked. "Where's my son? I...he was supposed to come back. I did what you wanted. I DID!"

Confusion passed between the officers. She saw it in their eyes and the dumbfounded expression wore across their lips, but it made no sense. Who else could get her a gun other than the police? Who else could see into her home and track her movements? Susan felt lightheaded. She put a hand to her forehead.

"Susan, just calm down." The officer smiled, changing tactics. "We don't want an incident and you seem very upset. Why don't we take a few deep breaths? Step outside for some fresh air?" The officer stepped up and his hot breath was in her face.

She shook her head, taking a labored breath. "No, I—I can't. It's, uh, dinner time."

He smirked, his eyes cruel. "I think you know that's over. Step outside so your daughter doesn't have to watch us slip the restraint belt on your neck. One way or another, you're coming with us."

Susan threw a glance back at her family. Marie was huddled tight against Jeff and is arms were tight around her like a blanket. Her eyes were shielded and he refused to meet her eyes.

She nodded, setting down the knife and heading to the door.

"Mom!" Marie shrieked, "No!"

"It's best you and your daughter sit and finish your dinner. Don't want those mashed to get cold." The officer grinned and it was the last thing Susan saw of her family before she stepped outside.

With two officers following closely behind her, Susan's nerves were frayed beyond anything she felt before. Her hands were shaking and her heart was palpating. Her legs felt so weak that she could barely walk, but still her mind churned, trying to find a way to escape her fate.

"Stop right there. That's far enough."

But, they were only in the driveway.

Her family could be watching. Susan closed her eyes, taking a few deep breaths as waves of dizziness claimed her. Her head swayed. She could feel her skin beginning to tingle and she chanted, *You are human. You are not mutant. You are human.*

"We're just going to take you in for a little therapy." He winked at her and Susan knew what they meant. They were going to lock her up. They were going to reprogram her.

But then what would happen? Would she be calm? Would she be okay with her son no longer in her life? Susan backed up and nearly tripped over the stairs to her porch. If she went with him, who would free Jake? "I can't—I can't go with you."

"We're not exactly giving you a choice. You have to come with us, Susan. Let's not do it the hard way." In his hand was the restraint harness.

She panicked, taking deep breaths but her heart was pounding so fast Susan couldn't breathe. The world was beginning to spin and Susan felt like she was floating outside her body. "I can't. I have to save my son. I did what they asked. I can't go with you until I see how he is!"

One officer grabbed at her, but Susan jerked away. While she was distracted, another placed a collar around her neck and she knew what would come next. The shock that was meant to subdue her. Keep her from turning into a monster. God help her, she wasn't a monster. She wasn't! A mother would do anything to protect her children. Tears in her eyes, she could barely see the officer as he tugged on her collar.

The color began to fade from her skin. She felt her skin begin to stretch up underneath her shirt. Her wings were trying to free itself of the cloth. All she felt was anger, betrayal and hate such as she never felt before. She would not go with them. No matter what happened, Susan knew if she went with them it was over.

Her body bucked, up and down, until the pole from the restraint collar came free from the officer's hand. "Get a hold of her! She's gone manic!" One of the officers screamed. One drew a gun while the other reached for the pole on her collar.

Susan bucked her body, throwing the handle wide. The officer dived for it, but missed as she dropped to all fours, aware her hands were claws and charged the officers. Their screams were mixed with gunfire, but the shots went wide. She tackled one to the ground, using her meaty paws to push the man to the ground. Her claws stretched in relief from years of being in hiding.

Thick nostrils on her nose were covered in tiny hairs that shimmered in the sun as she snorted a deep breath. Her mouth wide, she roared huge fangs protracted and she dug into his neck as if it were a big steak. Her big paws kneaded his stomach like a kitten in love, but she felt orgasmic as she feasted on her enemy.

Drawing her head back, Susan pulled off a large piece of muscle, swallowing the blood as it rushed down her throat. With the taste of human blood, Susan Monroe crossed a line from which she could not return.

Another officer rushed from the car across the street. Someone grabbed her tail. Susan grunted, looking over her shoulder. Her eyes were yellow, now like those of a bat, and protracted in the sun. She turned to pounce on him, giant wings flapping behind her, giving her air. Her feet curled beneath her she fluttered toward him.

He fell to the ground screaming, legs spread wide as he raised his gun. Susan growled so loudly that the trees rattled around her and birds flew to escape her rage.

The officer never got a chance to fire; Susan ripped through him like paper machete. Warm strings of meat hung from her teeth and the gush of blood flowed down her throat. Just like it always should have been. It tasted so much better than the juice they were provided. This was the meal of champions. She couldn't believe how shortchanged she felt. Never again, Susan promised herself. She wouldn't be a caged animal any longer.

Behind Susan there were orders, voices. Who did they think they were to give her orders? When she turned, her body was pelted with bullets.

Susan fell, her wings being torn into shreds by the bullets that continued to sweep through her body.

Roaring, her head turned, her claws stomping on the pavement. She snort, her head back as she reared in for an attack. Her victim did not move as she approached. He held his gun steady and fired one bullet.

Her head jarred back as the bullet broke through her skin and lodged in her brain. She remembered nothing as she fell to the ground. Her yellow-slated eyes shut for the last time.

Chapter Twenty-One

Wendy Reynolds was welcomed in the fishing hamlet of Summerset with open arms. She and Jake stayed in a cabin on the lake, with access to canoes, boats, and her new favorite thing to do, sun-tanning.

The summer house was arranged by Rebecca and the Dragon Rights and Protection group. But they didn't just get the house, they also got a trained bodyguard, and Wendy had her own personal nurse.

It was there that she lounged in a low-lying chair so the grass tickled her thighs while the wind swept across her cheeks. She wore a bikini top and jean shorts unable to button across her wide middle. She enjoyed the heat from the sun, beating down on her skin. Never had the warmth from the rays felt so good.

In New Haven, the protective dome kept out real sunlight, but out here, Wendy felt like a piece of cooked meat and she liked it. She loved the intensity of it, loved the beads of sweat that clung to her forehead.

Jake worked at a nearby convenience store, packing groceries and stocking shelves. Until he got back, Wendy had little to do other than relax. Ear buds fed her soft music as she drifted in and out of sleep. Only the hard jabs of her unborn baby stirred her every few minutes, but Wendy was able to stay in her dream.

A tap on her shoulder woke her. Wendy took off her sunglasses and pulled out her earbuds to see it was Sally Withers, the nurse Rebecca assigned to the house. She wasn't much older than Wendy and had a pageboy haircut. "Sorry to wake you, but it's time to check you again."

Wendy nodded and offered her arm. She tried to remain calm while Sally slipped the blood pressure cuff on her arm. So far all but one reading had been normal. The smile on her nurse's face said this one was normal too. "Are you keeping more fluids down?"

"Yes." Wendy answered simply. "The medicine you guys have me on is really helping. I've even been getting hungry again."

Sally smiled. It was warm and always put Wendy at ease. "That's wonderful. I'm so happy you're feeling better."

"It's a nice place. Here." Wendy saw a few houses across the sailboat-filled lake and not far a long hiking trail. "I can see us raising our baby here."

"It's a nice town," Sally agreed. "And Jake is fitting in nicely. He's doing better than we could have hoped." Sally shined a penlight into Sally's eyes and tracked their movements. "You're sweating. Do you feel feverish?"

Wendy shook her head, but opened her mouth for the thermometer. "It's just the heat."

When it beeped, Sally looked at the readout. She scowled. "You're slightly elevated. Nothing to worry about, but why don't you come inside? I'll get you some sun tea. I made it with peaches this time."

Wendy accepted Sally's hand. She wasn't so big that she couldn't stand up on her own, but she definitely felt like her baby was growing faster than before. Wendy knew it was expected to happen now, especially since it was part mutant.

They climbed the rickety back porch and went in through the rustic kitchen. The floor creaked as she slid the door closed. When she turned around she was hit in the face with a white T-shirt Removing it, Wendy saw the scowling face of Thomas Crane. He was a grumpy old fisherman in a black plaid shirt.

"Put that on. We don't need you flaunting how knocked up you are."

Wendy pouted silently, but put the shirt on. It clung to her baby bump. Thomas scowled at it. "You better take her shopping for maternity clothes. Respectable maternity clothes." Thomas picked up his cup of coffee and headed over to the kitchen sink.

"I don't have to hide that I'm pregnant here. Everyone already knows." Wendy argued. "They think I'm a college student, not some stupid high school kid."

Thomas downed the rest of his coffee. He stared into his vacant mug, a thick silence hung over the room. "While you're staying here in my home, you'll do what I say. I don't care if Rebecca thinks you're the messiah. You'll stayed cover up, do your chores, and do what you're told."

Feeling deflated, and suddenly missing Dad, Wendy watched him exit for the front porch, most likely to clean his hunting guns again. Sally spoke, "He really is here to protect you. He'll make sure we're all safe. You would look cute in some nice maternity clothes."

Wendy did agree. She just didn't like being ordered around by someone she didn't know. "I have almost outgrown everything I brought with me. I guess it's good I left New Haven when I did."

"Yes," Sally said listlessly, "good."

****

After dinner, as the sun set, Wendy could see the lights from across the harbor shinning along the water. It calmed her. After a stressful day of putting up with people she didn't know, she liked to sit on the old wooden swing and watch.

Wrapped in an old afghan, she swayed back and forth, taking in a deep breath of harbor water. Off in the distance a horn sounded and a chorus of boat horns filled the lagoon. Her hair swept past her face and she cradled her belly through the blanket. It looked like a basketball hidden beneath the layers of fabric and when her son kicked her, Wendy wondered what labor would be like.

What would it be like to be Mom to someone? What if she couldn't take care of him, hold him for the first time?

The back door swung open and Jake sat beside her. She took his hand and placed it on her belly. They didn't speak, and the silence was as comfortable as a warm bed. She snuggled against him, taking in the smell of his cologne, and closed her eyes. It was worth all the anxiety just to be close to him again. She missed her parents, but she hated pretending she didn't love Jake.

Jake slid his arm around her shoulder and they watched the sun slip behind the horizon. "It'll be nice," his voice broke the silence, "if we can do this every night, once the baby's born."

"It makes me happy that you think about things. The future."

They fell into silence again until the door opened. Sally stood there with the harsh glow of the kitchen lights behind her. "Come inside, kids, before the mosquitos rip you apart."

Wendy gathered the blankets around her and did as she was told. "I'll be up in our room." She slipped her hand away from Jake and her eyes smoldered with desire.

Jake moved to follow her, but Sally threw a dishtowel at him. "Your turn to dry."

"Later," Wendy mouthed to him silently. When Jake grinned wildly at her, she bit her lip and raced upstairs to get things ready.

****

"Faster," Wendy gasped, her head buried in her pillows while her hands gripped the pine headboard so hard her joints were beginning to ache. Her legs were split high against Jake's waist.

He grunted, grabbing her ass with both her hands, fingernails piercing her skin. Wendy's mouth fell open in a silent scream. While it felt like her hips might split from the force, her body began to spasm and she moaned in pleasure as the orgasm raced through her entire body. Her fingers shook. Her legs so fatigued she could barely place them down as Jake kissed her rounded belly.

"I love you," Jake took her face with his hands. They kissed, unable to part. His breath was hot and spicy like the dinner they ate out by the lake. On him, the spices tasted even better.

Wendy moaned, gripping his face with her fingers. Everything about him turned her on, and the bliss of being with him every day shut every doubt she had from her mind. "If you keep kissing me like that, we'll make love again."

"So?" His voice was huskier than usual, and her heart raced as he nibbled at her neck. He slid his hand down her thick waist and traveled between her thighs. "We're adults now about to have a baby. Who's to say we can't be together as often as we like?"

"I'm hungry." Wendy whined. "I'm going to sneak downstairs for a little snack."

Jake smiled, his face glowing in the moonlight from the open balcony doors. "Bring me back some chocolate if you find it."

Wendy agreed, and slipped on her blue pajama bottoms. She placed one hand on her lower back because it hurt so much these days, and placed the other on the railing as quickly she waddled into the kitchen. Walking was harder these days thanks to her widening hip joints. At least that's what her new friends told her.

The sun tea was in front of the refrigerator and Wendy pushed it aside; it wasn't what she was craving at all hours of the night. In her view was a blue pitcher of organ juice. Made from organic cows and smuggled out of New Haven by Rebecca Seers.

At first Wendy had just been curious. It tasted almost like a raw liquefied steak and should have been vile and gross, but for Wendy it was a gourmet meal. The first time she had it, Wendy grew so hungry she ate enough for two meals, but she hadn't been sick. It was the first time since getting pregnant that she hadn't puked.

Now she just had a small glass when no one was looking. Part of her wanted to drink more, so much more, but Wendy tried to stay in control. She didn't want to overeat or binge on juice made from cow organs. Her baby wasn't just mutant; he was human.

She poured her glass and quickly drank it, groaning outwardly at how good it tasted. Licking her lips, she poured another glass and downed it. Wendy leaned her back against the counter and used her finger to get the last bits of juice out of her cup.

When she opened her eyes she saw Thomas in the entry, studying at her.

"I was just…getting a drink." Wendy threw her cup in the trash.

"Uh-huh. I'm sure you were." Thomas turned to watch her head for the stairs. "Is there something you think you ought to tell us?"

She paused, hand on her belly where the baby launched into a frenzy of kicks. "I was just thirsty." He asked her something else, but Wendy didn't hear it. She just hurried up the stairs to Jake. When she saw him, she'd feel better. She'd realize everything was going to be okay.

Wendy wasn't pregnant with a monster.

Everything was going to be okay.

Chapter:

By early afternoon, the sun was high in the sky. With a trunk full of packages and bags, Wendy pulled her borrowed truck up to the convenience store. She really enjoyed her shopping trip in the city, but she wanted to show Jake how cute she looked in the jean overalls she bought. Her hair was even pushed back with a stylish bow headband.

"I'll wait here this time," Sally said. "Just pick up some fruit or whatever you want for breakfast."

"Okay." Wendy stepped out of the truck and the front door of the store chimed as she stepped in. Air conditioning met her face and Wendy was glad. Thomas Crane's stupid old truck with hunting traps in the back didn't have air conditioning or FM radio. He was supposed to be keeping her safe, but he didn't seem to consider the idea that the pregnant teen might be overheating.

"Claire!" Jake said from up high on a stock ladder when he saw her and waved.

She smiled with every ounce of her being. She went to say hello and was welcomed with a warm kiss and embrace. "Do you like my new outfit?" she grinned.

He held her at arms length to see. "Oh, you look fab!" Jake cleared his throat. "I mean, awesome. Wonderful." For a moment he rubbed the top of her belly. "How's he feel about your new threads?"

"Oh I bet he likes them." Wendy giggled, but turned serious when Jake's boss, John Miller, came to say hello. He wasn't too old, just in his thirties, and still had all his hair.

"Hi, John." Wendy suppressed the urge to call him Mr. Miller. She was trying to seem more adult, like a recent college student and not some underage high-school girl.

"It's good to see you again, Clair." Hearing her new name always gave her goose bumps. "I tell ya, this is a good guy, you've got here. He fixed my cash register and Travis Henderson's motorbike today."

"Oh, it was nothing," Jake blushed while Wendy grinned at him.

"Nonsense. You have a real aptitudes for fixing stuff. What was it your father does?"

"TV repairman," Jake said, and Wendy almost slapped him for it. She couldn't believe that lie every time she heard it. Jake couldn't keep the twinkle out of his eye.

John laughed into his fist. "I was going to ask Larry here, but now you've saved me the trouble. Would the both of you like to come to dinner tomorrow? Lisa's making steaks and wants to see you again."

Oh, steaks. Wendy's stomach grumbled. "We'd love to. I can bring something sweet for after."

"Oh, just yourselves. You're new in town and just getting on your feet, so just bring yourselves. Best get back to work. See ya, Clair." John gave her a wave before heading into the back.

"Me too. See you tonight." Jake kissed her cheek and headed out to the front.

Wendy couldn't hide the bounce in her step. They were making friends, real friends, even if they were older. Things were beginning to feel real and stable. She just wished she could tell her dad.

Chapter Twenty-Two

Outpost, Detainee Center

Time dragged.

Jenna bounced her heels on top of the metal desk, causing a metal *thang* to echo through the room. It annoyed her, but she hoped it would annoy the people watching her even more.

Why would someone want to frame her for Travis's murder? Maybe Laurel really did think their van was tied to the crime.

Maybe someone planned to pin it on her the entire time. Maybe she should have ordered fish instead of steak for dinner? Wondering like that always led her to trouble. She needed to get out and find answers.

She glanced at her watch and then coughed into her fist. "Time's up," she whispered, playing with her hair to disguise the fact she was talking.

Jenna hoped no one realized they were still wearing their comms. It was a rookie mistake not to grab them and it just proved to her that whatever was going on was huge. Laurel had her men distracted onto something big.

"I used my cell phone to check the status updates," Jameson said. Jenna wasn't surprised that he somehow managed to keep one of his cell phones. Some of them were so small, they could be hidden inside a body cavity. She usually thought it was gross, but tonight was finding it to be a bit of a relief.

"Something big—*big*—is going down. Half the Outpost poured out of here ten minutes ago."

Jenna heard the sirens. The room was secure, but it wasn't noise proof.

They fell into silence again, so not to risk getting caught. Ten minutes passed before Jameson spoke again.

His voice was hushed but there was no mistaking the excitement in it as he rushed on, barely catching is breath. "Vids show Susan Monroe killed Lawrence Stark. Point blank. Police approached her at home. Susan went manic. Killed two guards before she was taken down. Dead."

Jenna coughed into her hand. "Holy shit." She heard Dirk whistling through her comm. Never in New Haven 56's history had a dragon shifted and taken the guards out.

This was huge and if other shifters knew what happened, containment and curfew would be the first protocol they needed to take before the news spread like wildfire.

"They moved the vids off of the usual server, but left a trail. I found those SOBs like they left me detailed instructions." Jameson laughed.

"Tone it down." Jenna turned her head, scratching the side of her face. "Can you play it through the comm?"

It must have taken all of Jameson's willpower not to make an Xtreme ironing joke. Instead the static of a vid came through her speakers. She heard the rustling of clothing, heavy breathing from the officer, and then, "I did what they asked! I want to see my son!"

Susan's voice was high-pitched, squealing. The tension was so tight Jenna could practically see her going manic in front of them.

"Someone put her up to kill Stark?" Dirk asked. "Jenna, there's no way—"

"I know." There was no way anyone could have gotten to Susan, given her a gun or given or instructions, without the police knowing about it. They were police or had friends inside the department. Her skin began to crawl.

But not all the pieces fit. Jenna was beginning to think they were working two distinctive puzzles, but none were straight edges. She couldn't put all the pieces together. The muddled confusion of her mind made her want to stress-eat. One thing was sure, Susan Monroe never was going to see her son again. She was used and whoever put her up to it, knew it. It was—

"Crime of opportunity." Dirk sighed, finishing her thoughts even though they were rooms away. "I guess Outpost got Stark out of the way without looking guilty. Didn't rile the shifters up. Just have to keep Susan being put down under wraps."

They were talking too much. Jameson jumped in. "Should have taken Stark out a long time ago. He was a dangerous liability. He didn't know his place and he got exactly what he should have. Few months too late."

"Time to shelf this debate for another time, boys." Jenna said even though she didn't necessarily disagree. It was frightening to her that reprogramming never worked on Lawrence Stark, but they couldn't just make him disappear.

Other shifters would care, and Rebecca Seers for sure would bring it up to Congress, or anyone else who'd listen. And tabloids sold more magazines talking about shifters than celebrities. Most likely because the shifters *ate* all the celebrities. They always said that Hollywood was a dog-eat-dog world.

The latch that kept her locked inside the room snapped. Laurel stepped inside, and Jenna wasn't surprised that she came, but was surprised she was alone.

The acting chief wore a smug smile and crossed her arms in front of the chest. "Gotta say I've been dreaming of this day for a long time. The day where you sat down on that side of the table." Laurel took a seat across from her and Jenna thought it was a mistake. If the roles were reversed, she never would have lowered her guard that much.

"Your jaw hurt much?" Jenna smiled at the bruise that graced the lower half of her face. "If not, I can oblige you and do it again."

Laurel's eyebrows rose, but didn't bait easily. "The Chief always protected you, even after you went off the ranch. Sad as his death is, finally you're going to get what's coming."

Jenna fumed and looked away. No matter what she thought of Laurel, the truth was she was a good interrogator and already the bitch was under her skin. She tried to stay calm, but her blood pressure was changing and her stomach was growling with hunger. Never a good combination.

"Nothing to say?" Laurel teased her, bouncing a bottle of pills on the table. "We ran tests on these, but haven't been able to figure out what they are yet. No label." Laurel studied the bottle before rolling them across the table. "Why don't you tell me what they're for?"

Still Jenna refused to look at her as she flipped the cap and stuck a red pill under her tongue. "Condition I've had since I was a kid. Fainting spells, seizures. Noting to concern your little head about." Already she could feel the medicine going to work. Which meant she could think clearer, try to formulate a plan.

Forget she was a monster beneath her pasty skin.

"All right." Laurel's voice was terse. "I guess I should ask you about the Chief. What your motives are."

Jenna took a deep breath. "I loved the Chief. If something points to me it's a lie. Someone is setting me and my team up. I know you hate me, and the feeling's mutual, believe me, but you have to know my guys are good. If I was going around the bend, they wouldn't follow."

"Again." Laurel corrected.

"Pardon me?" Jenna asked, agitated, barely able to sit still. She put her hands on her jittery knees to try to calm them.

"If you were going around the bend. Again. Because it happened once before and you could barely be stopped. But those were shifters. Those didn't have rights, exactly. So it was easy to sweep under the rug. Easy for the Chief to look the other way, but I'm not the Chief. He wasn't a mutant. He's going to get justice, even if I need to extract it from you myself."

She was sure Laurel was playing her. The woman wasn't the type to go seeking her own justice. But if Laurel was that angry, maybe Jenna could find a way to work it to her advantage.

"What I think is that someone paid you to do it. Everyone knows you've been for sale to the highest bidder. I just thought you'd put a bigger price tag on the chief."

Jenna's face wore confusion as Laurel handed her a small PDA. On it was Jenna's bank account information. She recognized her number and her debit card transactions from the last job they were on, but what she didn't recognize was the twenty-five-thousand dollar deposit into her account.

"This is a lie." Jenna threw the PDA back at Laurel and stood up. She slammed her hands down on the table.

"Sit down, Sergeant." Laurel warned, standing up herself.

"Someone put this there to make me look guilty. I'll be damned if I'm going to let you railroad me."

"I said sit down!" Laurel screamed and one of her hands went to her hip. So she was packing heat.

As much as it pained her, Jenna sat down and crossed her arms. She pouted and made sure it was very strong. She glowered at Laurel.

"I'm not trying to railroad you." Laurel spoke softly. "I'm just going where the evidence suggests and it makes a lot more sense than someone paying you just to get you out of the way."

"Not if I'm that big of a threat."

Laurel laughed. "Your narcissism is classic."

"Well…screw you!" Jenna heard Dirk sigh in her head. He had been quiet for so long she wasn't sure if he was keeping score.

"You're pathetic."

Jenna couldn't exactly argue with that. Her ear chirped. "Wait a second, Jenna." Jameson sounded worried. It stressed Jenna out to hear it. "The quarantine's been lifted. The van—the van that looked just like ours is at the checkpoint now. It's being processed to leave. The killers are getting away and I bet I know where they're headed."

They needed to get out of there fast if they were going to save the life of two helpless teenagers and clear their own names in the process. No time to play nice anymore. For better or worse, they needed to escape now. But if she did, it was possible Jenna would never be welcome back into the Outpost. Or her team.

For Chief Travis, though, Jenna would do just about anything. Including saving the life of his knocked-up daughter who was in way over her head.

"I want to see Internal Affairs."

"Excuse me?" Laurel asked and from the look on her face she was aghast.

"Excuse me?" Dirk and Jameson echoed in her ear.

"You heard me. I have a right to see my representative. I think I'm being railroaded. Do you think I just got off the bus yesterday?" Jenna paused. "What am I, your Aunt Maple?"

Dirk and Jameson groaned. "Not the Aunt Maple."

"We're going to jail for sure." Dirk muttered. "I was banking on my pension one day, Jenna."

"We were headed there anyway." Jameson said. "Guess now we're getting the electric chair."

"I have a right to see him." Jenna pushed. "If not I'll push to be released and to get you removed from the investigation." She pressed her lips together in victory.

Laurel turn three shades of green. It was a good look for her.

"I'll…go page him. So help me God, this better not be a trick, Jenna." Laurel smoothed her jacket and pulled it down firmly. Something else was on her mind, but she didn't voice it as she turned and marched out of the room. The door slammed behind her and echoed through the room.

Jenna felt sickened to her stomach. How she was going to pull this off—get past whoever was in the hall, get together, and get to their van—without killing anyone? "Goddamn it," she muttered under her breath, reaching into her boot. She felt at the stitching along the inside panel and pulled on it with her fingernails.

It pulled easily, and she cursed the idea of ruining her favorite boots, but they were her favorites for a reason. She always hoped it wouldn't be necessary.

"Well?" Jenna asked as her fingers ran along the sharp edges of the hidden knife in her boot. Six inches of sharp and deadly steel.

Jameson sighed. "Lock hacks in place."

"Good." Jenna pushed the knife up the sleeve of her jacket while bent over the table. She shivered as the cold metal pressed up against her flesh, and wrapped her fingers around the handle. "Dirk?" She whispered. "You good?"

"Good, yeah. Ready."

Jenna stood, stretching her legs, and peered at the two-way wall mirror. If anyone was watching, she wasn't sure. "Do it."

Jameson worked fast and this time was no disappointment. Jenna stared at the door handle and waited for it to snap open. She wasted no time in grabbing it and slipping out into the hall.

Officer Tim Hornes did a double take, a manifest order in his hand. "Hey," he said, but was cut off when Jenna's fist crunched against his jaw. She pushed him down and kicked his crotch. He groaned, grabbing at the family jewels.

"Sorry for all this." Jenna grabbed the pistol at his waist, and jumped over his body.

Time to find her team. By the time she sprinted to the end of the corridor, red lights were flashing and horns were blaring.

Someone was watching after all.

Chapter:

Jenna ducked behind a wall and felt a bullet fly past her red curls. She grunted in frustration; she was close to the impound where the van was being kept, but kept getting cut off at the last minute. The reflective mirror at the corner of the ceiling revealed two officers advancing on her position.

She didn't want to kill anyone and so far had managed to pull that off. Her name was already mud, Jenna didn't want to make it any worse.

The metal door in front of her thudded with the force of several officers behind it. Jenna managed to fry the lock, but knew they would soon find a way to hack through it. And then she'd be back in handcuffs, thrown in solitary confinement, and she'd never see dear old Mom again.

Her gun was empty, but no one needed to know that. Not yet. Jenna put the gun under her chin, pushing so hard it hurt, and stepped out. "Get back, boys, or I'll blow my own brains out."

The officers, Jenna didn't know their first names but knew them from around the base, glanced at each other.

"We doubt you'll do that."

"Really? You want to chance that? If you're wrong you'll never—" Jenna took a deep breath. "—You'll never know what happened to the chief or why. Do you really want that kind of knowledge dying with me? It'd be on your hands."

"Dammit, Jenna," Dirk whispered in her ear. "I'm almost there. Couldn't you just hold off for one more second?"

"I'm out of time." Jenna gritted her teeth. Louder she said, "Both of you back up and let me pass or what happened to the chief, dies right now. NOW! And you'll never know who's next."

Their jobs would be on the line if what she said were true. They slowly backed up toward the chain link fence that led into the impound yard. The closer they got the more Jenna could feel the crisp air and her nose stung from the smell of gasoline.

"Back up against the fence." Jenna trained her gun on them.

It clinked as their bodies wedged up against it. Dirk, in position, handcuffed them through the links.

"How could you, Jenna? The chief stuck his ass on the line for you a dozen times."

She couldn't meet his gaze. For all the trouble and gossip she caused, this was the worst and Jenna didn't have the stomach for it.

Dirk opened the gate. They walked in time, their boots crunching on gravel. Dirk took her hand, but said nothing. Jenna thought about pulling it away, but didn't have the strength. She squeezed it and left everything unsaid as the spotlights overhead shone on them. Marking them for death.

Dirk groaned, jerked backward as he let go of Jenna's hand. She never heard the bullet whiz by, but saw his shirt was torn, saw him clutch at his stomach. Screams and her heartbeat echoed in her ear as Jenna knelt down beside him, grabbing at his arm. "Dirk?"

Bullets pounded on metal in all directions as Jameson's van came to a screeching halt in front of them, giving Jenna and Dirk the cover they needed.

"Get in, for the love of pumpkin-chunkin', get in!" Jameson hissed out his window and over the comm. Jenna was able to put Dirk into the van and slide beside him in one fell swoop.

The tires spun, grating against the gravel as Jameson punched it hard toward the Outpost gate. Lights from the checkpoint filled the van, making Jenna shield her eyes as her hand clutched Dirk's chest.

"Hold on!" Jameson screamed as the van rocketed forward toward the locked gate. Officers scattered for cover. The van, never slowing, crashed through the gate, bending it until the chains broke. Jenna heard the wail of sirens and tires peeling out against slick pavement.

The open road always made her feel better, but not his time.

Dirk gave Jenna a goofy grin. She figured it was the loss of blood, but then realized there wasn't any. Her hand should have been covered in the stuff by now, but it wasn't.

"You're wearing a bulletproof vest, aren't you?"

He gave her a wink. "Nice to know you still care though."

"Asshole." Jenna nearly spat at him. She punched him in the gut and took a seat beside Jameson.

Dirk groaned. "C'mon, it was funny!"

"Can you lose these jerks?" Jenna asked Jameson, ignoring the movement from the rear of the van.

"Doing my best, but it's like trying to be stealthy in a sperm whale."

Jenna nodded. "Do your best while I work on a secure line. We're going to need to warn Rebecca Seers about what's coming for her and for those kids. We may not be able to catch up with the guys framing us, but I bet we sure as hell we know were there headed."

"To kill the kids. Never thought that we'd be on the same side as her." Jameson raised his eyebrows like they just made a deal with the devil.

"That's still debatable. Until we blow the lid off this thing, we're going to need some allies. Let's try not to burn any more bridges." Jenna said more to herself than to anyone. "This van is marked for death. We need to ditch it and get something else. Up for the challenge? Rhetorically speaking."

"No more time for games. I get it."

Jenna was glad. Heading into the back of the van, she glowered at Dirk as he worked at a computer station. She was so angry with him for forcing an emotional response out of her. Stupid men and their tricks. What else was new?

"I opened that secure line you asked for."

She knew an apology when she heard one, but ignored him. Instead she took out her phone and used her speed dial function. Jenna set her comm to private, so Dirk and Jameson wouldn't be able to hear the rest of the conversation.

"I need to speak with Rebecca Seers. Tell her it's an emergency."

"I'm sorry, ma'am. She's not taking calls."

"Tell her I know she has Wendy. I know she has Wendy and something is coming for her. For her and that bastard baby of a mutant."

"Straight to the point," Dirk shrugged.

"We don't have time for anything else," Jenna said while she waited for Rebecca to pick up. Finally, her comm clicked, but it was the voice of Rebecca's secretary.

"I'm sorry, she's in a meeting." Her voice was strained in an obvious lie. "Can I get your number and take a message?"

Jenna gritted her teeth. "Tell her she'll have to answer for this and soon." Jenna ended the call and peered over Jameson's shoulder. "Make a course for Rebecca Seers and her little organization. I'm making a house call."

"It's going to take hours to get there. Hours we might not have."

"We don't have a choice." Jenna slumped into a seat.

Chapter Twenty-Three

"Go upstairs," Jeff closed the blinds in the front window. Behind him Marie cried hysterically. She cradled her waist like she did when she had the stomach flu. The happy girl, the one they named after his wife, was shimmering blue before his eyes.

She would go full dragon without an intervention.

"Marie!" Jeff snapped. "Go upstairs. Lock your door."

"She's dead." Marie whispered. "Mom—"

"Upstairs, sweetheart. Please." His voice begged her to move. Jeff knew it wouldn't be long until the police entered their home, but he didn't want Marie to see. She was just a kid. He had to hope she'd be spared. He had to pray that she wouldn't be treated the way Susan was. The way he was about to be treated.

Susan, the light of his life, was dead.

Jeff blinked his eyes and watched as Marie rushed up the stairs. When he heard her door slam, Jeff turned back to the window. Fear lodged in his throat and he peered through the blinds. Outside more police were arriving. On the grass, beneath a black plastic sheet, was his wife's body.

What she did, Jeff thought was impossible, but he witnessed it with his own eyes. It was like a nightmare playing out on his lawn. He saw how scared Susan was and how they cornered her like she was a wild animal.

Never before had Jeff seen someone take dragon form. It scared him when he saw Susan change and he was surprised at her strength and horrified at how she killed those officers.

Terrified that his wife was really a dragon.

They were all dragons.

Movement outside caused Jeff to move away from the window. Footsteps drew up his front steps. Jeff stood in the darkness of the living room. He waited for them to come to him.

The rustle of footsteps and heavy shouting of the police rushed him like a moving wall of sound. There were many bodies charging him, all in heavy cavalier suits with breastplates and protective helmets. "Freeze! Do not move, Monroe! Hands up!"

"Hands up!" Multiple voices screamed at him and Jeff couldn't focus on just one. Trapped in a whirlwind where multiple storms pelted him at once, he didn't know which way to look. His arms trembled as he lifted them.

They were wrenched behind his back and he was forced down onto his stomach. Handcuffs were snapped on. Jeff struggled to lift his head and his body was hit with an electrode stick. Electricity entered rushed up his back into his limbs and chattering teeth. He lost control of his body, convulsing like a suffocating fish on land. His head rocked and a scream of pain and loss left his mouth.

He stared at the grouping of boots all around him. Footsteps charged up the stairs and a door was shattered. Jeff cried, gagging on his vomit, and heard the screams from Marie.

"Daddy! Daddy!"

They forced him up, carrying him outside where the sun still shone. The flowers wafted in the breeze and Jeff wondered how a thing was still possible. The light in his world was gone; things would never be the same.

He was forced to a paddy wagon; when they opened the back, Jeff saw his neighbors and friends shackled in the back. A quick glance showed a record number of officers on his street. And in front of each house, a paddy wagon waited to be filled.

What would become of them? What would become of New Haven?

Chapter Twenty-Four

May 20th, 11AM
Crane's Cabin, Summerset

"I won't be argued with." Thomas Crane said with a level eye. "Neither of you are taking this situation as serious as it is. Before it's too late you both need to listen. Both of you sit down."

Jake and Wendy sat on the sofa, the look of chastised children on their faces. The pretty dress she got to wear for the first time was now the farthest thing on her mind as Thomas went on.

"This isn't a game. You are not playing house. Understand? Jake, as far as the world is concerned you are a monster. A monster that must be quarantined. You being out here is about the same as a lion escaping from the zoo. If people suspect, they will have you arrested, or worse. And you," Thomas glared at Wendy, "pretty dresses and making pound cakes—"

"You told me to look respectable."

"Keep your mouth shut when I'm speaking to you. You still act like a child. If you were my kid and pregnant I'd be worried, and I'm talking a human child. But this? You have any idea the undertaking you've decided on? That kid is what this entire country is afraid of and that makes them dangerous. They'll be afraid and not just of it, but of you. How am I supposed to protect either of you while you're going out on dinner dates?"

"He's my boss." Jake argued. "But we'll do what you say when we're there. Promise."

Wendy shot him a look. He was always so agreeable, always ready to listen to orders.

Thomas nodded. "Good. Follow the script and everything will be fine, but step out of line and we'll have no choice but to move you."

Wendy didn't want that. She was happy in Summerset. She wanted to raise her baby here away from prying eyes. Until it was older and then everyone could know the truth. Maybe the world would come together.

They promised to be careful. Then, hand in hand, they headed out to the car while Thomas watched through the blinds with Sally at his side. For a split second his hand grazed her ass. "You have any idea how bad this is going to get?"

"I do." Sally answered.

"She doesn't."

***

"Surprise!"

Wendy yelped as the small crowd of people leapt out from their hiding spots behind the sofa and love seats. The room was decorated in blue streamers and balloons. She covered her mouth and fought back happy tears. Beside her Jake clapped his hands together and Wendy realized he was in on it. A baby shower for her.

Her, and her half-dragon baby.

"I can't believe you did it all this," Wendy whispered as he gave her a light kiss.

Jake grinned. "Oh, it was hard to keep it a secret, but we wanted to do something nice for you."

"That we did," John gave her a warm hug. "Welcome, Claire. And congratulations. Babies are a blessing." He gave her a wink.

Wendy smiled and greeted people for what felt like an hour. Her head spun and she felt so overwhelmed as she was handed some punch, a plate of food. She saw the towering table of gifts wrapped in light blue paper and a wave of grief washed over her. Wendy knew her parents should be there and would be if the situation were different. She wished it were, but she loved Jake so much. Wendy was glad it was his baby, but knew how much her mom would love to have thrown such a shower.

And that it came from a bunch of strangers who didn't even know her real name made Wendy so sad. She felt like a phony, but she smiled through her tears and thanked everyone as she made herself comfortable in an oversized blue paisley chair.

The afternoon was filled with laughter, conversation, and present unwrapping. There were bags filled with delicate outfits and bundles of soft blankets. Sheets, towels, and bottles; Wendy got everything she would need for the baby's first few months. She was so grateful for everything and didn't know how to express it. Jake was there with support and hugs. His eyes were a mirror to her own.

The gifts loaded in the truck, Wendy sat and visited with the ladies while she waited for Jake to get back. She was eating another piece of cake because it was her favorite, chocolate. The men sat in the living room watching CNN. The way they were studying the screen it seemed they were very into politics, or whatever was going on. Wendy's dad was the same way and made her think of him.

Mary followed her gaze. "Oh, men. It's either world events or sports, isn't it? John's been obsessed with that channel since news broke about what's going on in New Haven."

Wendy's heart skipped a beat. She put her plate of cake down. "We don't have a TV at my uncle's cabin. What's...going on?"

Barbara rolled her eyes. "Something to do with those beasts. I try not to think about them. They nearly destroyed the world and we just keep them in those plastic things. I won't even come within ten miles of one of those bubbles. Disgusting."

Wendy bit her lip. She didn't know what to say.

"It's not about them. It's about the chief. Everyone's heard by now. There was an explosion. There's a talk it was an inside job, but I think it was the monsters. Only about time they'd kill them."

"Where?" Wendy asked, her voice cracking. "Which New Haven?"

"Forty-six or fifty-six. What's the difference?"

Mary ignored the question. "Congress will be reconvening to vote on a new bill that was just drafted. To get rid of the shifters. Forever. I'm not saying I agree, but this could be life-changing. Maybe finally the world will be free of the HI police force."

One of the women snorted. "Global police, they like to call themselves? More like career criminals who think they are above the law. Going anywhere. Stealing anything in the name of justice. Worse than the CIA."

Wendy felt sick. Her hands had begun to shake so bad that her fork rattled against her plate. She put it down. "I really would like to know, which New Haven."

Everyone's eyes were on her. "Are you feeling okay, Clair? You look kind of pale suddenly. Let me get you another glass of punch."

Wendy shook her head. She didn't want punch. She wanted answers! Throwing her napkin down, she slid her chair backwards and marched into the living room. "Which New Haven?" She demanded of the men. "Which one?"

John startled, blinking his eyes at her. "Fifty-six."

"What?" Wendy's hands shook as she pushed her hair from her face. "And, the chief, his family?"

"Dead." John said simply.

Wendy backed up, a shriek of a sob lodged in her throat. Everyone was watching, everyone saw, but she couldn't help herself. Why didn't anyone tell her? Why—

"Well, it took a pry bar, but I finally got everything into the back of the truck—" Jake stopped as his eyes laid on Wendy. "Clair, what's the matter?"

"My father's dead." Her words sputtered out of her mouth. When horror crossed his face, but not surprise, Wendy grabbed his shirt and shook him. "You knew? And you didn't tell me! How could you keep this from me!"

Jake looked like a deer trapped in the headlights. "We thought, in your condition—"

Wendy laughed, tears rimmed in her eyes. "My condition is exactly why you should have told me. Damn it, Jake!"

Slowly John stood from his armrest.

Jake eyed him with fear. "I'm sorry. We'll just be going. She's not usually so upset by the news." He took her by the arm, trying to lead her toward the door, but Wendy swatted him away.

She yanked her arm, her eyes widened and her lip snarled. "I'm not some hysterical pregnant woman." She pointed her finger at him. "You should have told me."

"I think maybe she should sit down," John said, getting between them. "Maybe you can both explain to me why she keeps calling you Jake, and why's she so upset about Chief Reynolds."

Realizing what she had done, horror set in Wendy's belly. She felt torn up into knots and felt the frantic movements of her baby, feeling her anxiety. "I—uh." Wendy swallowed. She felt so dizzy and lightheaded that she didn't know what she was saying, or doing. "I think I should go home and lie down."

"I'll take you." Jake extended his hand and begged Wendy to take it with his eyes.

Wendy reached for his fingers as someone turned the volume up on the television. Her eyes went to it without meaning to.

"—again the FBI working with the New Haven police force is issuing a bulletin for missing Wendy Reynolds. Missing since the night of the explosion, she may be kidnapped and being held under false arrest by whomever is responsible for the death of Chief Reynolds. Just released is a recent photo from her graduation photo taken earlier this year."

Wendy didn't need to see it to know what was going to happen. She took Jake's hand and they bolted for the door. *Don't look back*, she willed herself as she got into the pickup truck. Even when she heard John scream, "Wendy!" after her, she never looked back.

She cried all the way back to the cabin.

***

Wendy didn't want to look at Jake anymore. She didn't want to look at anyone.

So she packed her bags. She tore through her drawers, only taking what was necessary to survive. Thomas Crane would be happy with that, but probably not happy that she took a few baby outfits and baby blankets. They were so beautiful and the baby would need something. It didn't matter where it was born, it was going to need something.

"Wendy."

She turned her heard to see Sally in the doorway. Wendy busied herself with folding her clothes. "I don't want to talk to you."

"I know you don't want to. I know you feel betrayed. But we thought it was best not to upset you. I thought it best. Stress isn't good for a pregnant woman, especially one with blood pressure problems."

"I don't have a blood pressure problem. It was one reading."

"It wasn't just one."

Wendy gave her a dirty look. "More secrets then?" She slung her large duffle bag over her shoulder and headed down the hall.

"We're all in this together," Sally said as she rushed after her.

"Some of us are in it more than others. It's growing in me, not you. It's Jake's head on the cutting block. Not yours." Wendy stomped downstairs and saw the collection of bags at the front porch.

Thomas Crane was in the kitchen, readying some rations for the road. "You're right about that. I won't lie to you, Wendy, we're in a bad pickle. Your picture is everywhere. I didn't think they would release it. In fact, I was surprised they announced you were missing at all. Means one thing."

"What's that?" Wendy asked.

"They want you out in the open. They want to force us to run and catch us out there, off guard. It's smart, I suppose, since they don't know where you are. They are going to force others, like Jake's boss, to do their work for them. We have no choice but to leave. Like I said, it's a pickle."

Wendy scowled. "Are you saying...are you saying that the police, the people my Dad worked for, want me?"

"Not so much you as that thing growing inside you. Until you have it, you're worth more dead than alive. The New Haven police isn't known for its tact or for following laws. With them, there almost are none. They will do anything to make sure shifters stay right where they are."

His words hit her with the force of a truck. "Are you trying to upset me? Because it's working."

"No, I want you to be careful. On guard. What happened this afternoon can't happen again." His stare was level, intense, but not unkind. "We have a lot of ground to cover so we best head out."

Wendy nodded and watched Thomas pick up her bags before she left the cabin, most likely for good. The little rustic home had been perfect, she thought, for raising her child with Jake. But she hadn't known then that her baby got her parents killed. That the government would want to silence her. Maybe it had been a mistake, and nothing but a pipe dream.

If the baby kept her on the run forever and kept her from friends and family, maybe Wendy shouldn't have had it at all. Thinking those words made her heart sick with grief and as if to remind her of his existence, the baby kicked her hard.

"I didn't mean it," she said with tears in her eyes, holding her belly. "I'm sorry, baby. I didn't mean it."

***

Outside, John erupted from his truck and Mary followed close behind him. John grabbed Jake's arm. "Whatever is going on, Larry, Jake, whatever your name is, we'll help you. Just tell us.".

Jake didn't know what to do as he sat in the driver's seat of one of the blue pickup trucks in the driveway. He had to do what Thomas Crane and Rebecca Seers told him to, but he liked the Millers a lot. He liked living in town and having a job, he didn't want to leave. But he was told there was no choice; the FBI was probably already alerted and someone soon would be on their tail. If they wanted to have their baby, if they wanted to be safe, they had to go.

"I wouldn't hurt her. That's all you have to know." Jake swallowed hard, relieved when he saw Thomas put the rest of the bags into the back of the truck.

John's eyes threw accusations at Thomas. "You arrived here saying you inherited your grandfather's cabin, but you know, I never knew anyone who lived here before. Why don't you tell me what you're doing with these two kids?"

Thomas sighed, placing his shotgun into the front seat of his cab. "Mr. and Mrs. Miller, your nice people, I respect what you're trying to do. But if you care for these kids, you'll turn your back and let us drive away. Forget you saw us, at least for a day or so."

Jake got out of the truck just as Wendy stepped outside. She was beautiful, swelled high with his child, but her face was so sad. He wished she hadn't heard about her dad that way. Rushing to her, he took her hand and led her toward the trucks.

Mary intercepted them, blocking the passenger side door. "If you're in trouble, girl. Real trouble, tell us now. We'll get the police. Anyone who will listen."

"And if you're not, if you need a place to hide, we'll help you." John added.

Jake didn't know what to do, which adult to listen to. All his life he had been conditioned to follow the law, to always listen to authority, but now they were telling him different things and he didn't know which way to go, who to pick.

"I don't want to go," Wendy whispered, her chin quivering. She reached out for Mary's hands, "Please—"

"Now listen here!" Thomas yelled, reaching inside his truck and unlocking the door.

"I knew it." Mary whispered, yanking on Wendy's arm. "Stay with us. Have your baby here if that's what you want, but don't go with him. Whoever he is, he smells like trouble."

Sally threw her arms up in the air. "Everyone please calm down, please! Her condition is very serious. I am her nurse and I'm telling you, we have to go now without any more drama, before the stress does more damage than it's already done."

Jake didn't know what she meant by that, but knew he trusted her. If Sally said they had to leave, then they did. He opened the passenger side door and implored Wendy to get in. "For me, please."

After what seemed like an eternity, she did.

He let out a sigh of relief as Thomas pulled his shotgun from the car. He held it in a relaxed fashion, but the tension around the automobiles increased tenfold. "Now I'm a patient man, but know when I say we are leaving here, I mean one way or another. Stand back. And if you think of calling the authorities, remember I know where you both live. Where your children go to school."

Jake was shocked by the threat. But he got into the second truck when Thomas yanked on his collar. Using the rearview mirror he could see John physically restraining Mary from chasing after them.

After a few minutes, Jake turned around and saw Wendy crying in the other truck, but Sally was just driving straight ahead as if nothing was wrong at all. What had they gotten themselves into?

He wasn't sure that he fully trusted either of their guardians. At that very moment, Jake felt that he made the wrong choice and should have told his parents. That they should have stayed with the Millers. He just wanted the chance to do everything over again.

"Don't worry," Thomas broke the silence. "We'll regroup at the compound. You'll see her again soon."

But Jake had a feeling he wouldn't at all. He felt like he might never see her again, and that image of her crying uncontrollably, would be seared into his brain forever.

Chapter Twenty-Five

Dragon Rights and Protection Organization
Alexandria, Virginia

"You can't go in there."

The secretary was on Jenna's ass following after her with a clipboard, but Jenna didn't care. "Keep her busy, will you?" she said to Jameson or Dirk, whichever would listen. As long as it wasn't she who had to put up with crap from some nonessential worker doing what she's told. Meanwhile, a girl's life was hanging in the balance.

Jenna knocked on the door and pushed it open.

Rebecca jumped up from her chair and papers flew everywhere before floating down to the ground with the precision of a parachute. "You? Here I thought you were being held somewhere for murdering Chief Reynolds."

"I do not have the time or patience to throw barbs back and forth. Let's not do this the hard way." Jenna pulled her gun from her side and cocked it. "Bullet's in the chamber so you better damn answer my questions the way I need them answered."

Rebecca held her hands up. "I know they say you are unreasonable—"

Jenna tilted her head. "Do they? That's very understated of them. Where in the hell do you have those kids hidden? Is it here? By the lack of security outside, I'd say no."

Her chin quivered and her eyes darted while she thought of an answer. Rebecca wasn't the pillar of confrontation that Jenna thought she'd be. "Summerset. It's a small fishing village. Few hours away at best. I can send the coordinates to your phone."

Jenna nodded. "See, I knew you could cooperate. I don't like you, Seers. What you've done has set off a chain of events you can't undo. You shouldn't have moved them in secret. You shouldn't have moved them at all. You should have made her get rid of it. If you did, my life wouldn't suck and the Chief would still be alive."

Rebecca's eyes flashed with disbelief. "You really believe that? You really think they killed Chief Reynolds over Wendy?"

"What I believe is that the Chief was just collateral damage and the real targets got away. You're going to tell me the thought never crossed your mind? I don't buy it."

Rebecca glanced at her desk. Jenna saw the truth on her face.

"What's her condition?" Jenna asked. "If I'm going to save her ass I want to know what I'm walking into."

Rebecca stuttered, smoothing her hair back and her eyes wouldn't meet Jenna's. "Good. I get reports from her nurse. You know her. She works for your mother."

"Sally?" Jenna asked and felt the color wash out of her face. She snorted and shook her head, teeth clenched. "I can't believe your nerve, getting my mother and her camp involved in this."

"She was involved in this way before I was. Your mother is a pioneer."

"And an idiot." Jenna took a deep breath. "Thanks for the information. I'll let you know when the kids are safe. But if I'm lucky, maybe the men searching for them will come here and blow you first. Seems only fitting, don't you think?"

The shock on Rebecca's face made Jenna laugh. She stormed out and saw Jameson holding hands with the secretary, who, judging from her blushing cheeks, was eating every moment of it.

"Loverboy." She slapped him in the chest. "Let's make tracks."

"Where are we headed?" Dirk asked, jogging to keep up to her long strides.

"We're going to the country, boys. Break out the fishing rods."

New Haven High School, Basement Level
Security Clearance, Restricted

For a long time, Marie sat in darkness. There was nothing to see or hear. The only sound was her chattering teeth from the cold. Her naked skin stuck to the metal of the chair and her wrists were raw from how tightly the ropes were tied against her naked flesh.

Unaware how much time passed, her ears focused on the sound of footsteps and a metal door banging shut behind her. The metal cuffs around her neck kept her from behind able to turn. "Hello?" She whispered in the darkness, her throat hoarse from the cold.

A warm hand clamped on her shoulder. For a split second, Marie felt that everything would be okay. Before the needle slipped beneath her skin.

The darkness spun until there was nothing at all.

***

Marie was aware that her chin was buried into her chest with such a crick in her neck that it made her head thud with pain. Her wet hair was frozen in icicle chunks all around her face. Squinting, she looked across the dark room. She could see a pinprick of light opening in the distance. She tried to sit up to attention, to see what was happening, but was so cold that none of her body seemed to respond to commands anymore.

The light snapped into such a blinding light unlike anything Marie had ever seen before. Instinctual, her eyes closed, but still the light hurt her. She moaned, unable to look away, thanks to the bracers she wore. Trying to scream, an electrical pulse deadened her muscles through the bottom of her chair. It surged through her bones, chewed through her muscles, and put her through such agony, Marie wished for it only to end. She didn't care if they killed her, if they disposed of her, only if it ended.

It did end, in that moment.

And Marie was grateful.

But then a moment later it was back. Brighter and more intense than before. She did her best not to scream, not to give in.

Music flooded in around speakers unlike anything she had ever heard. The harsh sounds hurt her ears. Guitar riffs and obnoxious drum solos. When the men sang, they screamed. It wasn't music, it was torture. If Marie's hands weren't clamped to her side, she would have covered her ears. Time ticked by, hours maybe, or even longer. Marie could barely think from the constant pounding in her ears.

The music finally cut off, but Marie could still hear it vibrating in her head and feel it quivering the floor beneath her feet. Her dull, tired eyes detected a window opening to the room next door.

There was a metal slab in her view and beside it a man in a white coat, as if he were a doctor. But he scared Wendy, because she knew he was one of the worst kinds. He wasn't a mutant, like she was. He wasn't just a human being. He was one of the doctors who worked for New Haven. Probably did experiments on other mutants, just like they were doing to her now.

On the metal slab was a small frame covered up by a white sheet. The doctor peeled the cloth back enough so Marie could see the dead woman's face. It was the face of her mother. It was Susan Monroe. The one she was named for. The one Marie loved more than her own life.

"Mom!" Marie shrieked. Her throat burned, but the screams couldn't cease. Marie's wrists ached, but still she veered forward, pulling and straining against her restraints. Marie's neck strained against the metal clasps, but it was in vain.

The window slammed shut. A voice echoed through the room.

"Begin phase 2."

More cold air was pumped into the room, and then the lights returned.

It all started over from the beginning and Marie didn't think she would die. She wanted to die.

****

When the window snapped open again, Marie felt almost nothing. Even the pain she had felt the last day, the past hours, was no longer present. There was only a numbness in her mind and a tingling through her limbs. She didn't know how many phases she had been through, but phase five had been the worst, while phase six made her cry the hardest.

Marie blinked as she regarded the lifeless frame on the slab in front of her. When they pulled back the sheet, she barely reacted. "That's my Mom," she said flatly.

"She's dead." A voice said to her over the loud speaker.

"Yes," Marie repeated, listlessly. "But she's in a better place."

"A better place?"

Marie nodded. "Just like we all want to go to someday. Can I go home soon? I think someone needs to feed our cat. My mom used to do it. Before she moved on."

"Congratulations, Marie, on completing all the phases so brilliantly. We will see you get something to eat and see you home."

With a snap, all of her restraints were free. Marie used her hands to shield her eyes as the light gradually turned back on. Someone was beside her, wrapping her in a warm blanket. It was one of her old teachers from kindergarten. The woman had a warm smile. "You are exactly who we need you to be, Marie."

"I will be whoever you need me to be." Marie followed her. She was in the basement of the high school. The walls were lined with doors, each guarded with a police officer. Marie smiled at them for a job well done. She thanked them for their service.

Her old teacher led her to the second-floor bathrooms and instructed her to take a hot shower and get dressed. "We'll take you home soon. I'm sure your Dad can't wait to see you."

Marie couldn't either. She thought maybe she could make him a nice cake. Or maybe a pie. Apple pie was always his favorite. Since Mom wasn't around anymore, someone was going to have to take care of him.

■■

Marie felt grungy in the sweats they gave her. Never before had she been in public in anything other than a skirt, but her teachers assured her it was just temporary until she got home. Then she could change, make dinner, and unwind in front of the television. After a long day of school and extracurricular activities, Marie welcomed it.

Megan met her by the curb with a warm hug. "How are you, sweetie? Last I heard, they sent your Dad home a few hours ago. I'll take you home. I'm sure he can't wait to see you."

Marie smiled. Megan was one of her mom's oldest friends. She was sure one day she'd end up married to Megan's son. Too bad her mom wouldn't be around to see it. It was too bad, but at least now she was in a better place.

"She's in a better place now, you know." Megan said once they were seated in the car. Marie couldn't help but notice there were bruises on Megan's face, and on her neck there was a thin red line.

"Did you get tangled up in the clothesline again?"

Megan smiled. "Yes, I did. Seems to happen every few months, doesn't it?"

It certainly did.

Once home, Marie thanked her for the ride home and gave her a pleasant wave goodbye. She watched her drive off, surprised how empty the streets were. It was if everyone were inside. All the stores were closed and Marie didn't even see anyone inside the neighborhood parks at a time of year when all the parks were full. There was hardly anything fun to do in New Haven. Marie supposed the malt shops must have been extra busy that night.

Stepping inside, Marie let the door close behind her quietly. "Dad, you home?"

"In here." His voice was sad.

Marie felt so bad for him and rushed into the living room. He was seated in a recliner watching a *Scooby-Doo* rerun. Mom's favorite cartoon.

"Your mom's favorite." He said as if he read her mind.

She sat down on the armrest beside him. "I'm sorry, Dad. About Mom. About Jake."

"At least I still have you, kiddo. I love you, Marie."

"I love you too, Daddy." Marie leaned in for a warm hug. It lingered probably too long, Marie thought. Maybe he could sense that deep down somewhere, she was sad too. "I'm gonna go make us something to eat. Just like Mom would."

Marie excused herself, but not before she noticed the red marks on his wrist and his neck. Just like hers. Maybe this was normal, maybe this was life, but Marie doubted it. She wasn't sure she could ever bring herself to ask, even over a tall glass of warm milk.

Would she ever feel safe enough to be honest again?

****

After a wonderful dinner, Jeff did the dishes while Marie did her homework in front of the television. He could hear its soft whine over the running water and the meowing of the cat bellowing at his feet. Susan usually fed him milk at night, he remembered. So he took a yellow saucer from the cabinet and filled it up.

"Sorry, Harvey." Jeff scratched behind the purring cat's ears. "It'll take a little getting used to, but we'll find our groove."

The doorbell sent Jeff to the front door. When he answered it he was surprised to see his friend from across the street. "Billy? You're just in time for coffee, if you want some."

Billy's eyes were shifty, but he looked relieved to enter the home. "Thank God you're here. I saw your car, but was afraid that they got to you. They've already gone through a third of the town. Some of us are held up in the old church. The one Stark used. It has *special properties*."

"I can't go out." Jeff poured Billy a cup. "Marie's here."

Billy's eyes drifted to the living room. When he saw her, he waved. "Well, bring her with you. It concerns her too."

Jeff scowled. "She has homework and school in the morning. What's gotten into you?"

"This is more important than school work." Billy grabbed Jeff's wrist and pushed up the sleeve. Then, he inspected his neck. "Oh, gosh, they got to you." Billy backed up, fear in his eyes. He wiped spit off the corner of his mouth. "Damn it, Jeff, snap out of it. We need you. If we have you, others will join us. Susan would want a good life for you and Marie. If we stay here, we have nothing left. Not with the chief dead. Not with all the cops knowing we can take them out if we want to. We have to strike now before they clamp down on us. Or worse."

"Billy, I don't know what you think you know about Susan. Her death, while tragic, is just a hurdle we have to overcome. She's in a better place." Jeff grinned. "That's all that matters."

His friend set the coffee cup down unsipped. "I'm sorry you feel that way, Jeff. I'm sorry for a lot of things." Billy left without saying goodbye and slammed the door shut.

Marie came from the living room holding a notebook to her chest. "Dad, what did Billy want?"

Jeff didn't have the foggiest idea.

"Dishes are done," he said. "I know it'll take a while for us to get into a groove. Just the two of us, but it'll be nice, I think."

Marie agreed. "We'll get through it. I'm glad I have you." She hugged him, and Jeff slapped her back.

"I'm going to head up to the bedroom and lay a few things out for the morning. I'll be back in a few moments." Jeff grinned before and headed upstairs.

The bedroom was warm and quiet, with the shades drawn. The bed was freshly made and everything looked as it normally would, except Susan's shoe rack was empty and her closet was cleaned out. The town did it, to save him the trouble, and Jeff was grateful.

He pulled a shirt and a pair of slacks out for work the next day. He laid them on the bench beside Susan's old vanity. Her makeup and jewelry was gone. All that was left was the mirror and a few rings on the wood were Susan used to rest her morning coffee.

Jeff thought of the morning and everything he would have to do: make Marie's lunch, get her to the bus, head to work, grab the weekly rations. It all seemed so normal and relaxed.

He should have been happy, but there was a hole inside him. Almost like a growing wound and the longer he ignored it, the larger it seemed to get.

He didn't know what it was, but when he thought of Susan, he felt angry. Sad. But, he shouldn't be. Jeff needed to snap out of it. For Marie, for everyone. Jeff had to be the caregiver now and he couldn't do that without a level head on his shoulders. Work would notice if his performance was anything less than perfect.

Heading back to the door, something under the vanity gleamed in his sight. Probably a piece of trash, he thought, so he went down on his knees and stretched his hand under the vanity. Jeff was surprised to see Susan's engagement ring in his hand. Delicately he stroked the small diamond and then it all flooded back at him and knocked him over onto his butt.

Taking Susan out for their first float date at the malt shoppe.

Kissing her beneath the glow of the moon at the monthly open square sock hop.

The pleasure of taking Marie, and then Jake, home from the hospital as tiny newborns.

Before her death, Susan had been scared. Jumpy. But she always put a brave face on and Jeff knew. He knew, and for his part, he ignored it. Pretended noting was wrong. Even when everything was wrong. Susan knew then, what Jeff knew now, they were nothing more than pawns. And Susan, his girl, had been used by New Haven to kill Lawrence Stark. And then they killed her.

Jeff squeezed a fist around the engagement ring so tight it caused the stone to dig into his flesh. Finally he felt something other than calm. It was like fire in a pit, beginning to smolder.

A look of anger, of determination, of revenge, fell upon his face.

Chapter Twenty-Six

When they arrived at the Summerset cabin, the sky was twilight and the air was cool. Jenna inspected the perimeter of the area while Dirk investigated out front.

The comm in her ear chirped with his findings. "Someone's been here, Jen, and it wasn't Santa Claus. They left in a real hurry. Two set of tire tracks. Big trucks. And overlapped on top of them is a third set."

"Let me guess," Jenna said dryly. "A van, right?"

"Bingo, the lady wins a prize."

"Damn, we're still two paces behind." Jenna sighed, her eyes sweeping across the terrain. The cabin had a great view of the town and the harbor. It was far enough away so if there were trouble, the neighbors probably wouldn't have heard anything. It made her anxious. "I'm going inside to see if there's anything left. Anything that will tell us where they've gone."

Dirk's sigh had *argue* written all over it, but Jenna didn't wait around to hear it.

The door squeaked as she went inside. Downstairs was orderly, as if everyone would be back after running errands, but things were different upstairs.

Dresser drawers were half open and the closet hangers were askew as if clothes had been ripped off them in a hurry. One room had a few traces of medical supplies and saline, and there was an old blood pressure cuff on the bed. Maybe they had prepared for Wendy to give birth here, or maybe she was having medical problems due to the mutant in her womb.

Jenna thought that more likely and moved to the room across the hall. It was decorated in blue with a bassinet, a gentle mobile, and a half-hung wall border with stuffed teddy bears. She felt bitter about Wendy's innocence, that any adult had allowed this to happen. She was just a kid. To be thrust into the middle of a war between those that supported shifters and those that didn't wasn't fair.

Damn shifters. If the baby had been aborted, or miscarried before anyone knew, no one would be in this mess. But it was real now, a heartbeat and limbs. Probably a soul. Jenna was going to need to protect it and Wendy. If she could just catch them.

For the lives of her crew and for the Chief, she needed to make things right. But she didn't know how much of their lives would be intact when this was over. The vids over the Net made it seem as if Congress was two breaths away from destroying the New Havens.

But she was sure that government suits would pat each other on the back for saving a few budget dollars. The New Haven projects would be bulldozed for new mini-malls. People would forget. Makeup and plastic surgery would come back. And then maybe one day, it would all happen again.

Jenna sighed. She hated it when she thought too deep about this stuff. She wished she could just have a few bottles of beer and veg on the sofa downstairs. But every minute they were there was another minute that the police closed in on them. She didn't want a confrontation yet. Not before they knew where Wendy was. And why they had suddenly left. Leaving all of her baby's stuff behind.

She couldn't help but stroke the small blankets. They were so soft, for delicate skin, and made Jenna wish for simple times. How wonderful it must have been for Wendy, still excited about the future and everything it would bring.

Jenna remembered too.

Her comm buzzed. It was Jameson. "Come around to the back. We found an old shed. There's a stench."

Jenna's stomach tightened. "On my way."

She sprinted down the steps and out the back door off the kitchen. The backyard, set up for sunbathing, had a nice view of the summer harbor. Far off was the padlocked shed, with enough distance from the house to keep people from wandering off to it.

A nearby ax for firewood made quick work of the door. Jenna and Jameson pried the boards free. They were old and splintered, so dry that even through black gloves Jenna felt the sting of wood shards piercing through her leather.

With the boards free, they were assaulted by the smell of death, thick and consuming. Jenna covered her mouth on instinct while Jameson coughed. "Wendy?"

Jenna shook her head. The smell was so foul that whoever—or whatever—was there had been there longer than a few days. She bent and pushed some gardening tools out of the way.

Not really surprising from the smell, there was a dead body, but Jenna was surprised that it was a naked woman. Her arms were bound behind her back and her vacant eyes stared up. Jenna recognized them, even through a river bank of dried blood. It was Sally Winters. The middle-aged woman who always aided her mother.

The one who helped Jane Morgan give birth to Jenna Morgan.

In secret. In hiding.

"It's the nurse," Jenna said.

"If that's the nurse, then who's with Wendy and her mutant lover?"

Jenna didn't think she was going to like that answer.

Dirk's footsteps rustled the grass behind her. "Lots of local chatter online. Looks like the family running the local store, the Millers, threw a baby shower for a young couple, who flipped out when Wendy's photo was featured on the afternoon news. Before you know it, people at that party were calling the hotline. FBI's already mobilized. Once the red tape clears, they'll be here."

"Guess that explains why they left in such a hurry."

"News?" Jameson asked. "Who watches the news?"

"It's a fishing port, Jameson. Not exactly on the cutting edge." Jenna said. "So," her mind spun as she tried to piece everything together, "Wendy hightails out of there and come here. Tell her nurse imposter what's going on and the nurse forces them to move. To cover her tracks and to keep that baby for herself."

"Who do you think she works for?" Jameson asked.

Dirk stuck his head into the shed. "Damn. I hope when I go, it'll be with more dignity than that."

"It probably won't be."

Dirk gave her a look. "I already said I was sorry."

"Sometimes sorry doesn't cut it."

Jameson sighed. "Can we work on your issues later? Laurel's goons will pick up our track soon. I rather not have them find us here having a lover's spat."

Jenna agreed. "Let's head to the Millers. If they were friends to these kids, they might have more information than they know."

"Let's get moving before our photos are cast all over the evening news. Armed and *very* dangerous." Jameson grinned, but it lacked all humor.

"With a potato shooter? Mini-marshmellows?" Dirk asked with a trace of laughter in his voice.

But there was no laughter left in Jenna's heart. There were only hot stinging tears in her eyes. "Time for jokes is over."

****

"We're here to help the kids," Jenna explained to the guarded couple at the door. The home was quaint. Again she felt herself jealous for a simpler life. Wouldn't it be nice to forget this all and retire to a fishing village or maybe become a surf instructor off the coast of Hawaii? She always did like warm climates. "We want to help them, and we can't, without some direction."

The woman's stance softened, but John Miller stared her down, his arms crossed his chest. "I feel lied to, taken advantage of. Why should I trust you enough to tell you anything?"

They always started with the tough questions. "Because it's my job to help people. I've gone through a lot of trouble to track Wendy here. I need to get to her before others do. Her life and her baby's life are worth a little risk, don't you think?" Using kid gloves wasn't her usual tactic, but when you were a fugitive, choices changed.

John grunted. "You're with New Haven police, aren't you? And if I don't tell you what you want, you going to come in here? Bust up my home?"

Jameson cringed. "Some stories get embellished. We're not above the law. We just run perpendicular to it."

Jenna gave him a quick elbow. "What Officer Jameson is trying to say is don't believe everything you hear. A few bad officers doesn't make us all bad. We're here to help."

Something about what she said, softened him. John nodded. "Was she being held here against her will?" he asked and Jenna wondered why. What made him think that she was in trouble?

"Not that I'm aware of, but that doesn't mean she's not in trouble. If you know something, tell us. Before something happens to her and her baby."

"What about Larry?" Mary asked. "I mean, Jake. Why don't you care about him?"

"Wendy is our first priority, Ma'am." Jameson said.

"He's one of them, ain't he?" John asked. "Mutant."

Jenna really didn't want to answer that question, but to earn his trust, she did. "Yes. But he's not a threat."

Mary gasped and covered her mouth while John only nodded. "Suspected, once everything came out. How good he was with fixing stuff. Polite. Almost something old-fashioned about him. I liked him. Good kid." John sighed. "You gonna harm him when you find him?"

"No, just bring him back. His parents miss him."

John nodded again and Jenna felt like she had him where she wanted, soft and pliable thanks to Twenty Questions, nineteen of which she didn't have time for. "All right," he sighed, "we went to the cabin to try to stop them. It was quite the scene. Wendy, Jake, neither of them looked like they wanted to leave, but they forced them into trucks."

"They?" Dirk asked and the nervous twitch in his voice made Jenna's stomach tighten.

"The nurse and the guy. He's only been in town a few months. Seems fishy to me. Thomas Crane, he calls himself. He took Jake with him. He," John swallowed hard, "threatened us."

"How?" Jenna asked.

"He had a big shotgun, that's how." Mary's cheeks lit up red with anger. "He said he'd kill our kids if we talked to the FBI. Well, he didn't say it, but he inferred it."

That explained their reluctance. Jenna wanted to know who this guy was and fast. Jameson looked at her and took out his phone.

"We wanted to help them," John said. His eyes were warm and he wore worry lines on his face. "If they are in trouble, if they need a place to hide, I want to help them."

"Oh, John," Mary whispered.

They were good people. Honest and noble. Jenna forgot good still existed and her heart felt warm in their presence. "I'll do my best to help them. I'm sure you'll hear from them again one day. Right now, we have to find them." Jenna tried to make them feel better, but wasn't sure she had. Wasn't sure she could. Instead they headed back to their van, still shiny black and brand new from where they picked it up the night before, and for the main road.

"Marksmen?" Dirk asked.

"Sounds like it. A professional, whoever they are and whatever they want, we can bet it's not to knit booties for Baby Mutant." Jenna felt that they posed no immediate danger to Wendy, not until she gave birth to the baby, but the men following them wouldn't hesitate to take them out.

Whoever this marksman was, Jenna hoped he was good enough to protect Wendy, but hoped he didn't kill the only men who could clear her name.

Her phone rang, interrupting her thoughts. "Hello?"

"They haven't made it to your mother's compound yet. Any sign?" Rebecca's voice was a tight rope of stress.

"No. They're not headed there. The nurse you put in charge, Sally Winters, is dead." Jenna wished she could relish in shocking Rebecca, but couldn't.

"What? That's *impossible!*"

"Tell that to the stashed cold body in a storage shed out back. When was the last time you spoke with her?"

"Over the phone? In person? We sent her there six weeks ago to prep everything. Her last report was yesterday morning. Said Wendy was fine. All her stats were good. It's better than we expected because—"

"Because?" Jenna prodded with urgency.

"Because when we examined Wendy at our offices here, her blood pressure was already high. We thought the medicine was working. We thought—" Her voice was rushed, like a girl trying to get out of punishment.

"What you thought doesn't matter. Those e-mailed documents to you were forged by what is most likely two highly trained mercs, or assassins, or worse. Designed to keep you far away from the cabin." Inside her, Jenna's anger flamed. "You should have been here. Checking on her in person. That baby is your prize, so why weren't you here, Ms. Seers?"

"I have appearances to keep up. Do you have any idea what's going on? In the House? Congress? I have my work cut out for me already. The lobbyists trying to keep our country pure are pulling out all the stops. Meanwhile the Mutant Rights and Protection Act is under attack. If one more thing happens that casts a bad light on the shifters —"

"I know," Jenna said softly. "I can't stop that, but I can protect this kid. But first I have to find her. Do what you can to help the shifters and mobilize your people at the compound. They have to be ready for when I take Wendy in. We don't know what her condition will be when we find her."

"And Jake? What about him? Do you give any thought to him at all?"

Not since his mother went apeshit and killed Lawrence Stark and three of her fellow officers. But she didn't want Rebecca to know that. "We will do everything we can to save all three of them."

"Maybe I misjudged you, Ms. Morgan. Do your best and I'll do mine."

"You sure forgive easily considering I questioned you under gunpoint." Jenna had a lot on her mind and couldn't keep it to herself anymore. "From the looks of it, Wendy dreamed of the three of them being a family together. I'm pretty sure you always knew that wasn't going to happen. Too bad you let Wendy believe it."

Rebecca stammered. "It could too work. At a protective facility. The child is going to need love. Its mother is the best thing for that."

"While you run your tests and parade it in front of the press, politicians, showing them how 'human' it is, right?" Jenna didn't really want an answer and slid her phone shut.

Jameson gave her a sideways glance. "Don't forget to put your comm back on group."

"You have something to say?" Jenna asked, and not nicely.

"I'm just being paranoid, right? Since we're all one big happy fugitive party, if you're keeping secrets, I'd like you to stop. For reals, Jenn."

"I'm not keeping anything you need to know. Nothing that matters to this mission."

"Why doesn't that make me feel any better?"

A wave of nausea hit her. Jenna closed her eyes and counted to ten. "Listen let's head to the cabin and make one final sweep. We're going to need to make tracks before the FBI gets here."

"Is there food somewhere in your plan?" Jameson asked. "We can eat from the road. I saw a drive-thru on our way in."

"Burgers?" Jenna asked with hope.

"Burgers."

"Awesome."

****

Jenna didn't find much in the cabin. Her eyes lingered on the baby's nursery, even though it was Wendy's room that ached her the most. In her dash to safety she left behind mementos that were usually important to teenagers. Necklaces, pictures of friends, some makeup. She wasn't a kid anymore, not really. Now her mind was reeling with worry about her half-breed kid and how it led to her father's death. Jenna remembered how Wendy looked at Travis. It was the same way all girls looked at their father. The way she looked at hers, even after everything.

The way—

Jenna sighed and moved to the next room. Inside there were lacy bras strewn about and a pair of soiled work boots in the corner. Looked like Sally's impostor and her partner frequented the same room. She wondered if the teenagers knew or cared. Or were they too busy playing house to notice?

The first nights, she bet, were exciting, but by now the novelty probably had warn off.

She hated being thoughtful.

Jenna entered the baby's nursery. A number of cute outfits were in the small bassinet. There were packages of pacifiers, knit caps, and a few canisters of formula. Why the formula was left behind, she didn't know, but Jenna knew these things were important. So she found an empty plastic bag in the closet and packed everything away. Delicately, she took the clothes off plastic hangers and folded them before placing them inside.

The ones with dinosaurs on the shirts made her smile. Soft to the touch, they already smelled sweet, like baby's breath. She was going to bring it all along for Wendy. Give the girl some hope that everything would be all right. Babies were promises of renewed hope, a better future. Too bad it was damned from the start, but maybe if Wendy were strong, things would be okay.

Maybe.

"Jen?" Dirk's voice rang out as he knocked on the door. "We're ready to check out."

Caught off guard, Jenna stood and wiped a stray tear off her cheek. "Just, uh, packed a few things Wendy might need. For, you know."

"Baby." Dirk's eyes swept through hers. They smoldered with his usual intensity. Under his gaze Jenna felt naked, her soul exposed. "You okay?"

"Fine." Jenna saw Dirk was going to try to touch her arm, so jerked herself away. "I'm good. Just a lot of crap, you know?"

"You want to ... *talk* about it?"

The words sounded so foreign to her. Jenna rarely wanted to talk about anything, rarely wanted to let anyone in. But she was going to need to, and soon. When they took Wendy to her mother's compound, everything was going to come out in a frenzy. Jenna needed Dirk and Jameson on her side. She needed to control the situation, and she couldn't do that with a fleet of people around her, offering their opinion on who she was and what she had done.

Dirk stepped forward and caressed her shoulders. "You look like you're coming unhinged. What's the matter? You can tell me, if you want to."

"But, you think I won't want to, right?" She nearly cried when she said the words. Jenna had to get a grip. Usually she didn't feel so vulnerable, but being here, with him, and with the baby's things around the room..."

Dirk shrugged. "It's not like you've been forthcoming. You were gone for two years and I don't know why. Except for the dead shifters. And the hearing. But that only accounts for one year, not two. If you have something important to say, I think you know I'm here."

"For now." Jenna laughed bitterly. "Yeah, you're here for now. Til we get where we're going. Until you know the truth. About me."

"Just try me, Jenn. Maybe I'll surprise you." Dirk flashed his smile. Warm, inviting, lovable.

She didn't know what she was doing. She couldn't be doing this. Jenna needed to stop herself, but it was like she wasn't in control anymore and words tumbled out of her mouth that she never wanted to say.

"My parents came to me right before I was supposed to be getting dressed for our wedding." Jenna took a deep breath and watched Dirk's eyes darken. "They wanted me to know, before I got married and got pregnant, so they chose the worst moment in history to tell me, that my father wasn't my father. He raised me, but he didn't make me."

"I don't—" Dirk started, but Jenna shook her head to stop him. If she stopped talking now, she might never get the courage to say the words again.

"My real *father*. Was killed by people not much different from us. Then my Mom found out she was pregnant. Very sick and very pregnant, she met Alan, the man who raised me. He's a doctor, you know." Jenna paused for Dirk to say something, but he didn't.

Nervously, her teeth chattered. "Anyway, they hid my Mom, and together with Sally, the dead woman in the shed, brought me into the world. But I was always sick. Always had seizures, slips of time, and I would become so hungry." Jenna squeezed her eyes. "Only red meat could fill me up. Still like that today. But the seizures, the slips of time, Alan developed a pill to help. It evens out my blood pressure. It's not a cure, I don't think, but it helps keep me normal. Normal as I can be."

Dirk was still scowling. "I have no idea what you're trying to say. What's this have to do with our wedding and what's going on now?"

Her own breath pounded in her ears. "I can't take it back if I say it. I can't undo it." She gripped his shirt and pulled him close. She didn't want to talk. All she wanted to do was kiss him.

Dirk wouldn't oblige, his nose against hers, but his lips just out of reach. His voice was husky, his breath sweet, and Jenna just wanted to remember it; one last time. "Jenn, just tell me, c'mon. You're so close. Maybe then we can move on."

"We can't." Her lip trembled. "We won't. That's why I left. That's why I needed to get away. I knew that if you—" Jenna was cut off by his kisses.

Unable to resist being so close to her, Dirk grabbed her, kissing her with a tender passion she craved. His arms were strong, cradling her like he'd never let her go. And when they pulled away, barely away but enough so she could see Dirk's eyes, she was filled with such a fear inside herself that was unfathomable. This was why she didn't want him close, this is why she did her best to stay a bitch twenty-four-seven.

But she spoke the words for the first time in over ten months. The words she said only to Chief Travis Reynolds. Jenna always hoped to never speak them out loud again. "I'm shifter. I'm a dragon. I'm a damn mutant half breed."

Dirk's jaw went slack and his hands fell to his side. Jenna could feel the air in the room draw cooler, the space between them seemed to multiply and the fear inside her magnified. The look in his eye said nothing and everything all at once.

"When they told me, my life ended. I wasn't me anymore. But certain things made sense. The hunger, the fainting spells. My mom told me as a kid I was just sick. Didn't get enough vitamins. Until Alan, my stepdad, found a compound to help. I just thought it was regular medicine. I didn't realize. Not until they told me."

Dirk's eyes fell on her and reflected her own anguish. "You never suspected?"

She shook her head, trying to build strength. "Did you?"

His eyes were hard. "Then why tell you at all?"

"They wanted me to know. Before we started having kids. Put down roots. But it was too late," Jenna drew a long shaky breath. "Because I was already pregnant. I told my mom, the night before at my bachelorette bash. I was going to tell you on the sandy beaches of the Caribbean. But when I found out what I was, what it was—"

"You just ran off?" His nostrils flared and his eyes grew cold like she was a stranger. A perp. "You just—did you abort our baby and you never even told me? Did you?" The anger in his voice dared her to answer.

Jenna had bile in her throat and her heart felt like it was clamped in a vise. "You think I could? I left. I went to my parents' compound. The one where they search for a mutant cure. The one where I was born. I went there to have our daughter."

Dirk looked faint.

"But it didn't work out." Her voice was haunted. "It was harder than anyone expected. Something about me didn't like being pregnant. I was sick all the time and I knew in my gut, something was wrong. When she came, it was hard and fast. No one expected me to survive and she was stillborn." Jenna cried like she hadn't cried since that day.

The sob shattered every wall she built around her heart. "And then I went crazy."

Jenna took a deep, shaking break. Inside her heart quivered. "Grief, revenge, anger, post-partum swollen-breasts-with-milk-but-no-baby depression. I went out and started finding mutants and killing them. I didn't want to stop and didn't want to be stopped, not until the Chief came. Found me. Talked me into returning to the police, answering for my crimes."

"You were never going to tell me." The dark realization built like horror on Dirk's face. "Damn it, Jenn, she was mine. Ours, and you just shut me out like you always do. I should have been there. I should have—"

"What? Held my hand?" Jenna's eyes were wild. "Told me everything would be okay while I have their blood in my veins? While everything in me screams they are evil monsters and then I find out that's exactly what I am? I didn't want you to look at me like you are now."

Jenna turned her head away from his eyes. "I get it. Don't pretend."

"Pretend?" He snorted. "I'm sorry you think so little of me to think I couldn't have dealt with it, Couldn't have loved her."

He was living an idealized dream, like he always did. "And lose your life? Lose your job? We couldn't have stayed together, raised her, and kept things normal. If people found out what I am, what she was, we'd be Wendy and Jake. Is that what you would have wanted?"

"To be with you, to be a family, maybe I would have given it all away. But you never gave me a chance. You never asked. Screw you, Jenn. Screw you."

He slammed his fist into the door and Jenna's heart raced to watch his angry display, to see the hate in his eyes and the mourning in his voice.

Jenna bit her lip, tried to quell the sob building in her throat. "We need to pull it together to find Wendy and—"

"Work together like nothing happened? I don't get you. I don't get your timing or any of this. How the hell do you expect me to just act like nothing's happened between us? You were supposed to be my wife, and you were the mother of my kid, but hell, let's put it all aside because we have a job to do?"

"For Wendy and that baby. They're in trouble. She needs real medical care. And I needed to tell you because when you saw the compound—"

"I'd have questions. Yeah, I get it. I don't like it, but I get it. Anything else you want to tell me while we're at it?"

Jenna didn't, but part of her wanted to beg him for forgiveness. Wanted to tell him she loved him and would do anything to take it back. "Let's just get this show on the road."

Dirk stared at her, his eyes slit like coins, and studied her every breath. She broke the stare and glanced down at her boots. They were nice boots.

"Jameson's in the van doing some recon. Time to hit the road."

Her stomach rolled. Jameson, of all people, would probably tag him herself and throw her into New Haven to be conditioned. She hoped Dirk wouldn't tell him, but didn't think she had right to ask for favors. So instead she nodded and opened the bedroom door.

She found herself staring down the barrel of Jameson's gun. Her comrade for the last ten years spoke.

"They told me you were a mutant, but I didn't believe them, until now."

With a flick of his wrist the electrode collar shot out around Jenna's neck. It latched closed and she was gagging for air. He tugged it hard. Electricity surged through her body, racing from limb to limb, sending her slamming into the back wall. She fell to the ground. For the first time in her life, her skin shimmered.

Being a half-breed, only half of her shined in crazy patterns like she was a pair of plaid socks and her wings were nothing more than small nubs beneath her clothes.

But it was enough. She squeezed her eyes shut and heard Dirk holler at Jameson. Things would never be the same.

Chapter Twenty-Seven

When Wendy awoke in the car, the fog was dense and darkness tightened her. Through the thickness of the trees, she could see a glimmer of the moon trying to peek in. Glancing over, she saw Sally studying the road with both hands on the wheel. They hadn't talked since the last stop and Wendy hadn't seen Jake for the last two. It set her on edge.

Wendy struggled to push herself up and felt the movement of her baby as it too awoke.

"You're awake. Good. You needed your sleep, but it's good you're awake again. How are you feeling?"

"Tired. Foggy." Wendy said. "But safe with you."

Sally smiled at her. "Good girl. We'll be there soon. I'll make you something to eat and some tea. After a good night's sleep we'll decide where we are off to next."

"Where's the other truck? I don't see it?"

"Errands. They are picking up some supplies, but don't worry. They'll be along soon."

Wendy relaxed the rest of the way to the cabin. They drove through more trees than Wendy knew existed on the planet, let alone in one area. The roads turned left and right into the shape of the letter S. Beside the road, just off the path, were wooden rustic signs. Wendy couldn't see what they said in the darkness.

There was a single lamppost beside the cabin Sally parked next to. The patio looked overconstructed, with enough support beams to hold up an elephant and the doors were giant sliding pieces of glass. The building itself was towering, appearing to be at least two stories, with stone arches and an antique stone chimney. Inside no lights were on and Wendy wondered if anyone was expecting them.

Sally cut the engine and unlocked the doors. "Go easy getting out of the car. You've been sitting a long time. Might take awhile for things to respond."

"I've been on car rides before." But she yelped when she opened the car door. A cramp ran up her leg and settled along her belly. She felt like everything inside of her came together, hardened and then slowly expanded out again. "It was a cramp, I think."

Sally took Wendy by the arm and helped her out of the truck. "Walk around for a few minutes and take a few big breaths. You're probably dehydrated. I'll get you something to drink soon."

Wendy did what she was told, pacing in front of the house. She rubbed her belly to relax herself and then made a slow ascent to the patio door. She saw a small wooden box marked *keys* beside the entry way. It looks like this building was the main office and the rec center for the resort. Peering inside, Wendy could only see a small desk light on. There was however the flicker of a television and off in the corner an old wood stove burned. Wendy could make out tourist flyers beside the sofa and there was a warm-looking crochet rug nestled beneath it.

Sally came up beside her with her doctor's bag and an arm full of duffel bags. "My cousin's place. It's closed for renovations but he keeps watch. He's going to let us stay here until tomorrow. Until we think of something more long-term. It'll be a warm bed and good food."

Her smile made Wendy feel better as it always did, but she felt trepidation when the man came to let them in. His frame was small and his eyes were beady. He wore dog tags around his neck and twirled a toothpick inside his mouth. Goosebumps rose on her skin and her spine chilled. Wendy didn't like the look of his greased-back hair or the tattoos on his forearms, but as he unlatched the glass door, she smiled. She knew she had few options left.

"Is this her?" his words were slurred and he stepped back to eye her like she was a piece of meat on display, hanging from a butcher's window. Wendy stepped back without meaning to.

Sally rubbed her shoulder. "Easy, Jack, you're going to scare the poor girl. Why don't you go make her some soup or something?"

"Yeah," he sucked in air through her teeth and it whistled, "all right." He dragged his words out as his eyes lingered over her large breasts and protruding belly, but he left the room and Wendy relaxed.

"Sit down and put your feet up." Sally nodded to the sofa. "I can see your ankles swelling from here."

Wendy hadn't noticed, but they were a little inflamed. She did as she was told and thanked Sally when she was handed a tall glass. She hesitated when she saw what it was. Organ juice. It was Jake's juice, the one she had been sneaking since she left New Haven.

"Don't, okay," Sally sat beside her. "We know you've been drinking it. We know it makes you feel better. So drink it and don't feel guilty. It lessens your symptoms and right now we need as much as that as possible."

Wendy bit her lip and looked at the thick, red slop. It smelled good though and her belly was churning for nourishment. She took a tentative sip, wiping the corner of her mouth. Swallowing, the cabin came alive with smells of rustic pine, the crackling of the fire. Down the hall, she could hear Jack clinking together pots and pans as he whistled a little ditty.

She was probably just tired and not thinking straight, but she drank more. It made her feel like a freak show, a bloated uncomfortable freak show. Still, something in her felt better. Settled. It relaxed her enough to lay her head down on the sofa pillows while she absently stroked her belly and thought of her dad. And her mom.

Wendy remembered how she stormed off to meet Jake. She knew it was the last time she'd see her parents for a long time, but had been so angry with the fighting, with how Mom always accused Dad of everything. Like it was all his fault, but Wendy knew it was *her* fault. She was the one who had sex and ended up pregnant, so why did Mom have to go around screaming at Dad?

She left. She had to, but Wendy didn't need to scream at them. She didn't have to storm out and maybe she could have told them everything. Maybe. But, they never would have let her go without them. That's how parents were and Wendy needed to do this alone so she could be with Jake. But she hadn't realized they would die. If she knew someone was out to kill her, Wendy for sure would have told her parents everything, and taken them with her somehow.

Wendy moaned, waking when Sally sat beside her. Her eyes widened into narrow slits as Sally put her wrist to her forehead. It was cool to the touch. "Your fever's finally spiked. I knew it would." Sally sighed. "It picked a hell of a time to do it."

"Will I be okay?"

"Should be, for now. With some Tylenol. Most mutant woman break into a small fever toward the end. Just a little harder on you, that's all. Better get you to bed."

"Jake—"

"I'll send him along when he gets here. You need your rest. Think of the baby."

Wendy nodded and dry-swallowed two pills. She struggled to pull herself up from the sofa and Sally grabbed her arms and forced her to her feet. Wendy gave a soft laugh, and Sally guided her upstairs toward the bedrooms. Climbing stairs was hard on her back and her feet turned out like a duck. Wendy was out of breath by the time they reached the top.

"Everything's going to get harder now, so we have to be careful." Sally opened a door and Wendy saw in was a dim lit room with an ultrasound machine and various medical equipment. It was almost like they were expecting to come here.

Sally helped her in bed and then covered her up with a light blanket. "Sleep now. Tomorrow things won't seem so bad."

Wendy watched her go and listened to the door latch. Then she closed her eyes, begged that sleep would take her, and that her words would be true.

It wouldn't bring her Dad back, though.

She slept, but not soundly. Every so often her dreams were interrupted by the sound of footsteps. Underneath her door's threshold, the light was disrupted now and then by the shadow of a man's leg. Someone was keeping watch.

I'm in danger. Wendy thought, and her belly tightened.

***

Marshall Xavier Roberts, better known to his enemies simply as Crane, walked with purpose down the hall. Just outside Wendy's bedroom, Jack paced, looking anxious. His eyes were glazed over, drunk, and in his hand was a switchblade. He licked his lips before placing his hand on the doorknob and turned.

This wasn't going to happen on his watch. Marshall snatched him by the throat and threw Jack against the wall. Old portraits rattled and a vase of plastic flowers shattered onto the rug. "You better be rethinking that. No one bothers the girl, you got me?"

Jack squirmed and gagged for air when Marshall applied more pressure to his windpipe. He was a sniffling coward, just the type Marshall hated.

Maybe he was a lot of things, like a robber and a murderer, but he never raped a child and he didn't intend to sit by and watch. "You so much as make her nervous and I'll gut you and stick you in the icebox out back. No one will find you until next summer. Hear me?"

The fear in Jack's eyes was all Marshall needed to see. He let the boy go, but walloped him one between the eyes, just to send the message home.

Jack yelped, holding his nose with both hands. "What'd you do that for?"

"To make sure we're clear," Marshall rumbled. "Girl's under a lot of pressure. We need to make sure she's calm for now. Understand? Keep your distance and hands off. One look, Jack. One!"

Jack glanced at Marshall over his shoulder, fuming with rage, but he was small and Marshall was lethal. He headed into the bedroom across the hall and bolted his door shut.

Pleased, Marshall made rounds upstairs to make sure all the rooms were secure before heading downstairs. There was a common area just off the main office where he found his girl, "Sally." Most of the time she went by the name Marie, but hated to break character so that's what he called her. She was sitting in a pair of short shorts, no longer with the blond wig she wore around the girl. Her short brown hair was tousled as she sat on her heels and took a long draw from her cigarette. The way she bounced it told Marshall that she was nervous and agitated.

He didn't really blame her. He was calm, but he had assassinated senators and top businessmen. He was used to the pressure, relished it. The girl was young, hot, and eager for money. Didn't take more to convince her what needed to be done, that he could give her the world. It was still debatable if he would, but for now she was an ally. And a good toy to keep around.

He grabbed her hair to pull back her head and roughly kissed her neck. "You need to unwind, darlin."

"Not tonight." She grimaced and shrugged him off.

"It's the only thing I can think of when I can see your tits through your shirt." He knelt down on the sofa beside her and cupped her breasts in both hands, yanking on the nipples to elongate them. Kissing her bare shoulders, Marshall felt her relax as she snuffed out her cigarette. Sally always meant yes when she said no. She was the best type of woman to keep around and it was best to keep her distracted.

"What about the boy?" she murmured.

"He won't make a peep. Not until morning. Any doubts he's had about us, well, let's just say I convinced him everything will be fine. Tomorrow he'll be down for breakfast, he'll soothe Wendy's fears, and keep her calm til she has that *thing*."

Sally turned on her knees to face him and Marshall suspected that getting lucky that night was out of the picture. "If she has it. The blood pressure meds ain't working anymore. She's swelling up. I think she might be developing hypertension or worse. Pre-C." She fumbled with her pack of smokes.

"Well, you're the nurse, fix it."

"Nothing can fix that. Only thing is to have the baby. Barely eight months along. Not sure it'd survive. At least out of the hospital."

Marshall wiped his mouth. "For a human, but what about a mutant? I thought you were some sort of expert."

"I delivered lots of babies in New Haven 52, sure, but they weren't half-breeds like this. Most mutant babies are born in the eighth month, but it's not full mutant. It might not have a fighting chance."

"Then there goes all our money." He was thoughtful. "Tell me what you need and I'll get it."

Sally lit her cigarette. "Saline, steroids for Wendy. In case we need to deliver early we're gonna need to beef up that kid's lungs, but without an incubator—"

"Then we'll get it. Draw up a list and we'll get it."

"It's not going to be that easy."

"Hey, I never said it would, but if we can get the kid out and keep it alive long enough to sell it, we'll be rolling in it. Millions. We got a long list of people interested. Some high up in government. They'll pay well." He brushed her hair off the nape of her neck.

Sally closed her eyes and sigh. "How well?"

"Enough so we won't need to take another job ever. Then I'll take you anywhere you want to go. Tropical. Maybe even buy you our own island."

Sally eyes lit up in the way a little girl's would when she saw their first doll. She was gorgeous and the thought of money excited her to the point where her cheeks flushed and her breasts perked up. Money was a great equalizer when it came to mood and libido. Marshall wanted her right then, so he took her. Fast and hard.

***

Morning came quick for Wendy Reynolds. Once she stopped waking up from noise outside her room, she fell into a deep sleep. Then she blinked and it was morning, with sunlight streaming into her small room. There was no sourness to her stomach, or the feeling of bile rising in her throat. She just snapped awake, feeling refreshed and happy. Then the memories about the day before, about her parents, rushed back to her.

Wendy wanted to cry. She might have, had Jake not been sleeping beside her. Her heart skipped a beat and she stroked his cheek. His right eye was bruised. That was new. She wondered what had put it there. What happened to him since they parted last?

When his eyes opened, they were bright. Jake smiled. "I was afraid I'd never see you again."

Wendy couldn't help a few tears then. They embraced gently, but urgently. "Me too. I never want to part like that again. Promise."

"Of course I do. But Thomas was just doing what was best for us. To keep you and the baby safe. Me too. We need to respect what he says."

"That's the first time you've said that." Wendy rolled her eyes and resisted the urge to roll away and pout.

"Well before yesterday, it didn't seem too serious. I didn't know—didn't know people would react like that. And I want our peanut to be safe." He rested his hand on Wendy's large bulging stomach. He leaned down and kissed it.

Wendy wanted that too. She knew things were bad, worse, than she thought they were, but she hated to be told what to do. "I guess Rebecca sent him for our security for some reason. I guess we do need to trust him."

Jake grinned. "That's my girl."

"What happened to your eye?"

"My eye?" He echoed and touched it. "Oh, nothing. Just a little accident. I was getting some supplies. It was wet out and I slipped."

"Onto your eye?" Wendy asked with raised eyebrows.

"When did you get so suspicious?" Jake asked but was still cheerful. There wasn't a hint of duplicity to his voice.

"After everything, who can blame me?"

"Well, how about we go downstairs and I'll make you an omelet? With buttered toast."

"Yum, sounds good to me." When Jake offered Wendy help getting out of bed, she took it.

"And maybe, maybe once the baby's born. I don't know, how would you feel about going to look at rings?"

"Rings?" Wendy asked and felt like she might float away.

"Well sure, for our wedding. People who have babies are married. And I want to be with you forever, Wendy. I think for that we need rings."

She squealed like a little girl, unable to hide her excitement. Jake held her hair back, studying her face. Wendy knew she was puffy under the eyes and her jaw wasn't as defined as it used to be, but when he looked at her like that, Wendy felt like the prettiest girl in the world. "I think I love you, Jake Monroe."

"I'll take care of you forever. Whatever happens next," he promised. "Go get dressed and I'll meet you downstairs with everything you need for the day."

Something about him seemed different, but Wendy couldn't put her finger on it. She paused at the bathroom door. "Where is it we'll go, after here?"

Jake shrugged. "I'm not sure. Thomas will know. He always has a plan."

Wendy thought Jake found him as creepy as she did, but now he seemed docile as a puppy. "You sure you're feeling like yourself?"

"Oh sure. Spot on." Jake grinned.

You couldn't fake a smile like that, Wendy thought, and her nervous feelings subsided. She turned into the bathroom with duffel bag in hand. She decided on a quick shower.

While steam filled the tub, Wendy undressed and left her dirty clothes in a pile on the floor. Her reflection certainly had seen better days. With the dark circles under her eyes and the size of her popped belly, she felt like a freak experiment gone wrong. Part of her couldn't wait for this to be over, to have the baby, but another part was so frightened of the idea of giving birth, of raising a child, that she wanted to stay pregnant forever.

"You are just a host of contradictions," Wendy said to herself.

She enjoyed the hot water pelting against the sore spots of her neck and lower back. A moan of pleasure escaped her lips before she even realized it happened. She had been cooped up for so long in the car and nothing had ever felt as good as this. Wendy turned the water up as hot as she could stand, until it felt like the flesh might melt right off her. After her hair was drenched, she poured in her shampoo and scrubbed it hard. As she turned with her hands in her head, she could see through the foggy glass that someone was watching her. He had a wide stance, but Wendy couldn't make out who it was.

"I'll be right out," she called in a jittery voice, but the figure didn't move.

With suds running into her face, Wendy cautiously slid the door open and saw it was Jack, the cousin she met from the night before. He was standing with his mouth agape, a hand down his pants. His arm pulsed up and down with fervor, and he grunted as they made eye contact.

Wendy was horrified. Too sickened to move and her heart leaped wildly so that it echoed in her ears.

"Want me to come in there?" He slurred. "And you can finish what you started, baby. What do you say? Make ol' Jack come so hard, it'll rip you right in two."

Wendy's vision split so there were two bathrooms, and two Jacks. They came back together in a clap, causing her eyes to roll back into her head. She fell, her body seizing violently as her head smashed into the tile basin.

***

Barely able to open her eyes, the room spun. Wendy was back in bed and in a loose t-shirt, pulled up to expose her belly. It seemed to glisten in the darkness. Sally was there with her, prepping an ultrasound machine for a reading.

"Am I losing the baby?" Wendy asked. She could see two IVs were hooked up to her arm and she couldn't feel the baby move like she normally did when she woke up.

"Not if I can help it, hon." Sally said. "Thomas is grabbing an incubator, just in case. I'd feel better if we could keep the baby in you for a few more weeks, minimum. shifters have a different gestation than we do, but I'd feel better with a little more time."

"I feel really hot. Uncomfortable." Wendy shifted in the bed.

"Your fever's back. Won't go down." Sally sat beside her for a moment. "Your blood pressure is dangerously high. Protein has been in your urine for the past few days. Most likely you have pre-eclampsia."

Everything she said scared Wendy. "Can you fix it? Give me a pill?"

"Only one option. Give birth and then it goes away. So, I have you on steroids to help the baby's lungs mature as much as possible. We can give it as much time as we can. Or we can induce you now, and pray for the best."

Wendy took a shaky breath. "But the baby...?"

"Might not make it."

She blinked back tears. Then everything she had gone through, would be for nothing? Her dad, her mom... "He's important. He can change the world. I have to give him a chance, don't I?"

Sally looked at her shoes. "If that's your decision."

"Can we go to the hospital?" Wendy asked.

"We can't. If we do that, the people who killed your parents will find us. They'll kill the baby, all of us, if we're not careful."

"Is Rebecca coming? For the birth. I thought she'd be here by now." She thought of Rebecca and the words they shared at the compound. Now they felt hollow and false.

"She'll try. I've updated her on where we are. That's your decision, then? To give birth here?"

"I don't see another choice." Wendy said, as if she had resigned herself to her fate.

"We'll do our best to make you comfortable and I'll keep a close eye on your vitals. If it gets too dangerous, we're not going to have a choice but to induce you."

"Will I die?" Wendy asked. She wished Jake was in the room.

"Let's just...hope for the best. All right?" Sally placed the ultrasound scanner against Wendy's extended flesh. A few moments later, the baby's strong heartbeat echoed through the room. "His vitals are nice and strong." Her voice had hope.

Wendy felt some too as she gazed at the monitor and her fingertips extended towards it. "His head is down."

"Yes," Sally agreed, "won't be too much longer now." She turned the machine off. "I'll go make you some lunch. Bedrest from now on."

Wendy nodded her thanks and watched her go. As the door latched shut, Wendy buried her face in her pillow and cried.

***

Marshall's fist collided with Jack's head.

The base of Jack's skull crunched into the marble counters at the front desk. He didn't fall down because Marshall had a fistful of his shirt. His face was a river of blood; his eyes, two lost pebbles; his shattered teeth were shards of rubble.

"Stay away from the girl. Stay away from the girl, is that too much to fucking ask?" Marshall asked, throwing Jack down onto the bearskin rug and forced his knee into the other man's back.

He was right at mutant boy's feet, but Jake barely looked up. He couldn't because Marshall Crane told him not to. Jake couldn't do anything unless Marshall gave him orders. That was clear. It had been ingrained in him for over five hours, the same as his life had been in New Haven 56.

But now, he missed home. The world was too big and it was dark and scary. The only thing he liked about being on the outside was Wendy and cheeseburgers. He could have as many burgers as he wished and no one was around to tell him to stop.

But Jake missed the small town and the malt shops and his friends. He loved Wendy; sometimes when he was with her he could barely think of anything else but touching her. But Jake didn't want to have a baby. He really didn't, but what could he do? He got her pregnant and when you did that, it was like his mom always taught him. A man stands by his woman. A man loves his family. Babies were family, and that was that.

Tit for tat.

Babies were warm; they were the future. If Wendy had his, that meant she was his future. She would be a Monroe. So when Wendy sneaked word to Rebecca while visiting her dad at the Outpost, it made sense to Jake that he would go with her. You couldn't be a family if you weren't together. Kids needed a father. He had read about it in psychology class. Once you are a family, once you have kids, you don't come apart. The nuclear unit was more important than anything, almost more than the air he breathed. So Jake went.

He missed football, cheerleaders and sports. He missed home, Marie, and Harvey. Most of all, Jake wished his dad were around. It was more responsibility than he wanted. Jake had been happy living in Summerset, working for the Millers. But now he was stuck with a bunch of people he considered loonies. And Wendy? Well, from how everyone was talking about her, it sounded like she might die.

Jake blinked his eyes when the gunshot went into Jack's head.

But at least he didn't look up.

"Grab his ankles and help me." Marshall ordered.

Jake did, without a second thought. They walked out into the back off the deck and through a cluster of trees. The twisted path led them to a small lake where Marshall weighted Jack's body with stones and tossed him in. His eyes were gleaming with rage.

"Remember, it's your job to keep Wendy calm. You keep her calm, no matter what happens. You understand me? Answer me, for fuck's sake."

Jake nodded. "I'll always keep her calm."

"Good, now get back in that damn house and be useful. Clean up the blood."

"Do you know where the sponges are?" Jake asked.

Marshall rolled his eyes. "How about you start checking in the kitchen?"

It sounded like a good idea to him so Jake returned to the cabin. He knew where the kitchen was. It was where Wendy's toast still waited to be buttered. The chair was overturned where Marshall had sat up quickly when Jack announced that Wendy had some sort of medical problem. It worried Jake, of course it did, but he had to remain calm. He had to help Wendy.

He felt so guilty and knew it was wrong. Jake should be happy, but wasn't. He wished he had never left New Haven.

When he returned to the lobby with his bucket of solution and sponges, Sally was coming down the steps. "How's Wendy?"

"Conscious, resting. But tired. Not herself."

"Will she be all right?"

Sally looked away, fear in her face but avoidance in her voice. "I think so. With time. What happened here?" She gestured to the rug.

"Jack had an accident."

Her eyes became livid. "Where is he? Where's Crane?"

Jake pointed out the back, and Sally grabbed the small pistol gun off the counter and charged after him. "Wait here." She ordered.

He wondered if he should still clean up the blood. There was no one around to ask, so Jake got on his hands and knees and began to clean. When Wendy started screaming, he wasn't sure what to do, but knew screaming people often weren't calm so he went to her.

She was standing by the window when he entered the room. Her T-shirt was pushed out wide and low. Her eyes were blood shot and her hair was a bird's nest of knots. "What's wrong?" Seeing her like that jarred something awake inside him. He felt a stirring, like his eyes were fogged and now they began to clear after a storm.

She was sick. Wendy needed help. This was not her. This was not the girl he fell in love with in study class from afar. The way she smiled and laughed, twirling her hair around her fingers.

Carefree. Graceful.

Her eyes were void of happiness. Instead all he saw was fury and she gnashed her teeth at him. "Just frustrated. Angry. Didn't you care I had a seizure?" She asked, tilting her head to the side. "Sometimes I wonder if you care about us at all."

"I want to marry you. I told you."

"Because it's the right thing to do." Wendy huffed and waddled past him.

"There's nothing wrong with doing the right thing."

"If that were the case, you never would have got me pregnant at all. Now, I might die, but hey, as long as we do the right thing."

"Wendy—" Jake started.

She brushed him off. Her lips were caked with dry spit and her eyes were manic. "I'm going down to get some juice. He's thirsty."

"Let me help you," Jake rushed after her. She shuffled down the steps with one hand on the rail, while the other massaged her lower back. "I think you're supposed to stay in bed."

Wendy showed him the pouch in her hand. "I still have my steroids. Don't worry. Sally said she was going to bring me lunch, but didn't. Big surprise, no one around here does what they say they're going to."

Seldom had Jake ever seen her so angry. She tore open the fridge as if it offended her and the door whipped against the wall. She took out the bottle of organ juice and sipped some from the container. Wiping her mouth with the back of her hand, she chugged some more.

"It's good," Wendy said and put it back in the fridge. "I can see why you like it so much." Her eyes were clearing, her rosy complexion returning.

Vomit rose in Jake's throat and guilt crushed him like a rock. "I'm sorry, okay? I'm sorry that I did this to you. And that the baby is changing you so much. That it's putting you through all this."

"I'm sorry too." Wendy snorted and pushed past him. "My parents died. And for what? Who knows if it'll even be born at this rate. All we have are a nurse and a grumpy bastard to help us. Any week now I could be in labor and I can't even go to the hospital. Do you have any idea how scared I am?"

Frustrated, Wendy shook her head. "I wish...God, I wish I had aborted this *thing* and hadn't told anyone. But that's not possible in New Haven, is it? Because of guys just like you."

Jake had never felt so hurt, insulted. He didn't know Wendy could say such horrible things but he felt like it wasn't her fault. It was because she was sick. She was far angrier than he had ever seen anyone and he thought it might have been his fault. "Just come lay down and we'll talk about it."

"It? Talk about the baby? About how I don't want it. I don't want any of this? I want to go home. I want to study. I want to curl up in my room and be asked to take out the trash. I didn't think—didn't think being pregnant would be so hard. But it sucks, Jake, it really does."

Her eyes squeezed shut and as she sobbed, her chin quivered. Her mouth drew in a thin line, but a sob of grief and pain escaped out of the side of her lips.

"I'm sorry." Tears glistened in his eyes. "I wish I hadn't done it to you."

"I wish Rebecca were here." Wendy sighed. "She always made me feel better. It's like now that she has us on the outside—"

"That she doesn't like us anymore."

Wendy nodded in agreement. "Totally, yeah. Like she got her way. Now she just needs us quiet until I have our baby and then she can have her press conference. Parade us on display."

"I didn't know you felt this way."

"Well, I didn't know you did, either," Wendy huffed, crossing her arms above her belly.

"Then let's leave." Jake took Wendy by the shoulders. Every fiber in his being told him what he just said was wrong. He needed to stay put and he needed to listen to Thomas Crane, but he didn't want to. When he saw how sick Wendy looked and how upset she was, he just wanted to make it better. He wanted her to be healthy and happy, neither of which could happen in that stupid cabin.

"We can't leave." Wendy said. "Do you really think we could?" Her voice was renewed with hope, a light came on in her eyes.

Jake thought he'd do anything to keep it shining. "I saw where Thomas put the keys. We could take the truck. Get down the mountain and head to a hospital. No one can hurt us if we're out in the open."

Her eyes showed relief, but were filled with sorrow. "If you tell people who you are, they'll hurt you."

"Then I won't tell them." Jake said simply. "But you need a real doctor. Just come with me, please. Let's go have our baby somewhere safe and then, we can decide what we want to do."

"Oh Jake, I didn't mean what I said. I didn't really want to abort our baby." She cried and Jake kissed away her tears.

"Let's just go. You with me?" Jake grabbed the car keys off the table while Wendy took his free hand. He afforded her a small smile, but saw how tired she looked.

As they stepped onto the porch, gunshots rang somewhere off in the distance.

"Jake." Wendy whispered, filled with fear. But he said nothing, he just pulled her hand toward the pickup truck, urging her inside.

He started the truck and was aware of moving shadows through the rustling leaves. With the truck started, he swerved toward the main road and saw high-beam headlights gaining on them. His gripped Wendy's fingers. "You better put on your seat belt."

Chapter Twenty-Eight

Jeff opened the fridge, grabbed the organ juice that was lovingly supplied to his family by the government, and washed it down the sink. He didn't know for sure, but he suspected there was something in it to keep him docile and controlled. Something he didn't want any more. And neither did his friends.

Behind him came footsteps and a playful voice. "Hey, Pop." Marie never called him that before. "Are you taking the day off?" She nodded at his relaxed attire. "I know with Mom and all...but maybe our routine is important?"

"Yeah. We have arrangements that need to be made. I'm going to take you to Megan's for the day."

"What about school?" Marie asked with a frown. "I have tests."

"You can make up the tests."

"But, Dad," she whined.

"Enough!" Jeff snapped and then covered his mouth to keep himself from screaming. "Marie, I just need you to listen to your old man. Do you think you can do that?"

Marie nodded. "Sure, Daddy. If that's what you need."

"It is." He picked up her book bag. "C'mon, I'll drive you."

Jeff locked the front door, wondering if he'd ever see the old place again, and then drove Marie a few streets away to

Megan's home. He noted the bruises on Megan's face, but she smiled, a smile that no longer reached her eyes.

"Well, Jeff," Megan's voice was strained. "I do hope you have a good day."

"You too. We'll see you soon."

"Come inside for a few minutes," Megan said as she escorted Marie inside. "You can help Timothy find the sedan's keys. We're going to pick up a few more kids."

Jeff looked at the scribbling on the palm of his hand. Only a few more things to do. God help him, but he was nervous and scared. Did he really have the balls to do what he was planning?

"God forgive me," Jeff whispered, "if I'm wrong."

Chapter Twenty-Nine

Dirk watched Jenna morph right before his eyes.

He wasn't sure how he felt about it. Could barely even process everything she had just said about their wedding and their baby. Baby? Dirk's stomach rolled at the idea that he had been a father for a short while and never knew. All those months they worked together—hell, slept together—how could she never tell him, even just in angry grief, about what had happened?

When did Jenna Morgan get so good at keeping secrets?

She acted as though she were damaged goods, but Dirk didn't believe that. Never had. He saw a caring, sweet woman who put on a tough-as-nails charade, and time after time she proved she could do anything when her mind was set. But Dirk knew, underneath all that, that the anger wasn't her. Maybe it came from the mutant part of her, or maybe she was just angry now because she was mutant.

Jameson continued to drag Jenna down the hall. Her body dragged like a bag of potatoes. Except for her shimmering hands pulling at the collar clasped tight around her throat, as she struggled her breath. Parts of her were blue, but her hands and delicate fingernails were human.

He remembered kissing those fingers and sipping a diamond ring on them. Alert and wake, Dirk pulled his gun, released the safety and aimed it at the back of Jameson's head. Before he even spoke his colleague, his old friend, stopped moving. "Stop right there or I blow your fucking head off."

With precise steps, Jameson turned, holding the chain taught. You see what she is? How can you stop me? This is our job. This is what we do."

Dirk didn't have an answer. He didn't. Jameson was right. They did turn in shifters, but Jenna was different. She was their leader, and she was human most of the time. Hell, so were shifters. Suddenly the lines were blurring together and he hated it. He didn't know what to do or think, but knew for a certainty that he could not, nor would not, allow Jenna to be turned in like an animal. "Is this how you got the van out so easily? Made our escape? You made a friggin' deal with Outpost?"

Jameson wore a smug expression that made Dirk want to blow it straight off. "Damn straight I did. Laurel came to me, told me what she was. What she threatened to expose. New Haven would be in jeopardy if the world knew shifters could breed with humans. Like we're somehow the same. Do you want to live in a world where shifters are *citizens* and have the same rights as we do?"

Dirk didn't. He never did. "Did Laurel kill the chief?"

"For her part, she might as well have, but no. She didn't do it, but knows who did. Hell, we all do. Order came straight from the top. Mr. New Haven Initiative himself."

"And you're okay with this? The chief—"

"So a few eggs need to be broken to keep the system working. Make an omelet, right?" Jameson laughed. "I was supposed to tag her and bring her back here."

"And Wendy?" Dirk demanded to know. "Were you going to betray us there too?"

Jameson winked at him. "Bang-bang, brother."

"Laurel, the others were never after us, where they? They just sent you. Planted you by our side."

"Naturally."

Dirk's face raged with fire. "How could you, Jameson? We were a team. The three of us. We've been through hell and back. You were my best man."

"At least I didn't let the bride eat you on your wedding night. C'mon, Dirk, you're just shocked. But this isn't a woman. This is a beast. Like we've locked up a hundred times before. Look at her. Human's don't sparkle, they don't turn blue before your eyes."

Dirk shook his head, but he couldn't argue. He couldn't.

"Join me and we'll do it together. I know you already have the intel. You know where they went. I scanned it off your computer into mine. We'll leave here, locked Jenna in the back, and take out the teens. When Laurel meets up with us, we'll turn Jenna over. She'll be tried for killing the chief, and we go back to our lives, a little bit richer."

Dirk couldn't believe what he was hearing. He shook his head as if to clear Jameson's words from it. "She's *our* boss. *Our* friend."

"Yeah and she held a gun to my head just a few days ago. Call this payback, crazy-ass bitch." Jameson spat down on her. "What do you say, pal?"

Dirk surprised himself by thinking about it. He really was an asshole. "I can't let you take her, Jameson. If you try..."

"What, you're going to shoot me?" Jameson rolled his eyes. "You won't do it, I know you won't." He turned around, headed toward the stairs, Jenna dragging behind him. She strained her head to look back at Dirk. Her eyes shined their normal brown, lovely and deep. They were manic and begging for help.

"Sorry, *brother.*" Dirk gritted his teeth and aimed. He fired off a round into Jameson's arm.

Jameson's footing was lost. Dirk charged him, kicking him in the back of the kneecap to force him into the stair railing. He groaned, and when he tried to regain his feet, Dirk bashed his forearm against the back of his head. His nose cracked into the banister.

"Damn you, Dirk. Can't believe you would pick a damn monster over me."

"You betrayed us too. Jenna would have given your life for you before she'd frame you for murder." Dirk punched Jameson twice square in the face.

The analyst was never tough, never could take a punch. Jameson went unconscious and slid to the floor, but Dirk wasn't sure how long it would last. He made quick work of handcuffing him to the stairwell, and unsnapped the collar from around Jenna's throat.

She morphed back into her beautiful form, but her face looked more fragile, delicate, and there was only vulnerability in her eyes.

"Jenna," he said softly and put his hand on her shoulder.

She cried and did something he never expected Jenna Morgan to do. Rolling away from him, Jenna laid on her side in a fetal position, and her body trembled with huge sobs, crying into the carpet.

"It'll be okay," he whispered. "We're in this together. We just need to figure out what to do."

Jenna shook her head, but didn't speak. It seemed like she couldn't speak yet.

****

Jameson was awake and handcuffed to the railing by the time Jenna composed herself enough to go through his pockets. He bitched at her, which wasn't exactly that different than usual, but she couldn't meet his eyes. Didn't want to make a connection and see his contempt and anger.

No matter what he did, Jameson was her friend. Jenna relied on him more times than she could count. It just reinforced why she kept her secrets and why being half mutant was like wearing a scarlet letter.

"You guys are going to get me medical attention, right?"

Jenna grabbed his PDA from his pocket and stood, making sure she leaned on his bullet wound as she did it. Jameson howled at her, but his discomfort was ignored. "Here it is," Jenna said.

"What is it?" Dirk asked.

"Memos, records. See, Jameson," she said, waving the PDA at him, "I knew you'd want information on Laurel, and the New Haven council, just in case they tried to shaft you out of your reward. And you left it on our cloud server. Pretty easy to find for someone that has the passcodes." Jenna smirked.

"How incriminating is it?" Dirk asked.

"Oh, very. A order direct from Humphrey's desk to Laurel. Memos back and forth between them, and angry voice mails." Jenna pushed a button the phone and the voice mail played via speaker.

The chief is dead, but the daughter got away, but don't worry, I have the perfect scapegoat in mind so I can get the quarantine lifted.

Dirk raised his eyebrows. "That's enough to clear us."

"*And* put Alistar in the unemployment line."

Jameson's eyes were wide and he thrashed around. "Damn it, you can't do this, Jenna! If you go public with this, who knows what Congress will do. You'll be betraying the system. The system you've fought for your entire life."

"I didn't realize that system would frame us, me, and kill the Chief. Go after a teenage girl because they are scared of what she represents." Jenna shook her head. "I get it. You know I hate what I am, Jameson. It's disgusting. It's gross. If I could scrub off my skin, I would. But I'm not going to lay down and die. And I guess, well, I guess I don't expect them to either."

Jameson's eyes threw darts. "And if I had been a mutant? If I was half a monster, what'd you do?"

Jenna thought about it. "I don't know. But I'd like to think after all your years of service, everything you did for me, would mean more to me than that. Maybe the human half of you would mean more than the monster."

Jameson sneered at her. "You give yourself too much credit."

"And you gave yourself not enough. Goodbye, Jameson. Hopefully you'll be smart enough to cut a deal when they offer you one." The sorrow in her voice was thick as Jenna bolted down the stairs and investigated what Jameson was working on last. She found the real name for Thomas Crane, his bio, and a satellite location of a truck. She flashed the phone to "Dirk. "Find out where this is and bring it up on our GPS."

Dirk nodded. "Got it."

Jenna put the phone to her ear to make a call. "Rebecca, I'm going to send you some information on how to access my private cloud server. There's documents and files there. I need you to make them public immediately. Can you get a press conference?"

"If it's important enough. What's going on, Jenna?"

"I have information to clear our name. The plot to kill Wendy, the Chief, goes straight to the top."

"Well," Rebecca said breathlessly, "seems like I'm going to clean house."

"We're on our way to the kids now," Jenna said and slid into the driver's seat of the van. "Having Dirk send the location to your phone now. Has my mother's compound been mobilized?"

"They've already begun to move toward you." Rebecca paused. "What if they're too late?"

"Then we'll have a little talk about me." Jenna snapped her phone shut. In a moment the van was on the open road.

"You want to tell me where we're going, who we're up against?" She asked Dirk.

"A corrupt nurse from New Haven 52 and an assassin."

"Oh," Jenna said with her eyebrows raised. "Is that all?"

"Did you mean what you told Laurel? If Wendy and her baby don't make it, will you really out yourself?"

She gripped the steering wheel. "I'd owe it to them, I think. If I fail to save them. If I fail to protect the chief's daughter, I see little choice. Otherwise all these deaths and destroyed lives mean nothing."

Dirk touched her hand. "I'm sorry, Jenn. For all of it."

She nodded. "I don't want to talk about it. Not now."

"Then when?"

Jenna thought about it. "How about never?"

****

There were a lot of New Haven police officers driving through town and Jeff tried to remain calm so not to set off their alarms and detection units. He took deep breaths and parked his car in the full lot of the Bowl-A-Rama.

Reaching into the back of his sedan, he picked up his bowling ball case and carried it inside the dark alley. The smell of beer permeated the large, dimly lit room, but everything was silent and there was no one at the front counter. Stepping through the small entryway, Jeff entered the bowling area and saw the area filled with people standing in a circle.

Everyone's eyes were nervous and their hands were jittery as they sipped their beer. They acknowledged Jeff with a nod of their heads. He took the offered beer from Billy and sipped it. "It's a good day for some bowling. I finished my list."

"Me too," a haunted voice rang out.

"I dropped my kids off with Megan. They are going to run some errands. In the city square." The furthest point from Outpost, just in case. "She'll be heading toward Dolores's Scoops Ice Cream Parlor in thirty minutes." It was close as a mutant could get to the Outpost without actually being inside the enemy's den.

Jeff nodded and lifted his glass. "To our fallen family and friends then. Who are all in *a better place.*" They clinked their glasses together. Jeff finished his drink, thinking of Susan, his son, and then placed the empty tall glass down on the counter."

"We should start our errands," Frank said. "See you there."

Single file, they headed outside, one by one placing their glass upside down on the counter. Each of them exited the Bowl-A-Rama and marched through the parking lot. Across the street, Jeff saw an officer in a checkered rim hat watching them with concerned interest. He then talked into his shoulder, as if he were radioing in for assistance.

Jeff gave him a half-smile at him, then started his car and pulled out toward Main Street. At a red light, he unzipped his bowling ball bag and looked inside, not at a bowling ball at all, but of treasured mementos for the journey: pictures of his family, silverware his wife loved, and his daughter's favorite books. He had nothing else. With no possessions that were truly his, or money, Jeff was going in blind.

He hoped his rage, his anger for everything they took from him, would be enough.

Dolores's Ice Cream Scoop was a pink building with a pink-and-white-striped overhang. The window was decorated in glass drawings of ice cream sundaes and a neon sign flashed *Open* in swirly purple. Jeff pulled to the curb when he saw it and sat in his car, but the engine still purred. His eyes focused on the photo of his wife. How scared she must have been. Jeff blamed himself for being so big on the rules that Susan felt she couldn't come to him. Instead she did it alone, and she got herself killed.

Never again would he retreat after a long day to her warm embrace. Hell, Jeff didn't even know what they did with her body, but it was somewhere in there, inside Outpost. Maybe they cut her open, did an autopsy to see what made her tick, or would do experiments on her to find what certain chemicals would do to her insides. Irate, Jeff cut the engine, got out, and slammed the door.

The bowling ball container firmly in his grasp, he marched toward the tunnel leading to Outpost. There were two guards on either side and the entrance was blocked with red and white flashing lights intended to warn shifters away. Not that many made it this far. Just the idea of Outpost was enough to send most shifters to the shopping centers in need of new draperies or duvet covers.

Jeff marched with determination, heart racing like a storm of elephants. But so far the officers weren't afraid. They were composed, authoritative with their wide stances and arms clasped in front of them. "Is there something we can help you with, Mr. Monroe? Did you take a wrong turn?"

"Pretty sure you don't want in there."

Behind him, Jeff heard the rocketing chorus of a dozen and then two dozen car doors slamming. The sound echoed toward him and spun down the tunnel. "Oh, I'm pretty sure I do." By the time he finished the sentence, he lost all human thought and his large claw swatted the officer in the head. His large tail swiped against the other, breaking the man's vertebrae as he slammed into the rock wall with the force of a dozen elephants charging through open terrain.

Jeff continued into the tunnel, his wings flapping in time with the others behind them. Halfway through, their pace turned to a gallop and then a full-on run, as sirens blared and red lights flashed. Jeff tore off and was inside Outpost. A flap of his wing sent him high in the sky. His lungs expanded with new air that smelled dirty, unrefined, and not filtered like the air of New Haven. It felt like something in his mind snapped open, filling with painful memories, and his desires were stronger.

Even the air was laced, drugged, Jeff thought, to keep him tamed. But now he was out of control and nothing was going to be able to stop him.

At his side were a dozen shifters. Others took refuge on top of the large buildings, scoping out the area with their hungry eyes. Officers were coming with weapons and guns. Jeff knew it was time to strike. He dove through the air like a missile, diving and spinning toward the exit where the guards were posted. His mouth opened to receive its first taste of gristly human flesh.

***

They drove for hours through the mountains, Jenna pushing the gas as hard as she could without careening off the road. When they arrived at the cabin, it was already dark out and rain clouds were forming over the horizon like a looming threat.

Jenna and Dirk exited the van with their weapons drawn. Dirk went around the front while Jenna took the rear, to secure the perimeter. She wished she had their analyst, but that time was past. Now they were going to have to do things the old-fashioned way. She crossed a small wooden deck toward the windows that faced the front desk. And she smelled fresh blood.

Jenna looked down and saw her boots were slick in it. She followed the smear of red and found two bodies piled together. Each had a single shot to the head, execution style. She guessed they were Marshall Crane, the assassin; and Rachel Montgomery, the corrupt nurse expelled from New Haven 52 for smothering babies.

If they were dead, the assassins who killed the Chief were here. Which meant the kids were in danger.

Jenna slid the glass door open and stepped in. Her gun was at her side as her eyes swept across the lobby. It was dark and empty. Dirk came down the stairs. He shook his head to her unspoken question. "No one's upstairs."

"Shit." Jenna said and they headed back out the front door. It was raining now and they both surveyed the landscape.

"Only one truck," Dirk observed. He glanced down at the dirt, studying the tracks. "Hard to tell from the overlap, but it looks like someone left here in a hurry. They made a pretty deep rift."

"Can you tell which way they went?"

"That way, heading west."

Deeper into the mountains. Maybe they were being pursued. Maybe they were scared and had no idea what they were doing; that seemed the most likely. "Let's move."

"It's not a lot to go on, Jenn. Most of our equipment is gone. Jameson isn't here to run is complex algorithms. All we know is we head that way."

"Then we head that way."

"And pray we just run into them?"

"Pray they were headed toward the rental cabins. It's all we have to go on and if that's not where they were going, then they were headed toward a dead end. And might already be dead."

"Geesh, you're as upbeat as usual."

Jenna shrugged. "Nothing's much changed."

"Maybe not for you."

She cringed and Dirk apologized. "Forget it. Let's just move before we lose any more time."

In the van, Dirk seemed contrite, but booted up the small laptop. He used it to power the van's night vision scopes on the road. The rain was quickly washing away the muddy tracks and following them via technology was going to be impossible soon. Jenna was going to have to rely on luck and instincts to find these kids. But if she could find them, that meant that the people that pursed them could too. All of which added up to two dead teens and a dead baby.

Dirk was trying to read her expression. She could feel his eyes all over her, and it made her feel dirty.

"Keep an eye on those tracks. If they change I need to know."

"Sorry." He muttered and went back to gazing at his screen, but Jenna could tell he was distracted.

"Just say it," she blurted out with impatience. "Whatever it is, just say it so we can go back to work. I need you focused, Dirk."

"Excuse me, I'm still trying to digest a lot of things, all right? A lot of things make sense, but others? That we could be so close and yet you could keep from me that I was a dad? Awfully cold, Jenna."

Her fingers went rigid around the steering wheel. "I know that. That's why I kept pushing you away. That's why I didn't want to have this conversation."

"Because you were ashamed of the baby."

If he stabbed her with a rusty blade, it would have hurt less. "No," Jenna's voice cracked. "Because I was ashamed I was weak and handled it badly, all right?"

His voice was flat. "Were you sad? Or were you glad when she died?"

His words cut her deep and Jenna nearly slammed on the brakes so she could slap him. Instead she blinked back her tears. Everything she always said and did, well how could she blame him for feeling that way? "Did I hate that the part of her was mutant was me? Yes. I hated that I have evil in my blood and that damned our daughter to death. But no, I wasn't glad." Her chin trembled. "I carry her with me every day, always will. I was far from glad."

"I didn't mean to ... I just needed to know."

Jenna nodded, she understood it, but she didn't want to talk about it anymore. She slowed the van down and they crossed a wooden bridge. Crashed against a bent tree was a pickup truck, its hazard lights blinking erratically. Behind it was a van, just like their old one. "Shit." Jenna said, putting the van in park and hopping out.

She tore open the truck's doors. Both airbags were deployed and the windshield was cracked. The crash had been a bad one. She doubted either Wendy or Jake had driven before and their panic, combined with the rain, might have been a lethal combination. They likely left on foot, knowing they were being pursued.

"I updated our location with Rebecca." Dirk said at her side.

"Check the back of their van for flashlights. We're going into the bush. We have to find those kids."

Chapter Thirty

Wendy tripped over a tree root and fell. Her sneakers were thick with muck and she couldn't find enough purchase to stand back up. She was exhausted, but terror drove her on. In the back of her mind, she was aware of a pulsating pain through her abdomen and the scream for relief from her lower back.

Scurrying up the hill, Wendy grabbed at a root to pull herself up. Her limbs shook and her hands were so slick with mud, she slipped. She screamed, and Jake grabbed her wrist to stop her descent. Wendy clawed at his shoulder and he dragged her back to solid ground. "I can't do this anymore," she sobbed.

But they had no choice as they heard footsteps behind them. Streams of light zig-zagged through the trees. Jake took her hand, leading her further through dense trees and searing fog. The rain didn't let up, washing away the trail behind them and in front of them. In time they leapt over rocks and logs, and raced across a ravine. Ahead the mountain curved and grew even more steep; the rocks of the cliffs were razor-sharp. Wendy knew they had to find a way down the mountain. If they couldn't, her life was over.

She braced herself on the trunk of a tree. Leaning over and moaning loudly, she grabbed her belly. "Jake, I think something's wrong. I can't. It hurts too much."

"We have to." Jake gripped her side, a look of terror in his eye.

"You go." She whispered.

"Not without you." Jake clasped her hand again, only harder. He yanked on her arm until she cried and followed.

Voices and the rush of footsteps tightened Wendy's chest with anxiety. Jake quickened his pace, but Wendy trailed behind. He took her by the shoulders and hurried her along. Step by step he guided her, and in the distance, they saw an old abandoned shed surrounded by a fence with a simple lamppost outside. It was long burnt out, the bulb broken. Wendy and Jake rushed toward the building and barricaded themselves inside.

Their pursuers would find them. But Wendy couldn't help collapsing to the ground, using an old tire to support her back. She groaned, holding her belly taut, and felt what she knew was a strong contraction. She didn't think it would matter. They'd be dead before the baby was born.

Jake was frantic as he searched a nearby table. He came to a small metal box and laughed manically. "It's a CB crank radio! A CB radio! I had one of these as a kid. I used it to talk to the neighbors. We can call for help. We can get someone out here to help us." Wendy heard him begin to crank the handle and then utter the words, "Mayday Mayday."

But she didn't hear anything else. Her eyes rolled into the back of her head and her body began to seize.

***

"Mayday Mayday!"

Jenna stopped in her tracks when her phone beeped. She had set it to roam all open channels in the facility, but this was the first time it picked anything up. She didn't think they would get lucky enough to pick anything up. Especially a distress call. Her phone told her it was a CB transmission. "This is Jenna Morgan. Go." She said into her phone and nodded to Dirk. "Find the signal."

The boy's voice was rushed and panicked. "I need help. My girlfriend's gone unconscious. There are guys after us and there getting close, I can see lights getting closer. You have to help us, please!" His voice was shrill, which meant only one thing.

"Calm down, Jake. You need to take a few breaths and pull it together, understand? Are you hurt?"

"A little. How do you know who I am? Over."

"That's not important right now. I'm going to help you. Is Wendy breathing?"

"Yeah but she's in bad, bad shape. I didn't want to tell her. I wanted to be supportive—" The boy was beginning to ramble.

"It's okay. Deep breaths, remember? We have doctors waiting to help her. We just need to get you out of this alive."

"I've got it." Dirk said. "They're less than two miles away." He pointed toward a cliff. Too bad Jenna left her hiking boots at home.

"We're coming fast as we can, but Jake, you are might have to fend those men off until we get there."

"I can't," Jake whined. "I'm looking and looking for there aren't any weapons. I don't know what to do!"

Jenna's steps slowed down. "Jake, you are a weapon."

Dirk did a double take toward her. "Jenn..." He whispered, but she held up a hand to silence him.

"You know what you're asking me to do?" Jake nearly screamed. "If I do that, if I go after them, I might never come back. NEVER."

"I know and it's horrible. I shouldn't have to ask, but I do. You are the only thing standing between them and Wendy, the baby. If you want them to survive, you have to become a weapon."

"How, I don't know how. I've never...shifted." Jenna swore she could hear vomit rising in the kid's mouth.

"With the amount of time you've been off the juice and the amount of fear you're going to feel when bullets start flying, I think it'd be a miracle if you didn't." Jenna added softly. "Good luck, Jake. Hold them off, as long as you can."

"I sent a message to Rebecca," Dirk said when Jake cut his final transmission. "Hopefully the cavalry will be around soon enough."

"We better make a run for it. If we're going to make it up over that cliff, we're going to need all the time we can get."

Jake kissed Wendy's hands before placing them on her belly and then kissed her cheeks. He wanted to tell her he loved her, but didn't think the words would come out right. Besides, she still wasn't conscious, and there were now beads of sweat clinging to her face. Each breath seemed labored and he thought her time might be running out as quickly as his.

His fingers stroked her cheeks and remembered the first time he "accidentally" brushed against her. How Wendy once gave him money for lunch when he forgot his at home; and how she would smile at him during football practice. Back then it had all been a game and one he loved to play. The first time they snuck a kiss in the back of the school library had been the first time Jake felt alive. Every day they tried to sneak something and it was exciting, thrilling, but had been a game before the night on the field.

Then the game died. They just hadn't known it.

Heavy tears stung his eyes. He wished there was something more he could do, but there wasn't. He wished he hadn't slept with her that day and mostly he wished they had more time together. Wished he had more time. But now he needed to panic. He needed to stress himself out so that when the men finally approached the cabin, he'd be ready for them.

Jake thought of New Haven, his family, and how he would never be able to see them again. He thought of how much people hated him, hated the shifters, and how unfair his life had been. Even though he missed his town, Jake knew there were injustices and that people weren't allowed to say and do everything they wanted. If they stepped out of line, then they were conditioned. It happened to him once when he was a young boy, and he could still remember the chair and the needles they used to stick his body.

It wasn't fair that shifters were deemed as monsters when they were the strong ones. They had wings, they could fly, and were stronger than humans were. So how come the shifters weren't running the show? Maybe they should be. Maybe they should have won the war, but they didn't. Mostly out of dumb bad luck. Jake had never hated them before, he loved one very much, but looking back at Wendy's frail body, he began to. They were being hunted like animals and for what? Because humans wanted to kill them.

Jake wasn't going to let them.

As the rage built inside him, he clenched his fists and felt, for the first time, a fire burning inside him. He could hear their footsteps and he could see the flashlights so bright outside that it filled the shed with light. Then the lights dimmed and Jake knew they would be on him soon. Could he do it? Could he really protect Wendy? Anger and terror twisted in his belly so he couldn't distinguish one feeling from the next. His head begun to spin. Lightheaded, he grabbed the door frame with a shimmering blue hand.

Jake groaned as claws extended from his fingers. Instinctively he put his hands on the ground, gripping the dirt as the transformation continued. He snorted, shaking his clothes free with loud flaps from his wings. In his true mutant form, Jake barely fit inside the shed, which made no sense. Shifters did not get that big, that's what he was always told.

Using his snout, he butted the door open and stuck his long head outside. His yellow eyes blinked, seeing through the darkness perfectly. Two forms hid behind some trees. Each had a pistol.

He huffed, warning them off with a low growl, keeping his head low. Taking two ginger steps out of the shed, his tail smacked the door closed, shattering it into jagged pieces. The figures pulled further behind the trees, crouching. Jake roared a dragon's breath filled with rage and fire up in the air. The fire escaped his lungs, burning his throat and setting the leaves on fire.

One of the men ran, but Jake, with his wings flapping behind him, swooped in front of the man and landed on his chest with a thud. The gun was thrown clear and the man's sternum snapped under the pressure from his heavy clawed hoofs.

"Going somewhere?" Jake asked, but his voice was deep, guttural, unlike how he usually spoke. And shifters couldn't talk, not when not in human form. He didn't understand it. Neither did he have the desire to rip the man's throat out. Jake didn't want to eat him. He just wanted to stop him. Curious, Jake thought, but then a sound of a snapping twig caught is attention.

The second man was charging them, his gun drawn.

Jake howled. He took off running, his wings flapping with a quick breath. He swooped in and took the man in his jaws, but he held him lightly so not to kill him or even cut him. Instead he flew up through the night sky with his captor safely in his jaws, and deep inside his mouth Jake heard the man beg for his life.

He smiled so wide, Jake nearly dropped him. This was more like it.

***

It had been a long time since Jenna felt physical fear, but she was reminded then what it felt like.

The largest mutant she had ever seen in her life sat perched atop it, almost crushing it under its weight. Jake Monroe just wasn't a mutant, he almost looked like a dragon, with scales mutant in different hues of blue. She had never seen a mutant with a mane, but he had one and it glistened atop his head and under his snout like a beard. She felt like she was in the presence of a king and perhaps would have dropped to one knee if she were able to move.

Dirk pulled his weapon and aimed at the boy, the dragon. He was not as lost to his senses as she was. "Freeze!" he ordered, using his military voice. It woke Jenna up enough so she drew her own weapon and aimed for Jake, but she didn't want to fire. She wanted to know if he had consumed human blood first.

"There's a dead one over here!" Dirk screamed, glancing left.

"Bitten?"

"Unconfirmed!"

"Jake, if you didn't bite him, I need to know. I need you to come down here and change back, do you understand me?"

"I understand you." Jake said and Jenna was so shocked, she almost lowered her gun, but Dirk held firm.

"What the hell?" Dirk asked.

Jake swooped down from the ledge and landed with a hard thud in front of them. He bowed his head to the ground and opened his mouth enough so that the second assassin tumbled out. He was alive, but was unable to say anything coherent as he mumbled with tears streaking down his face.

Dirk secured the man and put handcuffs on him. But Jenna couldn't take her eyes off Jake.

"I thought you would want him for questioning," Jake said, but Jenna noticed his lips didn't move. But she could hear him. It was almost as if his thoughts were around her, echoing through the forest and the trees. When he spoke, the nature around him seemed to pulse with a shimmering white light.

"What happened to you?" Jenna asked.

"I don't know. I told you I've never changed before. For as I know, this has always been me."

"Will the baby be like you?"

"I don't know. I used to pray he wouldn't. Now, I think maybe it wouldn't be so bad."

Jenna wasn't sure she could argue with him. The dragon, Jake, didn't seem hungry for blood or lust for revenge. He was the most docile of any mutant she had ever met and there was something regal, even enlightened, about him. He didn't seem like a teenager. He seemed wise, like he was hundreds of years old. "I have to secure you. Return you to New Haven."

Jake laughed, squinting his kind yellow eyes. "I think you know, I can't allow that to happen, Jenna."

"Jen," Dirk's voice was caustic, "New Haven 56, it's coming over the wire now, it's burning. Mutants have revolted. They've seized the Outpost."

"Then I must go," Jake said. Jenna became afraid for a moment as he sniffed her. "Your scent is strange, but familiar. Almost like you were meant to be one of us."

Fear gripped her. "I can't just let you go. If you leave, I'll have no choice but to hunt you."

"You'll do what you must, just as I. Tell Wendy this was all for her. And that I am sorry, but I must help those like me. For our son. So he will not grow up like I did." Jake swooped up in the air and Jenna tracked his flight across the sky. Flickering across the moon like a dancing shadow, until he was out of her sight. The trees and mountains lost some of their luster, their beauty, in his absence and Jenna too felt a hole growing inside of her.

It was crazy, it was insane. But it was all true.

Jenna suspected she had not seen the last of Jake Monroe, and he just might well change the world. Change her world. But the rushing of footsteps behind her drew her from her thoughts.

Jane Morgan was a thin woman with tight red curls, just like her daughter. She carried her doctor's bag and a gun. Her mother always knew how to take care of herself, a trait she passed on to her daughter. "Mom," Jenna said, "it's about time."

"We all have our entrances to worry about, don't we dear? Where's Wendy?"

Jenna led her toward the shed and found herself sucking in her breath at the sighs of the girl, who was just beginning to regain consciousness. Her body was swollen with a child. and with fluid. She looked to be in extreme medical distress. Enraged, Jenna fought back angry tears at everything that caused this to happen. She stood in the doorway as doctors rushed past her to Wendy's side.

Jane peered into her eyes by lifting the lids and then rummaged through her bag. "Jaundice. Her liver's failing. Might be kidneys, too, from the signs of the fluid."

"Can you save them?" Jenna asked much too quietly for her taste, but couldn't talk any louder without betraying herself.

"We won't know until we get them back for a full exam." Jane gave Wendy two shots in her neck. "This will stabilize her enough for travel. Mutant sickness resembles pre-eclampsia. Your dad's made a lot of advances recently, but we still need to test it."

"I don't think she'll complain."

Wendy stirred with a moan. She blinked her eyes and looked around the room.

"Hello, Wendy, I'm Dr. Morgan. I'm here to help you and your baby. First, we need to get you off this mountain."

"I was having contractions. Where's Jake?" Wendy asked as two nurses took her by the arm and helped her up, leading her to an emergency gurney that was rapidly being assembled.

"He saved you." Jenna said. "And he's all right."

Wendy's eyes had many questions as they strapped her in, but there wasn't time to fill her in, and now wasn't the time.

Jenna turned from them and her mother's voice stopped her. "You're not coming with us, are you?"

"I have a prisoner to take into custody. Keep me updated. We'll come as soon as we can."

"Let me know. It's been awhile since you've been by for pot roast."

She supposed she had. Jenna smirked and left the shed behind, to where Dirk was standing with their prisoner with his phone. His phone was to his ear. He lowered it as their eyes met and Jenna saw something that made her uncomfortable. "Jenn, our New Haven..."

She stepped up to him. "What is it?"

He swallowed hard, his jaw clenching. "The mutants revolted. They've attacked Outpost."

Jenna couldn't believe it and their prisoner laughed. She glowered at him, twisting his arming behind her back and shoved her foot in his ass, forcing him to the ground. "Piss me off just a little bit more, and you're dead." His silence did nothing to calm her rage. "You killed our Chief. There is nothing stopping me from killing you when you resisted arrest. Right, Dirk?"

"Right." he said flatly. But Jenna knew he didn't agree.

Jenna forced the prisoner up and stuffed him in the back of the van. His eyes were smoldering not with anger, but with duty. "I did my job. What I was supposed to do. Only problem was, the girl got away."

Jenna slammed the door closed turned to Dirk. "Get us to the closest New Haven to drop this sucker off. Then we're on our own."

"Then where will we go?"

"I think you know." Jenna turned from him and headed toward the passenger's seat.

Chapter Thirty-One

Outpost was burning to the ground.

The insides were a ruin of dead bodies and a river of blood soaked through the pavement. Jeff placed his large feet on the chest of a woman—Laurel, he thought they called her—to keep her from escaping. She had a gun in her hand, but her fingers trembled so badly that she was unable to lift the weapon, let alone fire it.

Behind them, droves of cars whizzed by to make their escape out of New Haven 56. They would return to the world. Time to return to civilization, some for the first time. But Jeff knew he wouldn't be going. He had tasted, feasted, on more human blood than he had any right to. Jeff did it for Marie, for Jake, so they could be free. But now, all he wanted was more to eat. He didn't know who was going to stop him, but decided right then and there, he didn't care. First up: Laurel Kramer. She smelled of fear and was rich with fat.

She was going to taste really warm going down.

Jeff roared, sniffing the trembling woman, taking a deep breath, he could taste her scent as if he had already bitten her and it was delicious. Thick strands of saliva fell from his snout and he closed in for a bite.

"Stop!" The voice was deep and powerful.

Jeff turned his head away from Laurel and felt shifters all around him freezing in their spots. They all turned to face a majestic blue dragon swooping from the sky. It landed with precision, crunching the pavement. Its movements were royal as it flapped its wings closed and peered around the ruins of Outpost.

"We cannot continue this," Jake said, but his lips never moved. "You must stop. We must stop. Humans are weak, but are not our enemy. When we do this, we are our own enemy. You are all free to go, free to live, but we cannot feed on humans."

Being around this dragon, whomever it was, made Jeff feel better. More in control. He felt is anger subside and with a breath, he morphed back into a man. Falling to his knees, Jeff grunted and heard the grunts of dozens of more. The large dragon in front of him bowed his head down enough so he was eye level with Jeff.

His eyes were warm and kind. Jeff cried and took the large beast's head in his hands. The beast nuzzled his father's face with his giant nostrils and huffed against him. "Jake?" Jeff thought he cried all his tears, but renewed ones fell to his cheeks.

Jake cried, and in his father's embrace, morphed back into a human teen. His arms wrapped around his father and Jeff did the same. "Boy, I thought I'd never see you again."

"I'm sorry, Dad. I'm so sorry. I never should have left. Never." Jake gripped him hard, afraid to ever let him go.

"It's not safe here. We have to move." Jeff swallowed hard. "I have to tell you about your mother."

The New Haven 49 Outpost looked just like the one Jenna was accustomed to the last few years of her life, except it wasn't burning. But the one on the television monitor was. Every camera crew in a fifty-mile radius was parked outside and taking pictures.

While Outpost physically still stood in Jenna's mind, it was gone, and any hope that there was good in her was gone with it. A journalist was talking in the mist of all the carnage, but all she saw were fires raging and the blood running through the streets. This was what she fought to protect? This is what was in her?

Dirk gripped her hand. "You okay, Jenn?"

"Sure." Her voice was ice and locked far away. "I need to grab something from the van. Can I borrow your keys?"

Dirk's face grew with questions but he handed the keys over. Jenna thanked him without looking him in the eye and headed from the command center. Her feet crunched the pavement and the fresh air helped with her claustrophobic feeling as someone strode up beside her. Chief Montgomery, head of the Outpost. Beside the van, Jenna stopped and shook his hand.

"This mess, you have my word, will get cleaned up, Officer Morgan. As far as I'm concerned and the rest of my staff, you should be given an award."

Jenna nodded her thanks. "Don't bet on that yet, Chief."

Jenna slid into the driver's side and locked the doors, securing the seat belt across her shoulder. In the rearview mirror she saw Dirk running toward the van.

"Jenna," her comm buzzed, "don't do this. Let's talk about it."

"There's nothing left to talk about. I'm sorry, Dirk. You're too good a guy to drag down. Find that bitch Laurel and make sure she pays for everything she's done." Jenna turned off her comm and cranked the steering wheel. The tires kicked out rocks in a flurry, as she spun back out the way she came.

Who better than her to find and stop a pack of blood-hungry shifters? She saw no better way. As far as she was concerned, they were rabid dogs that needed to be put down. And when this was over, if they decided she needed to be put down too, so be it.

Chapter Thirty-Two

Wendy laid her head back and groaned as the van rocketed across rocky terrain on its way back to the highway. Every bump and turn seemed to emphasis that something inside her was wrong, breaking, and only getting worse.

"Take it easy," Jane Morgan said, and put a soft hand to her face. Her features were worn, like a side of a cliff that had weathered too many hard storms, but beneath them was a gentle beauty and kind eyes. "The medicine will start to work soon. You should feel some relief. We're headed to a hospital, of sorts."

She answered Wendy's unasked question. "You'll be safe there and we'll help you deliver your baby."

"How did you know where I was, who I am?" Wendy asked as they strapped a monitor around her bulging belly. Soon the back of the van was filled with the quiet sound of whoosing water and a fast pulsing heartbeat.

"We're friends of Rebecca's. My daughter's been looking for you, ever since you left New Haven."

Wendy was quiet while she thought, her hands resting still on top of her belly. "Ms. Morgan. I remember her. My Dad is—was—friends with her." She glanced out the window and watched the mountains whiz by. "She was looking for who killed him? Did she find him?" The question tightened a bundle nerves in her chest.

"We'll ask her together, when she comes to visit you. She said she would. Once she took care of some business."

"What happened to Sally?" Wendy asked.

Jane sighed as she unhooked the ultrasound sensor from the main hub against the wall. "I probably shouldn't tell you this, but you deserve to know. You never met Sally. Or Thomas Crane. Both of the people you knew were assassins. They killed Sally and were going to the same to you. Once you had the baby."

Her mouth fell open. Pain pelted through her. She didn't know what to say. They had seemed nice—well, maybe not nice—but seemed to genuinely care about her, and Jake. Why would they do something like that? "What were they going to do with the baby?"

"Sell it," Jane whispered. "To the highest bidders, and there were quite a few, or so I hear."

Tears welled in her eyes. Why was there so much pain and suffering being caused over her, and her baby? Wendy never wanted that. She thought the world would come together because of him. That long rifts would be healed. Her chin quivered. "I was such a fool. To think..." Her voice trailed off and her fingers dotted at the tears on her cheeks.

Jane pointed to the monitor. "There he is. Your son."

"Is he okay?" Wendy asked. For a moment, she didn't care at all if he was all right. All ready he had taken so much from her, even if it wasn't his fault. Even if he didn't know.

"Vitals are all good. Movement too. If we can get enough fluids in you to stop your contractions, I'd say we'd be in fair shape. Then we can just worry about you." Jane gave her a pleasant smile. "I'll just be a moment."

Wendy watched her go, feeling the pulsating kicks from her baby. She closed her eyes, and heard Jane tell something to the driver. "Put a little umph in it, would you? She's deteriorating."

Her eyes snapped open. Would anyone would ever tell her the truth again? Shivers ran through her and Jane returned with a blanket, as if she expected Wendy might be cold. "Thanks," Wendy couldn't keep the anger out of her voice. "I'm tired. Sorry."

"You've been through a lot. It's all right." Jane smiled. "I don't have much, but here's a juice box. We'll be at the compound in thirty minutes. We'll make you more comfortable there."

Wendy accepted it because she was thirsty and because she didn't want to talk anymore. She shielded her eyes as a blinding light filled the van from the front.

"Brace yourselves!" Jane shouted.

Jane leaned onto Wendy as the van crunched forward and collapsed onto itself, like an accordion, before spinning out of control. Wendy screamed and flew up out her gurney on impact before the van came to a screeching stop. The medical equipment and machines slid into her, bruising her legs and smacking her head. Horns blared, but there were no screams or voices. Whoever was driving the van was unconscious or dead.

"Jane?" Wendy whispered, her hand bloody and cut from the metal from a machine that punctured her. She used it to pat the doctor's back, hoping to arose her enough to get her to talk.

The doctor moaned and struggled to lift her head. "We have to move, before—" The sound of the rear door being forced open cut her off. Blinding headlights filled the van and Wendy cupped her eyes to make out the silhouette of a man holding a shotgun over his shoulder step into sight.

The closer he got, the easier his features were to make out. "Well, " said Thomas Crane, forehead spattered with blood, with a whistle through his teeth. "What we got is a pickle here, ladies. We better move."

"She can't be moved. She has to go with me!" Jane snarled and pushed off Wendy with a grunt. No sooner did she grab her gun, did Thomas aim his. They were locked on each other and the elder doctors gave the assassin a cold glower, revolted and unwavering.

Wendy looked between them, her eyes wide with fright. She pulled the blanket on her higher and wanted to slide underneath it.

Thomas chuckled. "Think we both know you won't shoot me, but nice show. Seems I teamed up with the wrong medical professional. I think I'll be taking you with us, being that this one looks about ready to pop."

Wendy clutched her belly. She bit her tongue to keep from moaning as her uterus contracted tight. It lasted longer than before and she had to blow out a slow breath, with her eyes closed, to keep herself from groaning.

Jane's eyes never left their assailant. "She needs a fully stocked facility. If she doesn't receive full medical attention, I can't say for sure either of them will survive."

"I seem to see enough equipment here. I think you can make do with the supplies I already have. Grab what you need, and remember if you try to run," Thomas stood closer and placed the barrel of his shot gun against Wendy's temple, "I'll cut the baby from her dead womb myself."

Wendy closed her eyes and trembled. She wasn't ready to die, but she didn't want to go with him either.

"That's not going to happen," Jane said defiantly. She raised her gun a little higher and fired at Thomas Crane right between the eyes.

He lurched backwards. His gun went off, the shot going wide and shattering the front windshield. Wendy screamed and shielded her face while Jane lowered her gun. "Show him to mess with a Morgan. We *always* fire first."

She stepped over him and unstrapped Wendy from her gurney. "It's not ideal, girl, but we have to get out of this van and into his truck. You think you can walk?"

Wendy didn't, but she nodded yes. Jane took one of her arms and slung it over her shoulder, helping the girl out of the van. When Wendy's foot hit the pavement below, she struck a rock and nearly fell. She grimaced and tightening quickened in her belly. "I'm not gonna make it, am I?"

Jane didn't answer as they hobbled to the truck. Their breath was both taken away when they saw its condition. The headlights were crunched and the truck bed was crushed into the cabin. The metal was disjointed and twisted as if melted by molten lava.

How Thomas had planned on getting them out of there as anyone's guess, but maybe he was the type who did things on impulse without a plan.

"Shit," Jane swore and strengthened her grip on Wendy's waist. She studied the horizon and then brought up her PDA. All Wendy could feel as pain surging up her back and then shooting down her legs. She tried to steady herself on wobbling legs.

"There's a restaurant less than a mile from here. Down Route 22. If we get there, we can radio for help."

Wendy's face scrunched. "I can't!" She sobbed, and wanted to fall over. If one more thing went wrong, she wasn't sure she could continue on. Jake was supposed to be here. That was the deal! She never wanted to do this alone.

"Hey!" Jane said sharply, forcing Wendy up. "You have to be strong for yourself and your baby. It is going to have a hard path in life, understand? You think this is hard? This is nothing. And it will only have you to protect it. Only *you*. You must be stronger than this. Must."

Her face was hard and her stare was icy. Wendy tore away from it. "Jake—" Wendy trembled.

"Isn't here." Jane was solemn. "He may never be here again. As unfair as it is, you are the one held responsible. You are his mother. So pull yourself up, ignore the pain, and let's get you out of here as fast as we can. Failure is *not* an option. Tell that to yourself, until you start to believe it."

Wendy nodded, sucked back her tears, and stood straight again. Jane took her by her side and they continued down the road. It wasn't until Wendy doubled over with contractions that Jane would allow them to slow down. Then she would rub the girl's back and while she was comforting, she never offered false platitudes. "The lights are getting brighter, we're getting close. C'mon, girl. I'll buy you something cold to drink."

It sounded good to her, and they continued down the dirt road until they came upon some trees and the bright shine of streetlights. Right in front of them as a gas station attached to an old diner named Silver Train. The inside was brightly lit and Wendy could smell beef. Oh, the beauty of red meat.

"Not far now," Jane said, but a surge in her abdomen caused Wendy to double over, grabbing onto a payphone to steady herself. Jane rubbed her back. "Breathe through it. Breathe."

Wendy tried, but she couldn't remember how and could barely remember what Jane had said. Her entire belly hardened; it felt as if it was contracted in a vise. Something inside her changed. She felt an intense pressure buildup and then a pop, almost like a balloon bursting. Wendy moaned and felt a heavy tinkle, then a gush of water pouring down her leg.

"Oh mercy," Jane muttered. "We need to get you off your feet. All this walking is doing more harm than good." She propped her shotgun by the front door and they stepped inside.

Almost at once the waitress, the short order cook, and two people sitting at the counter turned. Wendy could barely stand up and felt herself going slack against Jane's strong grip.

"Do you ladies need something?" The cook asked from his spot at the pass, a toothpick twirling in his mouth.

"An ambulance. We had a wreck. This girl's in a bad way." Jane said as she helped Wendy to a booth.

Every step caused her pain. Wendy could barely speak as she sat. All of her limbs relaxed, falling outward, and she leaned her head back against the red vinyl cushion, closing her eyes. She felt so hot and knew there was too much sweat across her brow.

"I'll ring them." The waitress went to the phone.

"Much obliged. A glass of water for the girl, if you could?" A moment later Jane fed Wendy a few delicate sips.

"I'm so hungry," Wendy said.

"Sorry, but you can't eat. Not if you're as close to giving birth as I think."

Wendy squeezed her eyes shut. "Will he be okay?"

"I wish I could make promises, but right now, let's focus on getting you through it first, all right?"

Jane stood as the waitress approached. "Ambulance is coming. Should be ten minutes to get out this far. There's a cot in the back, if she wants to lay down for a while."

"Thanks for your kindness. Wendy, come."

Wendy groaned as Jane tugged on her arm and was slow to get into the back, but she appreciated being able to lie down on the cool pillows. Even the lumpy mattress felt good to her. She took long breaths out her mouth and Jane waited for the contractions to pass before checking her. Wendy screamed, grabbing the side rails as she felt Jane's hand probing her insides.

"Eight centimeters. Looks like it's almost time to start pushing." Jane sighed. "That ambulance might not get here in time."

"I really didn't want to have my baby in a diner," Wendy said with a laugh.

Jane grinned. "Keep your spirits up. It'll help."

Wendy groaned, leaned her head back on the pillow and breathed deep with all her might. Jane rubbed her inner thighs to try to relax her, but still Wendy gripped the side of the cot like she might bend it in two. "Oh my God," she whispered and her teeth chattered uncontrollably.

"You're in transition. For some people, this is normal. Breathe through it," Jane instructed. "At least you have me. I was alone. Living in seclusion and I was afraid if the baby wouldn't come naturally I'd die."

Wendy looked at her as the contraction ended. "You?" A mutant baby? "Your daughter, Ms. Morgan?"

Jane nodded. "One mother to another, I'm sure you'll understand. We keep each other's secrets."

Wendy was shocked and didn't understand. She thought she was special, that her baby would change the world. Jenna Morgan hated shifters and hunted them. If she was a mutant and did all that, what hope of changing the world did her baby have? Had she gone through all this pain and suffering from nothing?

"My solution was to go on my on. To hide. Yours, well was very brave."

"Me?" Wendy asked incredulously.

"You faced your dilemma straight on. Went for help. It opened quite the can of worms, but you couldn't have known the hate that shifters inspired, not with being raised in New Haven all your life. The coalition will see your safe, and this baby, but first, we got to get it out of you, okay?"

Wendy nodded. "I bet Rebecca's drafting her press conference already."

"Twice." Jane smiled. "I'm going to go see if the ambulance is here yet." She stood, then froze. Wendy watched as she slowly raised her hands and a man with a gun shoved her back into the room.

"You're the lady on the news, I reckon. The one worth a lot of money. So I don't think an ambulance will be coming, after all."

***

Jenna throttled the stick shift and switched into second gear. Outside was dark and her eyes, while better than a regular human's, saw nothing but open road. They were on the service road, but most businesses wouldn't be open for hours yet. A few cars were on the road with them, but she passed them with ease.

Her phone rang again. Jenna held it up dismissively and saw for a split second it was Dirk, before sliding her thumb across it to avoid his call. It was like he and her mother were tag-teaming her, and she didn't want to talk to either of them.

Jenna loved her mom, she did, but her decision to shack up with a mutant, to want to "cure" them as though they had the flu, was crazy to her. Jane felt the same way about her, Jenna knew that, but there wasn't much she could do about it. After everything, Jenna couldn't change her core beliefs, and wasn't about to. Not even if her Mom and stepfather begged her too, for the hundredth time.

Jenna glanced down at her phone and the tracking software she had opened. She was getting closer. She just had to pray they wouldn't smarten up and remove their bracelets. They wore them all their lives and she had to hope against hope that they wouldn't even think of it. She just needed them to stay together in a single group. And so help them if they were feeding when she got there...

Jenna slowed down the van as she drove past a grocery store. It figured that the mutants would flock to somewhere so suburban, so domestic. What was more small-town than your local fast food burger joint? Nothing she could think of, and that's where she parked the van, close to the back exit of the kitchen so they could sneak out the staff. After that, if she blew the entire place to Kingdom Come with herself inside, Jenna wouldn't care. She was tired of the fighting, the hiding, the lying. She was ready for it to be over. So if one of those mutant bastards got her before she ended him, Jenna was going to make sure no one got out alive.

Through the back of the van she went, picking out a gun and a grenade. She snapped it on the belt of her jeans and desperately tried not to think of her team. Jameson, the one who betrayed her and Dirk, the one who never would. She hated the idea of losing them. No matter if she never said it, she needed them.

But that was over now.

marched toward the restaurant and knocked on the metal door leading into the kitchen once before pulling it open. She was met with surprised faces. Some were older, but most had the pimply sheen of teenagers. She flipped open her badge. "New Haven Police. On official business. Everyone out."

"No time for questions. Unless you want to end up mulched beef." They ran outside like frightened children.

Jenna surveyed the kitchen and headed toward the counter. Ducking down beside the deep fryer, she saw a bunch of men and woman clustered in booths. They talked in hushed voices, warming their hands on cups of coffee. From the way they shifted in their seats, Jenna suspected they were second-guessing their decision.

There were children sitting in the corner, munching on french fries. They were talking excitedly, like they were on a field trip. She hadn't thought of children, but they were all monsters. They all were responsible for the deaths in New Haven, whether they had been part of it or not. She also knew that the dozen she saw out there, weren't all that escaped. There were others, out there, and she needed to find them all. A scared mutant was a dangerous mutant. Plus, Jake Monroe wasn't part of the group. Wherever he was, Jenna had a feeling others would be.

Her stomach tightened at the thought of seeing him again. She wasn't sure what the right move was, but knew somehow he was important. Could she kill him? Should she?

Maybe instead of thinking, it was time to act. Jenna stared at the gun in her hand. She firmed her grasp on it, turning it over. Could she really do it again? After all those sleepless nights when she promised herself she never would again?

Jenna stood, took a deep breath. No one saw her yet. Not one twitched muscle in her direction. She raised her gun, her breath was hurried and her hands shook, but still she aimed her gun at the back of a little girl's head. It was better to take the young ones out first, get the hard stuff over with.

The bell jingled at the front door. Shifters screamed and Jenna saw Dirk charging her. She aimed her gun at him. "Get out of here, Dirk! What the hell are you doing here?"

"Looking for you, since you won't answer your phone. What the hell, Jenna? This is your answer, to go crazy again? After all the shit we just went through?"

"It's not going crazy, it's called vengeance. Now get out of here before you're too involved to step away."

"I'm all ready too involved." He stepped forward, hands up. "I won't let you do this. Throw your life away again, for nothing. They are not worth it, but you are. You get me? You are worth a lot more than a pile of dead mutants."

Jenna laughed but it felt bitter. "How can you say that? You know what's in me? I'm no better than they are."

He shook his head, tears in his eyes. "That's not true and I think you know it. You might not believe in you. But I do, Jenn. Always have. Even when you left, with no word, I always knew, you were the one for me. Don't blow our last chance away on them."

She lowered her gun, lip trembling. "So you'd really be able to look past me, what's in my blood, who I am?" She punched him in the chest. "Don't you dare say that, Dirk. Don't you dare! If you say that, and I walked away for nothing, for nothing..."

Dirk stepped in front of her and took her gun. She stared up at him, his kind eyes, and felt the pull to kiss him. Like she always did. But she didn't fight it, like she usually did. This time she leaped at the chance, leaning forward until her lips met his. Hungrily he kissed her back and for Jenna, it was as if all the walls between them were gone. She could hold him again, be with him, and she did. Jenna clung to him like her life depended on it and felt warmer, more whole. It felt as if part of her healed just because he loved her.

The mutants were gone. Jenna knew that, but in that moment, listening to them rush out, Jenna couldn't care. Dirk kissed her again, breathing against her cheek. She wished for only a few moments to be lost in him forever. She buried her face against his neck, knew there was so much to talk about and do, but in that moment she wanted nothing more than to just breathe him in.

Jenna did not get her wish.

Dirk's phone was ringing and he brought it up as Jenna cuddled against his chest, and his free arm squeezed her tight. "Rebecca." His voice was tender against her ear.

Jenna snatched the phone from him and scrolled through the messages. "Wendy and my mother never arrived." It looked like Jenna should have taken her mother's calls after all.

***

Jane couldn't believe their luck. What kind of backward hick part of the country where they in anyway? "You realize she is very close to having this baby right here? If it dies, it's worthless. To everyone." Her words were harsh, but with her gun outside, she saw no other alternative. Behind her Wendy's breathing was rushed every few minutes. If the teenager didn't start screaming soon that she needed to push, Jane would be surprised.

"We called the New Haven Initiative. They're sending someone for her and the baby. It's a monster, right? Be placed inside one of those bubble towns? Then we get our money. They told us not to let you leave, by any means necessary. This," he said, pointing the gun in Jane's face, "is necessary."

Jane stared at it and realized she had no choice but to deliver the baby. She always told herself get from moment to moment. This moment she was alive and the next moment she might come up with a plan to escape, but right now, there wasn't any such plan. Wendy was in no condition to run. At the moment the girl was barely conscious, and for the good of the child, Jane needed to deliver it there. She would have to worry about where it ended up later.

"I'll deliver the baby," Jane said, seeing how pleased her captor was. "But I'm going to need a lot of towels. And hot water." She returned to Wendy, whose eyes were glazed and from her breathing, a new cycle of contractions were beginning. The girl's hair was thick with sweat and Jane smoothed it back. "I know you're scared, but we're going to get through this. Take it one breath at a time."

"I can't, not with them watching." Wendy glanced toward the door.

Jane glowered at them. "Do you mind?"

When they had more privacy Wendy grabbed Jane by the shirt and pulled her close. "Once it's born, I need you to take the baby. Run. Don't let New Haven take it," she whispered.

"Wendy," Jane's eyes grew wide. "You're his mother."

"I'm in no shape to run. I *have* to protect him. Which means *you* need to promise me."

Jane swallowed hard. "That's not what I meant when I said that. It's not what I meant, darling."

"If you can get the baby away from New Haven, you have to take it. Please," Wendy begged and Jane agreed, if only to give her some peace as the cycle of birth continued.

Hours passed as Wendy's contractions became so intense that they drew the attention of the wait staff. The girl was exhausted, and screaming, but not advancing as well as Jane would have liked. She got the girl on her knees, rocking back and forth to try to get the baby to descend, but Wendy only cried in agony. "Please, God," she moaned, "don't let me die."

Jane seconded that prayer, but not aloud. If the girl managed to birth the baby, it'd be a miracle. Her vitals were weak and she was exhausted. She steeled herself for an emergency C-section. One that was sure to leave Wendy dead.

She could feel the top of the baby's scalp. "It's right there, Wendy. It's right there. All we need is a few good pushes and we can get him out, I promise you." Wendy's arms shook from holding herself up, but she couldn't respond. All she did was cry.

Outside Jane heard the sound of sirens. Seemed the cavalry had arrived and there was nothing she could do anymore as police swarmed the restaurant. It wasn't the state police, but they wore badges that appointed them as part of a secret security panel for New Haven, the ones that took orders from only Alistar Humphries. Which meant they were dirtier than pigs in mud.

"Step away from the teenager, Dr. Morgan. We have a lot of questions for you and your organization's involvement in all this. Harboring a known mutant baby? I think you know the punishment for that."

As she should, Jane thought to herself. She put her game face on as she faced them. "I think time to do that would be later. Right now this girl is about two minutes away from giving birth and I would like to see the baby born successfully first. I know New Haven doesn't care, but if it doesn't, it'll kill the girl and it will die inside her. Any issues with me saving their life?"

"We have an ambulance."

Jane shook her head and behind her Wendy screamed. "I think you can see we won't make it."

"I need to push!" Wendy bellowed, lifting her head off the pillows, her teeth gritted together like a vise.

Jane did by holding both of Wendy's feet in the air. For next several minutes she saw nothing but Wendy, guiding her breathing and her pushes, as she struggled to move the baby through the birth canal. The shrills of pain were intense and from the amount of blood Wendy was losing, it was hard for Jane to see if they were making any progress.

Wendy collapsed onto her pillow between contractions. "I feel like I'm gonna snap in two."

"Sssh," Jane whispered, "save your strength. Next push will be up in just a few seconds."

The girl's breath quickened and Jane could see the contraction playing out on her face. Taking a deep breath, Wendy pushed as long as she could. Between her legs, was a crown of black hair. "Keep at it," Jane ordered. "Push, push! C'mon, girl!"

Wendy screamed, keeping her chin to her chest.

"Stop, stop." Jane took the baby's head in her hand. She cleared its mouth. It was smaller than Jenna had been by a long shot, but its features were perfect and under the blood, beautiful. "A slow, controlled push on the next contraction."

Wendy nodded, and bore down. Jane slid the baby's body free, but it wasn't breathing yet. Small for a mutant, but about average size for a human newborn, she wasn't sure if it was all right. Maybe it had come too soon. Just as she was about to say something, the baby's limbs jerked and he cried that shaky newborn warble.

His mother cried too. "He's really okay?" Her voice was so quiet, Jane barely heard her.

"He really is." Jane wrapped the baby in the soft linens offered to her by the waitress. With the umbilical cord cut, she brought the baby over to Wendy and placed him in the crook of her arm. Wendy was beaming a new-mother smile but she was still in bad shape. She was still bleeding and her arms were too weak to hold the baby herself without assistance.

"You go clean him up for me?" Wendy said, but her eyes said something else.

Jane took a breath. "Yes. Then we get you to a hospital. You need medics."

Wendy kissed the top of her baby's head. Her chin trembled. Jane hoped she could hold it together as she took the baby from her and turned to the New Haven security officers.

"Where do you think you're going?" their leader said. "We'll clean the baby up at the hospital."

"I don't want his eyes to get infected." Jane lied. "His face needs cleaning. He's a preemie and is going to need extra care."

The officer nodded, but the one beside him snorted. "Like it's going to matter in the long run."

Jane knew. She quickly slid past them and followed the waitress toward the bathroom. In the woman's hand was a small key. "Never heard anything about a baby's eyes getting infected after birth."

"I'm sure you haven't heard of a lot of things," Jane said coolly. "Like decency and morality."

The waitress snorted. "It wasn't my idea. Once Dale gets an idea in his head..." She pointed down the hall. "Bathroom is on the left. Straight ahead is the exit to the back. This," she put the key in Jane's free hand, "is the key to my sedan. Try not to wreck it."

She left Jane speechless, thankful, but speechless. She didn't try to thank the lady. No time. With a nod of her head, she left and headed outside where the sun was beginning to come up.

Inside the sedan she found an old blanket, wrapped the baby in it, and started the car. As she threw it in reverse, Jane searched for her PDA. She was going to need a lot of help. Soon that baby would be hungry. And the type of milk it wanted, Jane couldn't buy in a store.

Dead ahead she could see the police were already hurrying toward their patrol cars. She prayed to God someone cared enough about Wendy to see she that got to the hospital.

Her phone buzzed and she saw it was her daughter. In the end, she always came through.

Chapter Thirty-Three

While Wendy gave birth, Jenna's van rocketed over the terrain, the headlights bobbing, illuminating small rocks along the side of the road. So far, no sign of Jane or Wendy. Jenna gripped the wheel and floored the gas. She had to catch them. Everything she went through couldn't be for nothing and Jenna refused to lose her mother.

Refused.

"No answer, Jenn." Dirk said softly, Jenna's phone in his hand.

"Try again." She was edgy, angry, but tried not to be with him. "Keep trying until she answers."

They drove along and the road curved as they came to a bridge over a small ravine. The headlights shone on a metal hubcap and then a wrecked van. Jane's van.

Jenna cut the engine and hopped out in one swoop, turning on her flashlight. "Mom!" She screamed, and tore forward. She nearly tripped over a leg. Using her flashlight she saw that the leg beyond to a man whose face was blown off. She tapped his forehead with her foot and more blood spilled out. She scrunched her nose as the scent made her stomach rumble with hunger. Disgusted, vomit rose in her throat and she swallowed it back while Dirk went through his jacket pockets.

"Looks like a shotgun blast."

Jenna nodded because that's all she could do as her mind reeled. "My mother's preferred weapon of choice."

Dirk flipped through the man's wallet. "Guess who? Our popular resident gun-for-hire." He tossed it to Jenna, who gave it a glance before her eyes swept over the scene. The truck looked more like melted-down metal than a vehicle. And inside the van the gurney was empty. Medical equipment was scattered everywhere. And her mother's fallen hat was on the ground.

Jenna touched it and her light illuminated sheets of the cot. They were stained with blood droplets. She bit her lip. "Where the hell are you?"

"Jenn," Dirk said from the front, pointing to a second body. "These guys are dead. On impact is seems from how his face is one with the dash. Hard way to go."

Jenna nodded, lost in thought. "So," she said, "Thomas with his impeccable intelligence rams the van to reclaim his prize. My mother shoots him. Gets Wendy out and then what?" She hopped down from the chassis and back onto the rugged mountain. "Which way would they go?"

Dirk glanced at his phone, bringing up his GPS.

Jenna walked down the road, shining her light on bushes and twigs. In the mud she saw the impression of knees and a set of hands, like someone had fallen. Wendy, she guessed. Her stomach tight, she continued on, staying on the main road until it split. A green rest stop sign pointed south. It was only a few miles away.

That was where she would take Wendy, and then radio for help.

"Jenn, Silver Train diner is only two miles from here. Gas, food, phones."

"Let's get back on the road. We might not have much time." Jenna ran to the van, slid in, and shifted into reverse before Dirk closed his door. "Call the police. See if anyone has called in distress."

Dirk was already on the phone. "We'll find them, don't worry."

Jenna knew her mother was capable and could handle herself, but taking care of Wendy and her unborn baby would be of utmost importance. Jane would put her own well-being last, and while Jenna admired her mother's strength and sacrifices, she didn't want her mother to die for a mutant baby. If something happened to her, Jenna didn't think she'd ever forgive herself.

"I should have went with them." She muttered. "Damn it, Dirk." Tears filled her eyes and Dirk squeezed her hand.

"FBI is running the show now," Dirk said to her, then spoke on the phone. "Agent, I'm glad to have connected to you." Dirk took a breath and listened to the person on the other end.

"Ha, New Haven jokes. *Love* it. Listen, we're on the same side. I know you guys think we have carte blanche to do anything we want, but right now our goals are the same. I need to make sure a woman and a pregnant teen are all right. She's in severe distress."

Jenna's heart wrenched at his words. Dirk really did care and she had been so blind by her own hate of the shifters that she didn't see it. Damn her blood, and her mother, for putting her in this position. She thought if she saw her mother again, she might punch her between the eyes. Thinking about it, made her feel better.

She glanced at Dirk from the corner of her eye. He was listening and nodding. "Several in custody? Who?"

Jenna took a deep breath and steadied herself.

"Okay, keep us up to the date on her situation." Dirk slapped his phone shut, running his fingers along his lips. "Jenn—"

"Just give it to me straight, Dirk."

"Wendy gave birth at the Silver Train under duress. Some guys there recognized her from TV and they were going to sell the kid to the highest bidder."

Jenna took a sharp intake of air. Damn her mother and her luck for trouble. "And *Mom*?"

"Your mother took the baby and escaped, taking a waitress's car. She was seen going west. If we hurry, maybe we can catch up."

Relief washed over her, but it was brief. "There's a but in there somewhere."

"There were New Haven police on her tail. Special Forces, straight from Alistar's private task force."

They passed the Silver Train Diner and Jenna accelerated, continuing west. This was the road that would take Jane home toward Chicago. If New Haven hadn't already killed her and the baby, that was. Jenna could see her mother, defiant in the face of certain death, even as she stared down her would-be assassin. Her mother was too good for that. If only Jenna could make her understand how much her life was worth.

"Wendy?"

"It's bad, Jenn. But she was taken by ambulance. They are headed to the hospital now. They'll call us when they get there."

"Call my mother again," Jenna said.

Dirk complied and this time, he got an answer. "Jane? Hold on."

Jenna snatched the phone from him. "Mother, how do you get yourself in these messes?"

"Probably the same way you do, dear. I need your help. I have New Haven on my tail and I can't shake them. I need you to intercept."

"We'll work on it. Can you send me your location to this phone?"

"Doing it now."

"Good." Jenna took a breath. "When you see us coming, keep going. Don't look back. We'll catch up with you later just get that baby to your compound. Is it...is it all right?"

"So far he's sleeping, but he needs food, Jenna."

"And you'll get it the food it needs. Just keep going." Jenna hung up and handed the phone to Dirk. "Work on a way for us to cut them off. We'll never catch up from behind. I don't care if we have to turn this van into an all-terrain vehicle, we have to get there before New Haven overtakes them. Or uses their rumble strip."

They fell quiet while Dirk worked and Jenna drove. Each minute felt like an hour until he handed her the phone. She studied the gravel roads and the off-terrain paths she would have to travel to cut them off. Looked like there was a guard rail and a wrong-way highway trip in her future. People were always saying she was on a suicide mission.

Jenna took a hard left and the van rocketed down a path designed for bikes. When her phone chirped she scanned it with laughter and handed it to Dirk. "This just in: Rebecca Seers's press conference, and evidence has been presented to the Department of Justice. New Haven Police authority has been suspended outside the bubbles. And an arrest warrant has been issued for good ol' boy Alistar Humphries."

Dirk whistled. "Straight to the top. That Rebecca works fast."

A few more hard rights and a hard left sent them careening in what felt like a circle. Jenn pressed her foot to the floor and the van rocketed through the trees and crashed down on four tires onto the open road. The van buckled, nearly tipped, and Jenna gripped the steering wheel for support as Dirk braced himself on the dashboard. She read his look of surprise. Maybe he thought she was crazy, but he kept the thoughts to himself, so Jenna pushed on.

She straightened the wheel, her eyes straining through the trees that lined the road. The roar of traffic was growing louder and she could make out headlights through the trees. Dirk glanced at her phone to pinpoint Jane's exact GPS location. "Drive three minutes this way, cut across the highway, pass the divider, and we're golden!"

"Be your chance to be a crash test dummy."

Dirk laughed and shook his head at her. "I love you, Jenn."

"I'll say it, if we survive."

Jenna timed her driving and waited almost three full minutes before turning right. The van bounced over some small rocks, sailing over a ditch and landed on the highway. Traffic was light for a rural highway, but horns wailed as she cut a few people off and merged with the flow of traffic. Jenna made a hard left across the divide, using the gaps in the guardrails the cops usually reserved for u-turns on official business. The van rocketed across and Jenna cranked the wheel, doing a one-eighty.

She yelped and slammed on her breaks as a beater vehicle barely escaped, horns wailing. The crew of cruisers behind the car convinced Jenna that she had found her mother. The cruisers' brakes squealed as the vehicle rolled toward the van at an alarming speed. The seat belt wrenched Jenna's shoulder.

Jenna looked outside the window and saw the cruisers sliding sideways right toward her. She didn't feel ready to die, but knew it might be coming. Jenna said a prayer, and undid her seat belt, and felt someone yanking her backwards out of the rear door. Jenna fell with an *umphf* onto the ground, on top of Dirk. The van skidded toward them and they scampered on their knees into the ditch.

They watched as the van's twisted metal slammed down the street with the two police squad cars. They rotated as a unit down the stretch of highway like well-trained dancers, twirling in the moonlight. The tires squealed and sparks flew from beneath the engine. Jenna almost expected them to catch fire or explode, but they finally stopped, turning slightly left before hitting the guardrail.

Dirk secured her in a hug, his forearm wrapped around her neck, and kissed the ruffled hair atop her head. "You know how to show a guy a good time."

She spun on her heels to face him, adrenaline surging. Her hand pulled on his hair and forced his lips down to her to meet his. His arms grabbed her shoulders, spun her around and up off her feet. Jenna squealed, biting his lip. A big smile played across her face.

"It's been too long since I've seen you smile, you know that?" Dirk's eyes glinted and for a moment all Jenna felt was happiness. She almost forgot what it felt like.

"I love you." Jenna said. "And I hope it was worth the wait."

Dirk touched her chin, licking his lips. "You're like a fine wine, Jenna. You get better with age."

Her mind consumed with thoughts of love, they rushed over to the squad cars. Jenna threw one of the squad car doors open. Inside were two disoriented officers. One was bleeding and the other barely conscious. "Gentlemen," she said, "you are hereby relieved of duty."

The driver groaned and turned his head. His eyes were mere slits. She could see muscles throbbing as his forehead swelled, right before her eyes. "Screw you."

Jenna smiled. "We'll keep you company until the ambulance gets here. Then I think the Justice Department is going to have a few questions."

She slammed the door shut. Over the horizon, the sun was rising. The orange hues danced through the trees and she thought morning had never seemed so beautiful. It was one of the longest days of her life and not one she wanted to repeat any time soon.

Dirk looked at her as he stood guard beside the trooper cars. She smiled at him, shyly, wondering what he was thinking. When he grinned, she knew, and she felt it too. Things were going to be better than they had in a long time. Life wasn't perfect. New Haven's future was uncertain. But now they had each other.

The only thing left was for Jenna to wrap up her investigation, write a report, buy a baby gift, and visit Wendy Reynolds. Yeah, her day wasn't going to get any less busy any time soon.

When her phone rang, Jenna was feeling chipper. "Officer Morgan."

"Officer Morgan, Sergeant Lynch from the state police."

"Sergeant Lynch, are you calling with an update on Wendy?" Jenna asked, walking away from the commotion .

"Yes. I regret to inform you, the girl was pronounced dead upon arrival. I'm told her organs were in failure and she lost too much blood to be saved. I'm sorry. I've heard you were a good friend with her family."

Jenna nodded, tears obscuring her vision. She thought she might have said thank you, but wasn't sure. She slid the phone closed, and fell to her knees.

When she started crying, Dirk was there with her, but Jenna might as well have been alone. After everything, she failed her promise to the Chief. She guessed now that the promise was going to have to fall to someone else.

To a yet-to-be-named half-shifter baby, halfway to Chicago by now.

Epilogue

The lab was dark.

They kept it this way so that she couldn't see. The confines of her cell were small, with only a cot to keep her company. Through the hours that turned into days, it was her comforter and her friend.

The drugs they pumped into her body kept her asleep. Her consciousness drifted. She remembered only men in white sneakers, talking in hushed voices.

And needles.

So many needles and so many tests. She didn't know why or to what end they serviced. She could barely remember her name.

Her hair was dirty. Like jungle vines, they clung to her face. She moaned, barely able to move off of her pillow. Her wrist, with puffy and dark blue veins, fell slack and dangled off the mattress.

Who was she? What was her purpose and why did so many people she didn't know what to hurt her.

Her eyes rolled into the back of her head. She was on the cusp of another seizure, thanks to their medicine. Thanks to everything they were trying to do. But, she didn't know what that was. They told her things, whispered things to her that made no sense.

What was it they called her?

Her mind begged for a savior. Someone to come and find her. She used to have a mother. Someone that always took care of her.

She was a mother too. To a dead baby.

Her body seized. Her body slammed the bed frame into the concrete floor. Her hair flew past her eyes and the sound of an alarm and the rush of footsteps rushed to greet her.

She saw their lab coats and the insignia of New Haven on their lapels. She grabbed at one, consciousness ripping from her brain. "Help me," she begged.

His eyes were kind and warm. His expression was nearly blank. It reminded her of Jake.

She grimaced as a needle pinched into her arm. "Ow," she moaned, going slack in his arms. She could see, but could no longer move.

"It'll okay," his whisper against her cheek relaxed her. He smoothed her hair back and his skin was soft, "Wendy, it's going to be okay."

Printed in Great Britain
by Amazon